Alexander Johnstone Wilson

The Rise and Progress of Sir Timothy Buncombe, Kt. and M.P.

An Extra-Moral Biography

Alexander Johnstone Wilson

The Rise and Progress of Sir Timothy Buncombe, Kt. and M.P.
An Extra-Moral Biography

ISBN/EAN: 9783337099442

Printed in Europe, USA, Canada, Australia, Japan

Cover: Foto ©Raphael Reischuk / pixelio.de

More available books at **www.hansebooks.com**

THE RISE AND PROGRESS

OF

SIR TIMOTHY BUNCOMBE,

KT. AND M.P.

THE RISE AND PROGRESS

OF

SIR TIMOTHY BUNCOMBE,

KT. AND M.P.

AN EXTRA-MORAL BIOGRAPHY.

BY THE AUTHOR OF

"THOMAS WANLESS, PEASANT."

———

MANCHESTER:
JOHN DALE, STRETFORD ROAD; AND ABEL HEYWOOD AND SON,
56 AND 58, OLDHAM STREET.
LONDON:
SIMPKIN, MARSHALL AND CO., STATIONERS' HALL COURT.
1886.

PREFACE.

———

CRITICS of my story, "The Life of Thomas Wanless, Peasant," demanded my name in varying tones of menace, remonstrance, or entreaty. "Here is a fellow daring to say, anonymously, what is in him," some said. Others cried, "shocking," "monstrous," "cowardly," and what not.

I take the present opportunity to thank these kind, earnest, virtuous, or angry persons for their most flattering curiosity, and to assure them that it is hard to deny a request so widely made. One consideration alone prevents me from yielding to the promptings of a—let us hope—pardonable vanity. These critics have not told me their names. I am, therefore, as much in the dark as they are; but, I hereby give them the assurance that when they reveal their great secret, I will not withhold my little one.

That, surely, is a fair compact, and after volunteering to make it, I hope to hear no more complaints on this head. In the book I now commit to their wisdom my faithful friends will, I trust, find many better inducements to indignation—virtuous or other.

H. A.

Weissnichtwo,
 1st April, 1886.

INDEX.

THE RISE AND PROGRESS

OF

SIR TIMOTHY BUNCOMBE,

—— KT. AND M.P. ——

CHAPTER O.

PEDIGREES OR PARENTS?

As a rule biographies of great men begin with an account of their ancestors. It is a fashion to which there can be no objection, yet I have an impression that I must beg to be excused in this particular instance from following it. That the notable hero of this remarkable history had a father I do not deny, but, this granted, it would, nevertheless, I feel sure, be a gross disregard of Sir Timothy's wishes on that head were I to occupy much space in dealing with the uninteresting fact. A man's father, in short, need not necessarily have aught to do with a man's ancestors. If, therefore, I am to pay strict attention to chronology in this history, the important facts of Sir Timothy's descent ought to be recounted, if recounted at all, much later on. As for his mere parentage, long ere

the hero himself came forward to the footlights of the
stage of life, and shone glorious before the eyes of men, it
had faded into shadowy obscurity.   On the other hand,
in proportion as Sir Timothy developes into a great
public man of potent purse, an ancestry may be said
to emerge for him, and take shape, so that when, at
length, those mysterious personages of the College of
Heralds come to trace out his pedigree, they will find the
materials ready.   It is not their imagination but their
constructive skill which they would have to exercise.

But we are a long way from that happy time, and I
merely allude to it in order to show how serious a
blunder would be committed were I to follow the beaten
track.   It would be impossible thus to attain a just
appreciation of Sir Timothy's character, or to measure the
depth and energy of his talent and persevering quest of
wealth and honours.   Indeed it is, I feel assured, contrary to nature, and possibly to truth, in so many
instances, that it surprises me revolt has not gathered
head against the parentage.   Loyal allegiance to chrono-
logical sequence compels us to recognise it as a remarkable fact that men who emerge from the darkness of
poverty into the day glory of wealth do not at the outset
bethink themselves of claiming kindred with some
mighty slayer of the middle ages, or liege of that magnificent appropriator of other men's goods—Norman
William.   They wait until they themselves have man-
fully by modern recognised methods attained fame as
consumers of the fruits of other men's husbandry.   In
their youth I have known several pushing "money

making " men, as they are designated, resign themselves with a certain degree of patience to the inconvenience of possessing a humble father, or mother, or both. But when success is assured, when the sacks are full of gold, and the man feels himself rich, the necessity for something better in the way of origin becomes imperative. Out of the thaumaturgic past of heraldry there emerges "an ancestry" before whose imposing array of names mere birth and parentage are, and deserve to be, held of no account. Is there a Bruce in the world, be he grocer, jerry builder, or cheap drapery retailer, who, when wealth crowns his long success in dealing with mankind, does not feel called upon to claim descent from the Scoto-Norman King Robert, and adopt for his own use the boastful motto *Fuimus?* Rare indeed is the moneyed man to be found who, though robber true, contents himself, like General Juno, with the glory of producing descendants. No, ancestors are what all men desire whose hands have prospered in the getting of gold. Give me " ancestors," each one says, for without ancestors, be they never so worm-eaten and musty, there is no respectability here below.

Need I say more to justify my desire to observe a due order of procedure regarding Sir Timothy Buncombe's parentage? Consider the matter well. Behold him as he is to-day, a prosperous man, fortune's ball at his foot, the possessor of a knighthood, hopeful of yet higher honours to come. Already this man is in the great transition state which would make it most difficult for me to give a, to him, satisfactory account of his origin and ancestry. His ancestry, in short, is in process of evolution. He himself never by any chance speaks of his youthful days or of his actual origin. The friends of his boyhood, if he ever had any, have all disappeared. Amongst those taking that name who surround him to-day, tales float vaguely about conveying hints of great descent obscured by misfortune. The astonishing Sir Timothy himself encourages that kind of thing, but so far from definite and consistent is his information that legends the most contradictory are now current about his immediate origin. According to one account, his father was a poor half-pay captain who, when past middle age, married rather beneath him and died in poverty. Others will gravely tell you that their friend Sir Timothy had the misfortune to be fathered by a clergyman—a poor curate of excellent family somewhere in Wessex— who married early and died young, leaving a wife and half-a-dozen infants to the tender mercies of the hard world, and harder mother Church. No doubt these and similar legends arise from the indeterminate character of Sir Timothy's own ideas upon the great ancestry question. From the most recent indications, however, I am inclined to believe that he has at last made up his mind to accept a military origin, and to cover up any apparent hesitation or discrepancy in the legends by assigning holy orders either to the half-pay captain's father or to that of his wife, Sir Timothy's mother. Still of this I am by no means sure.

And at this point I am met straight in the face by another important consideration. "This is all very fine," a voice I hear exclaims. " No doubt you are quite right to postpone details of Sir Timothy's officially certified ancestry, till the necessary authenticated documents are before you. You can suppress them altogether for all most people will care ; but if you know the real genuine truth about Sir Timothy's birth and parentage, it is your duty to tell what you know. It will be dishonest if you don't." There, I confess, is a difficulty which had not struck me. Of course I know quite well where Sir Timothy was born, and all about him. I should be unfit for my task as his biographer did I not ; but then it occurred to me that, as Sir Timothy would not like the story told, I had better hold my tongue. The question now is whom shall I obey ? I do not want to wound Sir Timothy's feelings too much, and at the same time, quite naturally, rest assured, it goes against the grain a little to seem to be a party to anything which smacks of prevarication. " Tell the truth," the same voice dins in my ear. But shall I? What becomes of all my excellent precepts just this moment carefully transcribed for the printer in an " execrable small hand " as my envious detractors aver ? I cannot find it in my heart to put my pen through these, and yet—yet it would be such a delicious bit of innocent scandal to lift the curtain which Sir Timothy has so carefully drawn over his early life. And why did I go so many times to Berborough, if not to gather material from which to compile what that poor old schoolmaster of mine used to call " the true facts ? " Ah ! the remembrance of those journeys, and the delightful little incidents and circumstances I fell upon at Berborough decide me. I will take the plunge. To the winds with your pedigrees and your parsons and captains. Sir Timothy, I defy you! I fear you not. You shall stand before the world, not what you desire to be considered, but what you have been, what you are.

There! am I not heroic as that perfect gentleman, new style, my Lord Capanbells, when he tweaked his political leader's nose for the first time? Happy as he too am I, for I hate conventionalities. Of what use are the stilted formal records of a great man's life? He accomplished this, he attained to that, was honoured in something else, his humble duty he conceived to be to amass so much wealth withal, and when the day's work was done no man loved better a good dinner and a glass of old port. Faugh! away with these dullards. Never mind the scoundrels of old, let us speak of the——. Hum! I have lost myself again. Really this is too much in the manner of the just mentioned distinguished descendant of a last century man-eater of talent, now so deftly gaminising our political manners. Sobriety becomes me better. I will leave preliminaries, and to my task. This most veracious history shall begin at the beginning.

And, accordingly, as this chapter counts for nothing, nothing shall it be. That will be considered an innovation, and, in a biography, perhaps it is ; but our weather prophets have given the example, and I do not see why they should claim exclusive property in their invention. Nought is a very good figure wherewith to number a chapter of a book that may possibly be no more to the purpose than a prediction in a weather chart.

CHAPTER I.

OF the facts set forth in the following pages there can
be no reasonable doubt. I have verified them. There
is not a special correspondent or press interview con-
cocter in existence at this present moment who has
taken more pains to crystalise and adorn vague hear-
say or gossip than I have. Sir Timothy Buncombe may
not like it, but I know the truth; and knowing now
likewise my duty, the truth shall be told in the way that
best pleases myself. Facts are facts, come by them how
a man may. And amongst the most important of the
facts with which I shall have to deal, it seems to me we
must rank the birth of the great Sir Timothy himself.
This event occurred in the important east coast seaport
of Berborough. At the time of its occurrence, which
was a few years before the first Reform Bill let loose
democracy upon our most noble oligarchy to demand
from it, much to its disgust, sundry forms of outward
respect for certain precepts of the moral law of Moses,
the honoured mother of this wonderful boy was in
possession of a small baker's shop, in a back street of the
town. Either at that time, or soon after, this little shop
became noted in the locality for the excellence of its

mutton pies. This shop, I have ascertained, exists still, although, such is life's uncertainty, " Buncombe pies " are no longer sold thereat. Sir Timothy himself put an end to that trade by purchasing, with some of his earliest acquired surplus wealth, the right of the then occupant to use the name. Rumour says that he gave about five times as much for it as his mother had obtained when she sold out and retired from business; but that may be slander.

Regarding Sir Timothy's true father, I must confess, little was to be learned when I undertook this severe labour. Happily, however, we are not much concerned with him, or for that matter, with any Buncombe of the family except Sir Timothy himself. The old man, I take it, had little or nothing to do with the baking business, which was conducted by his wife. I am able, however, to assert without fear of contradiction, that he had been a soldier, had risen from full private to the rank of sergeant in a foot regiment, and escaping death in the field, had retired at last into civil life, blessed with an excellent thirst and a pension of one shilling and six-pence per diem. Furthermore, it appears to be true that this battered defender of his country, in the quarrels got up by its supreme land-grabbers, was not a native of Berborough, and had no relations there.

It is doubtful, indeed, whether he ever had had any relations beyond the inevitable father and mother— shadowy individuals, possessed, it may be, with a spirit of gloomy pietism, for they had named their child Jeremiah. Jeremiah Buncombe—there stands the man. Not a man who wept and wailed much himself, but the cause, alas! of many Jeremiads uttered by his wife. For "Old Sergeant Bunny," as he was called, made up for lack of relations by the abundance of his pot-house companions. How he behaved with them I gathered from the lips of an ancient beer-shop keeper, who declared to me on his " most solemn ' Davy ' " that he had known the old sergeant " more'n forty year agone." Amongst other statements made to me by this man was the following : " I recollect," said he, " as little Tim "—that's our hero—" came reglar to fetch his owd feyther hum at ten o'cluk o' neet for the first fortnight o' every month. Th' owd chap drank steady, day in and out all that time, 'ee did. Then his pension money giv out and 'ee wor kind o' sober like, let aione drinks from chums, till next pay day. His owd 'oman never giv' him a brass farthin'."

Should this garrulous old tapster have told the truth, must we not forgive his son, Sir Timothy, for endeavouring to get himself another father ? Yes, let us be merciful, for how many of us are there who would like to swop fathers with some other fellow we know, if we only could. Better no father at all than this old sot. But do I believe the bar-keeper's tale ? Dare I throw over on such testimony all the gentle legend of the retired, poverty-struck half-pay officer ? Indeed, I fear I must. A strong suspicion, amounting almost to certainty, possesses me, that the tale of Sir Timothy is a mere poetical version of the bar-keeper's prose. And how about the clerical ancestor ? Ah ! there conjecture alone avails me, and I can only hazard the guess that some venerable progenitor of Serjeant Jeremiah, the " poor half-pay officer," may have been a methodist hedge preacher. Be that as you like—I have no prejudices in the matter—there is little room to question my tapster's tale. The "public" he kept had been his father's, and he himself had bibulously lived in it all his life. Beer had soddened him, no doubt; but his memory of this long-dead past was clear enough, and he was able to describe the serjeant in a way that left no mistake possible.

"Rayther a tallish man 'ee wor," my friend continued, growing loquacious over the second quart of "old and bitter," "'ee went limp, limp, becase 'ee wor left fut lame. A bullet 'it un in t' eel at th' battle of—of—blow me if I can tell ye the battle it wor. My mem'ry's a gettin not worth a pint o' fourpenny! Well, anyways, 'ee be a cripple, an' I mind 'ee had bleery eyes an' wor a'most blind, an' th' nose on 'is face wor sort o' dirty brick red like, all along o' snuff and liquor. An' 'ee told rum yarns of th' fights i' furrin parts—werry rum. Let me see, I recollect one in pertikler,"—

"Ah, do you?" I struck in. "Well, never mind it now, I'm very much obliged to you for what you have told me. I had heard of the old serjeant, you see, and was given to understand you had known him. So I just took the liberty of calling upon you to make sure, as it were, that there ever was such a man."

"Ever wos such a man! Lord bless ye, yes ; acoors there was. Ay, an' didn't 'ee swear at 'is boy Tim in style—him as be a big wig now—wen t' kid coomed to fetch un o' nights. His cusses was summat hawful, sir.

Never heerd th' like, 'cep once wen a dectective cove nabbed a confidence trick 'federate in this 'ere bar; 'ee wos sittin' a'most wer ye be, sir. Gad, 'ee did let his tongue go that un. Well, owd Serjeant Bunny did th' same, but th' baarn never let on as 'ee heerd un, and ony wen blows seemed a comin' did Tim wake up. He dodged th' owd un's stick as nimble as a street hackrey-bait. It allus ended in Tim's shoutin' round th' door jamb, 'An' ye doant coom hoam wi' me sure's death I'll fotch t' mother.' Heh! heh! Th' serjeant nivver went agin that threat for all th' game his set made at un. Ah, dear!" added the ancient, with a wistful glance at his nearly empty pewter, " them wos rum times, sir—werry rum. Eh! wen dee'd 'ee, sir, did ye say? Let me see. Why, it must be nigh five and thritty year agone, sir. Folks did say as his owd 'oman—she was a hard un and no misteak—a'most starved un. She ketched un a priggin brass for drink; but it was a stroke as knocked him over at th' finish."

Such are the main features of this ancient man's recollections—faithfully reported, I flatter myself, in a style that might do credit to the most expert manufacturer of newspaper flapdoodle now bestriding this moral world. More I need not add. The tapster, hoary bivalve of the beer shop, has sufficiently introduced the retired "half-pay officer," and it is our duty to turn to the mother. A Frenchman would have put the latter first, but we know better how to treat women in this country. For *place aux Dames* our manly tongue has no equivalent. Nevertheless, Mrs. Buncombe must be noticed. She was a woman of importance, and, as has been related, made famous mutton pies.

But with the utmost possible desire to present her to the myriads of readers destined to consume this book, I am unable to do so. A graphic mother-gossip to play fellow to the interesting beerseller, did not, I will swear it, exist in all Berborough when I was there, and Mrs. Buncombe died before the days of cheap photography. If any travelling scissors artist ever took her silhouette, that memento of his skill and of an excellent woman, has been lost. My tapster had seen her, of course, and bought pies from her honoured hand ; but, boy as he was, the image of the woman never appears to have imprinted itself on the sodden tissues of his mind. He thought she was of small stature, and was certain she was stout and dark-haired, and that her voice was sharp and shrill, as was to be expected from its constant exercise. A husband such as she possessed would naturally develop the vocal capacity, and try the temper of the best of women. I have not the least doubt myself that her display of virtue was overpowering. By the mere force of contrast between her own sober industrious habits, and the wasteful, idle drunkenness of her husband, Mrs. Buncombe must have been driven to look upon herself as a woman with few equals. The more her husband wasted, the more she would pinch and work and save, and the more likewise would she dwell on the superlative excellence of her character. The habitual want of any recognition of these far shining good qualities on the part of her husband, would, it may be hazarded, produce no sweetening results on her temper, and the self-assertion necessary to cause the least glimmer of the truth to enter his muddled head, would naturally develop with use, until it affected her intercourse with the entire household. Perhaps, therefore, it is just as well that I am not in a position to bestow much information upon the reader concerning this remarkable woman. Her virtues have died with her, hidden in the unmarked grave, where Sir Timothy—mere Mister then, and comparatively poor—laid husband and wife together, thankful, shall we say, to have wound up the low affair of his parentage.

There were more children than Timothy — several more of both sexes I was told. Some of these are said to be still above ground, but where and how employed, it does not concern my purpose to say, even if I knew, which I will not assert too confidently that I do. This much, however, may be admitted. Not a single man or woman of the family ever raised head above the level of the common herd, save Timothy alone. Before the mother died they had all left Berborough, except himself, and he alone remains our triumphant hero—the man who has succeeded. It would be beneath the dignity of this narrative to concern ourselves with failures. Timothy was, as he deserved to be, his mother's favourite from the first. She may have had a dream about him, or he may have early learned to flatter her, or it may have been a chance humour. It is useless to fathom the cause now, but the effect lives and is visible still in the person of her noble son. Because his mother loved him above her other sons and daughters, she gave him a better education than they. When the others went to work, departed young to go their several ways, among the ever surging press of fools who fail, Timothy continued at school.   Berborough Grammar School was the place that possessed the honour of superintending his education. There he picked up sundry shreds of classical lore, and a knowledge of arithmetic, which stood him in good stead in after days.

As a schoolboy Timothy gave little indication of his future capacity for great estate, but, if the legends still current be true his boyhood did not belie the talents of his after years.   He never got into scrapes, although often the cause of affliction to others.   Studious after a fashion, young Tim was likewise in some ways an idler, though never caught idling.   His most noticeable characteristic, perhaps, was a power he had of picking the brains of his schoolfellows, and of appropriating to his own use the fruits of their laborious studies.   Games of strength and skill he cared not for, but at games of chance his smartness cost his mates no small share of their slender allowance of pocket money.

CHAPTER II.

PIETISM AND PROGRESS.

SOMEWHERE about the age of fifteen this education was
brought to a close by a very natural event. Timothy's
thrifty mother had heard that a shipbroker in the town
wanted a smart lad as messenger and general office
drudge. Timothy, it occurred to her, was a smart lad,
and as he would one day have to earn his living, he
might just as well begin at once. Prompt action followed this thought. The boy was inspected by the
broker and accepted on the spot. A joyful boy was he.
The shipowner was an expanding man in a large way of
business, and had once and again made clerks in his
office partners in the firm, as preliminary to a mortal
and everlasting rupture with them. Timothy then, was
delighted, for he had already begun to dream of a greater
future than was embraced within the range of the
mutton pie fame. It was, therefore, with high hopes
that he entered on his duties, throwing his primers
behind him.

But his mind soon underwent disillusionment. To be
office messenger for Mr. Brown, Mr. Silas Brown,
Deacon Silas Brown, to arrive at the full glory, was all
very well, but to be office fag to all the clerks was not

so well. Timothy resented the way these clerks treated him with all the force of his nature, but he was much too prudent a lad to disclose his feelings. No : he bent before the blows and kicks distributed freely for his benefit ; answered meekly, when sworn at, and strove his best to please everybody. He was a supple lad in short, but holding hard to a fixed idea, even when most doubled up. Come what might, kick and curse who might, Timothy had entered that office resolved to get on, and he did get on. The very hatred which his meek sycophancy inspired amongst the clerks in a sense assisted him in getting on, endowed him with a determination to show them one day what he could do.

Amongst the maternal duties which Mrs. Buncombe of the pies had in great measure neglected was the inculcation of religious dogma. The good lady, not discerning perhaps, what she could get by it, never went to church herself, and put no constraint upon any member of her family to go, so that it would have been hard to say whether she leaned most towards the establishment or towards dissent. And her son was naturally in this indeterminate condition of mind when he became an inmate of Deacon Silas Brown's office. Not long did he remain in that unregenerate state. Deacon Brown was a "leading pillar," a "shining light," or something of that sort, in the most ∙fashionable Independent Chapel of Berborough, With that intuitive genius which afterwards so distinctly marked off Timothy Buncombe from his fellow men, the lad no sooner ascertained the truth about his master in this respect, than he decided to go to that chapel likewise. Without in any way seeming to thrust himself forward, he dutifully attended divine service twice every Sunday, and filled up the afternoon by going to the Sunday School, which he found to be an institution specially under the patronage of his employer.

As Master Timothy had perhaps calculated, "exemplary" behaviour of this kind on the part of a youth whose "spiritual education" had been notoriously overlooked, soon began to attract the attention of Mr. Brown. The deacon took a fancy for the quiet well-behaved lad, and, when opportunity arose promoted him, because, being young, he was obtainable cheap.

Thus it came about that before he had attained the age of twenty-one, Timothy Buncombe had risen to be chief of the outward freight department of the office, a post which brought him into daily contact with all the Berborough merchants who had goods to send abroad. The duties of this post Timothy fulfilled with so much cleverness that his employer began to be quite proud of him. The pious deacon considered the lad as in some sort of his own rearing, and grew to repose a trust in him which his past experience of clerks and of clerk partners, had made him vow—Mr. Brown always vowed, never swore—he would never place in any human being again.

Nor was it at the office alone that Timothy throve and advanced. From being a sweet-tempered Sunday school scholar who might perhaps shed a tear, but who never hit the boy who stuck pins in him, or peached in public on the sneak who dropped cayenne pepper down his back, Timothy had developed into the position of a teacher, equally sweet tempered and "exemplary." He attended week-day prayer meetings too, and led the tenor voices in the choir on Sunday, with an unction of look and manner that proved most edifying to more than one old woman of the flock. "He was such a nice good young man," they said; "and to think what a poor 'ome he had."

Ay, there was the rub. This matter of "'ome" was the one supreme trouble of Timothy's life at that time. His father was indeed gone for good ere this, but the mother remained, still in her pie shop. The fame of those mutton pies Timothy began to look at in the light of a direct personal insult to himself. It lowered his social "status" in the eyes of the well-to-do Christians of the fashionable dissenting flock, among whom "his lot had been cast," to be known as the son of a pie wife in a back street in the poor quarters of the town. In the eyes of the best scented and most expensively dressed godliness which shone in dazzling humility, an example to the congregation, this was a damaging circumstance there was no getting over. Had Mrs. Buncombe been poor, and come begging and whining round the flock in her poverty, something of this vulgarity might have been forgiven. Timothy could in that case have figured before men as a living example of the democratic charity and brotherly love of the independent order of Christians. Mrs. Buncombe, however, had enough for her wants, and scorned church and chapel alike, and her son was therefore a brand saved from the burning indeed, but one all too hot and smoky to be familiarly handled.

As Mrs. Peregrine Wipple, the wife of the senior deacon of the chapel put it to her friends, "How can I invite this young man to my monthly tea parties when I have four daughters all unmarried, each of whom, by the blessing of the Lord, will take a portion of three thousand pounds to the man as has her."

How indeed! Until he got his mother out of her shop, and out of the way, Timothy's matrimonial chances were as good as nothing at all among the daughters of the sanctified well-to-do. Oft and again was this truth "borne in upon his spirit" as he saw himself left out in the cold, and had it not been for the success which his piety brought him on the office side of his career, it is doubtful whether Timothy would have possessed the strength to persevere. To be meek in the office in the cuffing and kicking days was easy compared with the task now set him at the chapel. Happily his blood was not of the boiling sort, and in submitting to be condescended upon by the big people of the congregation, Timothy was at least acquiring the first principles of the art of condescending to others for his own future use.

His office successes consoled him, did I say? Well, they did; yet, strange as it will seem to intelligent students of this model biography, Timothy had still an uneasy time of it with his brother clerks. They no longer, of course, struck him with fist or foot, but their tongues often smote full as sore. Reprobates that they were, these clerks called his meek piety "humbug," and they lost no opportunity that rudeness could give, or malice create, of indicating their perverted view of what they vulgarly described as "Young Bunny's lickspittle toadying to old 'Skin-'em-alive.'" Much of this low-class ill-will may be ascribed to jealousy. By the time he was twenty-three, Timothy had become the confidant and right hand man of Deacon Brown, his employer, leaping into that position clear over the heads of men old enough to be his father. What more natural, then, than that these men, being unregenerate, should hate him, speak evil of him behind his back, and throw open or covert sneers at him before his face.

The very "exemplariness" of the young man was a standing reproach to some of the supplanted. They persisted in getting drunk now and then on festive occasions; Timothy drank water. They were not always scrupulously clean in morals; Timothy avoided "strange women" as the Levite avoided the man fallen among thieves. Most of the younger clerks—half-a-dozen, I believe—laid bets on horses, boat races, or regattas. The words "bet," "wager," "sweep," &c., were never heard to pass the lips of the holy young man, who was his master's delight. Timothy, in short, was a perfect being, whereas his fellows were quite ordinary creatures. So they misunderstood him, and made things rough for him when they could. One day, when an irate old skipper called him a "snivelling young hypocrite" in the office, these reprobates broke into sounds very like a muffled cheer.

But drags of this sort did the young man good after all. The more the demi-gods and goddesses of the chapel condescended, the more the clerks of Deacon Brown's office jibed and sneered, the more determined did Timothy become to be even with them—in his own way and time. To, as it were, throw down the gauntlet to the gilded saints at the chapel he zealously organised a "young men's society for Bible study," which assembled on Sunday mornings at ten. Of this class he took the lead, and in "expounding the Scriptures" to it he acquired additional glibness of tongue.

At the office no counter demonstration of this kind was facile, but as a means to an end, Timothy took increased pains to possess himself of his master's business secrets. This he succeeded in doing to an extent which Mr. Brown never suspected. No letter escaped him, a glance at the page of his master's private ledger, the tone of voice with which a remark would be dropped in the ear of a caller, any and every clue Timothy laid hold of for increasing his web of knowledge. And he was so meek and soft looking amid all this prying that his master trusted him more and more, which was a strange thing enough in so great a player on the gullibility of his fellow men.

Deacon Brown was one of the most militantly religious men in Berborough, and a professed teetotaler. Nevertheless, he kept a bottle of brandy in a cupboard in his room, and he had by no means a high reputation for uprightness among his trading neighbours. He ought, therefore, to have been suspicious of Timothy Buncombe, and the more that young man struck the zealot's attitude, the more should he have been on his guard. This, at any rate, is what you and I think we should have been. But we pronounce in haste. The deacon confided in Timothy, not because he believed in his expressions of piety, but because he considered the young man simple enough to think that they were genuine and that they would wear. To his mind Timothy's pietism was an unsophisticated thing, the product of a raw, enthusiastic, innocent mind. Hence his confidence ; but had he been aware that Timothy knew all about his brandy bottle, and his little tricks of trade in the shipping line, his views might, no doubt, have been what yours and mine would be.

CHAPTER III.

MARRIAGE AND MISCALCULATION.

FROM the course of this narrative it will be clear to the reader that Timothy Buncombe was at this period of his life both sharp and sly. I do not wish to combat that view of his character for one moment, and yet it must be admitted, however reluctantly, that the young man was not sharp all round. He had his weak side, and it was to be found, I think, in the determination he had so early arrived at to get on in the world, somehow. His eagerness, in this respect, caused him to be rash at times, and, as this history will shew, led him into more than one unfortunate mistake during the course of his active life.

The first of these mistakes consisted in taking to himself a wife. The Sir Timothy of to-day hints in his open moments, I believe, that this has been the only mistake he ever committed. Be that as it may, Timothy did unquestionably perpetrate the blunder of marriage. I do not excuse him for so doing. It may have been chapel morality, with its desperate severity on strange women and lean purses ; it may have been sudden passion, I cannot quite say. Nor indeed are we concerned with aught save the great fact, and how it occurred.

The motives of the smart, pushing young man, were without doubt, mixed ; but then an eminent dissenting divine has taught us that all men's motives are so. Timothy therefore cannot be censured on that ground alone ; nor would it be wise, perhaps, to censure him on any ground hastily, as you must see, when all the history of this blunder is known to you.

First of all, the isolated position of the young man has to be duly weighed. Since first the silk clad matrons of the flock overlooked him, he had to some degree risen in the social scale.   At the age of twenty-three he was earning one hundred pounds a year, exclusive of perquisites from shippers, insurance agents, and such like. His mother too had sold her pie shop, invested the proceeds and other savings in an annuity, and retired along with her youngest daughter to a snug cottage about twenty miles from Berborough, so that though the Buncombe pies still commanded fame, Buncombe's self was in no wise connected with them.   Nevertheless, the stale odours of his low origin hung about him and kept the "'omes" of Deacon Wipple and other rich holy persons of Goliath chapel closed to him for all practical purposes. Timothy, through no fault of his own, let us admit, had consequently to seek his society in lower social grades, where wealth might be, but where refinement certainly was not.   Need I say more to justify him in falling in love with the buxom round cheeked, giggling, ignorant, vain little maiden, Miss Penelope Drabble? Did I say fall in love? Forgive me ; the language is conventional, but in this instance, perhaps, inapposite. Timothy

liked the lass, but loved her guineas—in prospect—
more.

Of actual wealth Miss Penelope had none. She was
an orphan, and resided with an uncle and aunt, who
had no child. This uncle, Mr. Bob Cutler by name,
kept a dingy, not over clean, chandler's shop on the quay
of the outer harbour. It had not a high reputation this
shop, but that was entirely because of its owner. Mr.
Cutler traded much with sailors, with the skippers of
small coasting vessels, and the like. In the course of
business he had acquired a reputation for exacting high
interest, and for smuggling propensities second to none
in Berborough. But Mr. Bob Cutler had never been
caught by the authorities, so that the only definite
product of this reputation was an increase of respect on
the part of his immediate neighbours, by whom he was
reputed to be wealthy. It was an obvious inference
deduced from his long success as a trafficker in questionable goods with questionable men. Outwardly, however,
the old ship's chandler was just the same ill clad, rough,
swearing, untidy fellow he had been thirty years before.

Had the matter depended upon him, Mr. Timothy
Buncombe, the primly proper young man, would never
have committed the mistake of marrying Miss Penelope
Drabble. The orbits of the two men could never have
crossed. All the blame of this mishap must rest with
Mrs. Cutler and the girl herself. Both of them attended
chapel regularly every Sunday, and Miss Penelope—her
aunt called her Penny, "for short"—effected the conquest
of Mr. Timothy Buncombe in her capacity as a member

of the chapel choir. Her noisy habit of continuous loud giggling first attracted his attention, and then he heard of her money. After that he paid more attention to her until the giggle was for him subdued into a purr. By and by the habit grew up of seeing the young lady home from the choir practisings, and that in its turn paved the way for invitations on the part of Mrs. Cutler, to stay and have a bit of supper. Insensibly a friendly intimacy was established with the entire household, even Mr. Bob Cutler himself condescending occasionally to abuse radicals and parsons for Timothy's benefit.

Were the "inward truth" of the matter known it is probable that Mrs. Cutler would be found to have done her best to entangle this modest, innocent young man with her niece. Gossips did allege this to her credit or debit, but without other proof than that supplied by the old woman's extreme graciousness of bearing to the "dear young man who alleys looked so pale and interestin' like," and by the unquestioned fact that she, good woman, had poor relations of her own—Penny was her husband's niece—to whom she not unnaturally wished some of the usurious smuggler's hoard to pass. Penny once out of sight, it was possible that she might be out of mind when Mr. Cutler's last will and testament came to be made.

I am not sure, though, that the gossips of that day did know of this motive, for Mrs. Cutler never vaunted her blood relations, but Timothy Buncombe had plenty of scope for suspicion of her motives in after years. At the time he engaged himself to wed Miss Penelope he knew nothing at all. On the contrary, his mind was more and more fixed upon the lift in life the marriage would give him, for he had heard the old uncle swear at tenants behind with their rents, or demanding repairs and so on, expressions which increased the ardour of his affection more and more for the lady of his choice. Visions of a partnership with Mr. Silas Brown would rise before him and set his bosom aglow with such a fierce heat that he deceived himself, and felt convinced of an overpowering affection for his betrothed. In the pale auroral light of his day dreams she sometimes appeared to him almost beautiful, whereas he knew in his duller hours that she was in a manner commonplace, her private adventure ladies' seminary varnish notwithstanding.

A more surprising contrast, indeed, than these two people presented then and ever afterwards could scarcely be imagined. Mr. Timothy was tall, rather dark, and thin. He had a sharp, prominent nose ; a high, lumpy, but rather retreating forehead ; small, glittering, gery eyes ; a large, but firmly lined, mouth, with small regular teeth, and a square, massive, though remarkably short, chin. His arms were long in proportion to his height, five feet eleven inches, and his hands were thin, with tapering bony fingers.

Miss Penelope, on the other hand, was, as I have already remarked, short and stout. The most imaginative of male bipeds could not have held her to be a beauty. At her then age of nineteen she had a fresh clear complexion, no doubt ; but her enemies, and rivals perhaps, in the choir were not unjust in declaring that

she had not a good feature in her face. Not even her
eyes were good. They were largish, but without glow,
and of a pale kind of brown that promised early fading.
As for her other features, to take them in order, her
forehead was low and round, not square ; a heavy thatch
of frizzy, brown hair hung over it, hiding the parting
often, and bestowing on her a slightly unkempt look.
Flattish bright red cheeks but ill supported this pent
house-like upper storey. They were in keeping, however, with the nose, which was not flat exactly, nor yet
true pug, but stunted and knobby. Fleshy lips, that
were always wide open to display large, strong, and ill-
arranged teeth, and a round fat chin, with a dimple in it,
completed an inane sort of countenance, prepossessing
merely in its freshness.

Her habit of giggling always when young men were
near, earned her the reputation of merry-heartedness—
a reputation her wooer accepted without demur or
question. I dare not truthfully avow that he troubled
himself much with any of the qualities of his bride,
mental or physical, so far away was he in the land of his
dreams, during his courting days. Only when the die was
cast did Mr. Timothy ruefully open his eyes to the fact
that his wife was, in spite of the seminary varnish,
ignorant and underbred ; ignorant, not merely of polite
learning, but of the commonest attributes of housewifery ;
so indescribably ignorant, that when they returned from
their honeymoon he had to instruct her how to make a
cup of coffee. Her plan, and she asserted it was her
immaculate aunt's, was to put ground coffee in the cup

and pour boiling water over it. When the mixture settled, if it did settle, the beverage was ready.

Attempts at instruction on small matters of this kind soon disclosed to Mr. Timothy Buncombe that he had been rash in setting his bride down as a good humoured woman. To his amazement he found that she was petulent, wilful, impatient of the least contradiction, full of the spirit of grumbling, and above all, jealous of her skill and knowledge just where she possessed least of either. In short, Miss Penelope Drabble, when metamorphosed into Mrs. Timothy Buncombe, approved herself the spoilt child of her vulgar old uncle. Like him she was whimsically obstinate, uncouth in manners and speech, and credulous of absurdities as any witch worshipper of the middle ages. If now and then a faint suspicion of all this did cross Mr. Timothy Buncombe's mind before marriage it was instantly swept away by the remembrance of the good stroke of fortune he was playing. His wife would have money. Ah, how sweet that phrase sounds in the mammon believer's ear! Fairness compels me, however, to call the reader's attention to the young man's complete ignorance of the society of cultivated, well bred women. Far down in the scale as his bride was, she was higher by several degrees than his mother had been. That hard working woman used the language of a trooper when her temper was active, which was generally, if we can believe tradition, all day long.

When all is said I still feel that this marriage of a great man is a thing not to be lightly got over. He

must have been infatuated after all with the girl, else,
how on earth did he come to neglect the money question
when the wedding was decided upon and the " 'appy day"
fixed ?   Perhaps Mr. Bob Cutler's large way of talking
lulled his acquisitive instinct to sleep.

But it is no use : I really cannot account for this
weakness on the part of so great a man.   All I can plead
in his behalf is that he never did the like again.   "Love "
may have been in the case—love of a sort—and over
sanguineness ; ignorance, too, of Mrs. Cutler's designs on
behalf of her own relations.   It is a painful subject
altogether, which I would fain avoid.   But alas ; there
stands the hard fact—Timothy Buncombe got married—
not secretly in a hole and corner way, but openly in the
full blaze of congregational publicity and newspaper
advertisement.   There, in Goliath Chapel, on a bleak
December morning, the youthful couple stood and vowed
eternal love.   It was a Saturday morning.   Timothy had
obtained a few days' holiday for the purpose of getting
the matrimonial knot tied.

But bleak as the day was it did not prevent the chapel
from being attended by a tolerably large crowd of
witnesses.   Old maids were there, and young, sighing
over the lost past, dreaming of like scenes in the near
future.   Some, perhaps, stood there to gaze upon the
burial of a hope, for Timothy Buncombe was as
popular as all pious young men are in chapel flocks, and
may have been loved in secret by more than one sweet
maid.   These bade him farewell in their hearts, and sent
him parting gifts.

Indeed, for a poor man, the number of the marriage presents showered upon Timothy was quite surprising, especially when it is considered that the ceremony took place before the days when such presents are levied upon the friends and foes of brides and bridegrooms with all the unpitying ruthlessness of parish taxes. Shall we see in this phenomenon also " mixed motives ? "

You can if you like. I say nothing, but in my own mind have no doubt that both Mrs. Deacon Wipple and Mrs. Deacon Brown, with other pious matrons who had daughters to marry well, felt deep gratitude to *their* Providence and to Mr. Timothy Buncombe, that for them all danger was over. That they should express this gratitude in little gifts to the happy pair, was, you will allow, only natural.

From one cause or another the presents were numerous. Timothy's employer presented him with a handsome chapel hymn-book with tunes, bound in French morocco. It had a long pious inscription on the fly-leaf. His Sunday morning Bible class subscribed together, and gave him a huge inkstand, in imitation cut glass, with plenty of brass ornaments about it, and a penholder warranted unusable. A suitable inscription adorned this present likewise. One old lady admirer presented the bridegroom with a Bible of the S. P. C. K., bound in roan. Even the minister of the flock himself felt moved to " bestow his mite," as he put it, which mite consisted in a copy, price two shillings, of the " Evidences of Christianity," by some unknown American Divine. As for the bride, gloves and pocket-handkerchiefs were showered upon her by the dozen pairs, and pin-cushions and anti-macassars; and from the uncle and aunt a pair of fifteen-carat gold earrings and a silver-gilt brooch set with pebbles. When the newly-wedded pair came to add up these possessions, products of the " love " of their friends, they found that, besides the articles I have enumerated, they possessed two bibles—one a cheap family bible—five pencil-cases, say silver, four hymn-books, two "Sturm's Reflections," and three "Bogatzky's Golden Treasury;" a thimble, also silver, and nearly a dozen "ladies' companions," or other similar pocket books for the new year.

Altogether the wedding was a triumphant success from every point of view, except one. The most pious and truth-speaking devotee, male or female, in the whole flock could scarcely lift up voice and assert that the pair were well matched. As the two stood by the pulpit, listening to the ceremony which was to make them one, they presented a great contrast indeed, but not a match. The tall, dark, sallow-faced, clean shaven young man bent over the stout little ruddy woman in front of him as a gaunt fir-tree might be imagined to overshadow a gaudy poppy.

" But, bless your heart, looks aint nothing at all to do with 'appiness." as Mrs. Cutler dogmatically asserted twenty times a day to her neighbour gossips when discussing the chances and prospects of her " darling Penny " as the wife of this tall, ascetic-looking young Christian professor. And she may have been right. Had other things been equal, it is possible that Timothy Buncombe and his wife might have jogged along in the quietude of provincial obscurity till their journey's end. But then there would have been no occasion to write this history ; there would have been no Sir Timothy, perhaps; nothing great and resplendent to record. A good wife, even a well-to-do wife, might have lulled ambition to sleep.

As matters turned out, the blasting of Mr. Timothy Buncombe's expectations—not in the woman, she was at best quite secondary in his imagination—but in regard to the cash proved just the spur required to impel him on his high career. The foolish young man—I write it in sadness—had indulged his fond imagination with the pleasant hope that the warm-hearted uncle would present him with a thousand pounds at least to start the world with. It was a hope destined to suffer cruel wreck. When the newly yoked pair entered the cab which was to convey them to the station after the wedding breakfast had been duly consumed, Mr. Cutler followed them, and thrust a five-pound note into the bridegroom's hand with a wink, and a " Here you are, my boy, go and enjoy yourselves, and this'll 'elp pay the reck'ning. By-by: 'eaven bless ye both."

They were going to Harrogate to stay from Saturday night till the following Wednesday morning, so that Mr. Cutler had evidently decided not to allow them too much latitude of purse. But he slapped his nephew-in-law on the back so cheerily as he pushed him into the cab after his bride, and waved his hand so demonstratively as they rolled away, that when Timothy examined the note he felt little surprised. This is an earnest of what is to

C

come, he thought. Still, five pounds was rather little, unaccompanied as it was by any promise of more.

More! There seemed to be no thought of more even when the pair came back and commenced housekeeping. A week passed, a fortnight, and no money came, nor hint of money. Timothy grew sulky, then cross with his wife, then in a rage with himself, and finally took a resolution. He would procure by softness and guile, as it were, what had been denied him by right. Raging at his wife he found led to no good result whatever. It only served to reveal to him the fact that she likewise had a tongue, and a sharp one, too. Therefore he took the soft way, and smiled and spoke gently as of yore.

By this method he soon resumed such an ascendancy over Mrs. Timothy that she was ready to play the beggar for him with her uncle. This also turned out a poor speculation. Mrs. Timothy wept, Mrs. Timothy raged, Mrs. Timothy objurgated and made herself a torment to the old man, and all she got by her labour was a miserable fifty pounds, doled out reluctantly, note by note, over a period of nearly six months, by the hard-fisted wretch. At the end of that time the aunt intervened, and plainly told Mrs. Timothy that "if this 'ere yapping after her 'usband's 'ard won savin's wasn't dropped," she, Mrs. Cutler, would forbid her the house. Oh, the chagrin of it! Gloom, despair, disgust ; what passion save love and pity exists in human hearts that Timothy Buncombe did not feel when this threat reached his ears. For this had he married a dowdy, as, in his rage, he called his wife—for this, oh, horror, wrecked his prospects in life.

Let us leave him to his meditations and curses. The pen I possess is not strong enough to depict the conflict which raged in that great man's soul at this time. Here was he, barely twenty-four years of age, a married man, with the prospects of having a family, settled down in a miserable little cottage with a stupid wife and a salary of one hundred pounds per annum, with small prospect of its ever reaching two hundred pounds. Contrast the actual fact with the day dream, and imagine the mind of Timothy Buncombe if you are able. If not, do as I do, leave him alone.

He had only one hope left ; Robert Cutler, Esquire, landlord of working-class tenements in bad repair and overcrowded, ship chandler, money lender, and dealer in smuggled goods, must die some day, and then the money he hoarded might come to Mrs. Timothy. Alas! so relentless is fate, even this hope did not last out the first year of wedded life. In one of their now frequent tiffs his wife, his "Dear Penny," let out some of her aunt's family secrets. " She had two nieces, three nephews, and ever so many cousins among the miners of Forgeshire," said Mrs. Penelope, " and she declares as how she'll make my uncle leave all's money to them if we don't mind what we're about."

This was the last straw. Speechless over it before men, Mr. Timothy, pious still and " exemplary," could only pray out his grief. At the next weekly prayer meeting he is reported to have held forth in this strain :

" Oh, Lord God, this is a wicked, wicked world. It is full of the habitations of horrid cruelty, which man would hide even from Thine eyes, oh, Lord God. Men are possessed with greed, and hoard up gold instead of looking to the welfare of their souls. The poor are oppressed that some may walk in the vain show of ill-gotten wealth. But Thou knowest all things, oh! Lord, and in Thy sight the darkest secrets of man's iniquity stand revealed clear as the sun at noon. When Thou dost choose to exert Thy might all wrongs shall be righted and all the oppressed set free."

"A beautiful prayer," the devotees said, and so it was, no doubt, because the heart of the speaker was charged with his own wrongs. The Cutlers, husband and wife, were his oppressors, and in his devotions he cursed them. To the old women of the prayer meeting, this was a beautiful, because a sincere prayer, one that quite justified the observation several of them made that the dear young man's marriage seemed to have developed a deeper vein of piety in him than he had ever shown before. The Dissenting divine was right. Men's motives are mixed.

Timothy had married for money, heeding not the woman much, and lo! the woman was now everything. It might have been so had the cash come with her, for these gilded marriages mostly bring the despised woman to the first place, whether she be hid in sacks of gold or not. It is with the woman, not with the fortune, the husband finds he has to do.

CHAPTER IV.

A FOUNDERED SHIP, AND JONAH IN THE WHALE'S BELLY.

PROFOUNDLY interesting as the study of the earlier development of Mr. Timothy Buncombe's character is, I must, nevertheless, leave him for a time, to expand as it were in darkness and silence, enjoying what domestic bliss was open to him. This I feel to be necessary, both for the reader's sake and my own. A too painfully minute portraiture might be disagreeable. Besides, at this point it becomes necessary to the proper understanding of the great man's future career, that a closer acquaintance should be made with Timothy's employer—Mr., or Deacon, Silas Brown.

Considering indeed the deacon's own peculiar greatness, it is to no small extent a slight upon him that he has been so long neglected, left unintroduced, as it were. In his own esteem, at all events, Mr. Brown was one of the greatest men in Berborough, and decidedly the most important member of Goliath chapel. If not exactly wealthy, he was reputed to be so, and he laid much stress upon the claims to consideration which this repute gave him, not merely amongst his brother merchants, but, above all, at the chapel. There his standing grievance

consisted in not being senior deacon. "Old Wipple"
held that position in virtue of his years, and of the
unquestioned length of his purse. In Deacon Brown's
eyes, therefore, his senior was little better than an interloper, but mercifully the long-pursed provision dealer
lacked one great gift which Mr. Brown considered that
he himself possessed in a degree excelling most preachers
of the Word. Deacon Wipple could deliver extempore
prayers in a style that afforded much edification to the
faithful, but he could not make a speech, whereas
Deacon Brown was able to harangue by the hour. This
was an immense advantage to the younger man. By his
tongue power he was able to thrust himself forward on
all public occasions when speeches were in demand. On
emergencies he had been known even to occupy the
pulpit, and to deliver a discourse there, which, if it did
not exactly edify the flock, at least gave the envious
much to sneer at. Their malevolent comments gratified
Deacon Brown perhaps as much as praise would have done.
A man must be something to be worth back-biting.

Deacon Brown's gifts, however, shone most conspicu-
ously in the Sunday school. There he reigned in unob-
scured splendour, with no deacon of the batch to meddle
with him, surrounded by a troop of obsequious "teachers"
and overawed scholars. So great was his power that he
never scrupled to interrupt the routine of lessons in order
to bestow upon the assembled youths of both sexes an
address from himself. He called himself visiting superintendent, and came to the school when the spirit
moved him to make a speech.

"It struck me this morning, dear brothers and sisters in the Lord," he would remark, "that I should like to say a few words to the young of the flock to-day, and, if you are agreeable, I am ready."

Of course they were agreeable. Had they spoken the truth they might not perhaps have admitted that they loved much to hear Mr. Brown, but they would assuredly have owned to loving what they were pleased to call teaching less. Truth, however, was not in question, so the teachers pressed around their dear visiting superintendent, and abetted him in his whims. Acquiescence is always easiest to the mass of mankind, especially acquiescence which earns a fee. A ready obedience to the desires of Deacon Brown meant frequent invitations to patronising family teas, and "social gatherings" at his house—"my unpretending 'ome," he called it.

Tradition in Goliath chapel still retains some memories of these Sunday afternoon exhibitions of oratory, and if that fibbing old jade lies not, they were wonderful in their way. Usually the deacon discoursed upon a parable, or an event in Old Testament history; but no matter what the ostensible theme might be he always worked in the same peroration, delivered in a wheezy voice, as if the speaker's soul were stirred within him by emotions too deep for tears. "Repent, my deeyar children, repent, and fear the Lord, and you will be kept as the apple of His eye. Ah! my deeyar young friends, repentance is the most blessed thing on earth, for without repentance we cannot get to heaven to sing among the angels of God." Such was the burden of his homily always.

In personal appearance Silas Brown was not forbidding. He was a stout-built man of middle height, fat about the stomach, but by no means repulsively so. The most characteristic feature about him was his hair, which was thick and grey, and cut so short that it stood straight up all over his head like hog's bristles. This gave the man a bull-dog look, and the effect was not lessened by the rest of his face. He had rather a flabby countenance, and it was endowed with large prominent eyes, furzy eyebrows, and a wide, irregular mouth, whose fangy yellow teeth looked least pleasant when seen in their owner's times of holy mirth. Mr. Brown's forehead was an ill-shaped dome, and he was very proud of it, because a phrenologist had told him that a high forehead meant benevolence. Possibly it was in order to confirm the effect of this benevolent feature that Mr. Brown cut his hair so short. The hard, bristly, grey stubble that stood thick and defiant all round the dome, gleamed at a distance like a halo round the ruddy brow, increasing at once the apparent stature and the awesomeness of the great deacon. Minus very thick-soled boots and erect hair he might have been considered dumpy.

One great addition to Mr. Brown's gifts and graces which never failed to strike terror into the hearts of young offenders was the habit he had carefully cultivated of rolling his large prominent eyes hither and thither and all around when speaking in public. They rested nowhere, those eyes of his, and while they rolled the heavy eyebrows worked convulsively up and down.

But why elaborate this description, when, thanks to the events impending, we can look at him in the life as he habitually stood, moved, and spoke when the spirit of homilising was upon him in the Sunday school. The memory of his last harangue survives still in musty corners of Berborough memories because of what followed it, and strange to say it formed a link in the chain of Timothy Buncombe's life. But for that speech Timothy might have been still an obscure father, not of a "family," but of mere "straddling bipeds" like himself. This is how it all happened.

Late one Saturday night Mr. Silas Brown had received intimation of the loss of a ship of his in the Baltic. For reasons to be disclosed, he had been anxious about this ship, and it may be inferred that any news, even the most sorrowful, was a relief to him. That his emotions were profoundly stirred by what he did hear, I do not deny, but neither dare I assert that they were emotions of profound sorrow. Ships had been lost by him before, without his having been known to weep. On all such occasions, however, he had taken the earliest opportunity to "say a word to the dear children" of the Sunday school, and late as the hour was when the sad news reached him this time, he felt that so excellent a habit must be adhered to.

Next day, accordingly, he appeared in the school-room soon after classes had commenced, and intimated to Mr. Timothy Buncombe—still a diligent teacher—and to the other assiduous young Christians, that a grievous catastrophe had befallen him, whereby he was " moved in spirit to pour forth his soul in a short address to the dear little ones." Of course the teachers were agreeable, and it is to be inferred that the scholars felt no reluctance, for when the word passed round to suspend lessons and arrange classes, the room was filled with a cheerful bustle, in the midst of which Mr. Silas Brown ascended the superintendent's desk.

Once in the desk the great deacon felt himself above the human ruck. For a moment he sat down, and drew off his black kid gloves. Then he stood up with a jerk, stretched his arms, unbuttoned his ample frock coat, pulled down his shirt cuffs, puffed his cheeks out once or twice, like a man just emerging from the water after a dive, and rolled his eyes around, and worked his beetling eyebrows in the usual Jovian manner.

These preliminaries over, he extended his right hand above the assembly, and in a voice of thunder cried, "Silence and attention, all of you, I am going to begin."

Silence immediately ensued, and for full half a minute the deacon enjoyed it, working his countenance all the time. Then the right arm went forth again, and in a voice which was apparently husky with emotion the orator began :

" My deeyar children, the subject on which I propose to address you this afternoon is Jonah—Jonah in the whale's belly, my deeyar children." Then in sharper tones : " You all know who Jonah was, don't you ?"

" Yes, yes," came from various parts of the room.

' Who was he, then ?"

"A prophet, sir," cried several voices.

"That's right, my dears. Jonah was a prophet, a man of God. Ah! shall we, my dear children——Hey, Harry Weardale, you attend there, sir. Put down that book and listen to me." This in stentorian tones which contrasted grotesquely with the wheezy unction of voice that preceded and followed, but these effects were a peculiarity of Mr. Brown's oratory.

Without the least gradation, with scarcely a pause, the address was at once resumed. "Jonah, my deeyar children, was a man of God, and God sent him with a message to the wicked city of Nineveh. And what was that message ; can you tell me?"

"He'd destroy it, sir, if they didn't repent," said a boy near him.

"Who would destroy it?"

"The Lord, sir."

"Ah! that's right—quite right. Ah! my deeyar children, Nineveh was to be destroyed. What a sad thought. But——. Eh, Miss Maggs, I am sorry to have to mention it, but really unless you can manage to keep your class quieter, I feel that I cannot go on. Look at that little rascal in the corner ; he is wriggling about like—like ;—sit still, sir, will you?"

"Please, sir, it wasn't me, sir. Ben Snell's sticking pins in my leg, sir. Boo! hoo!" howled the boy alluded to.

"Ben Snell, you rascal, stand forth here. Turn him out in the middle of the room, Miss Maggs." A pause while this order was executed.

"And now," the honey tongue resumed, "attend, all of you, to the word of God, my deeyar young children."

But I must not repeat the whole speech; it would be fatiguing to both reporter and reader, and after all the interest of it lies in the climax.

The sample given, too, is good for the whole. It was, throughout, a mixture of mock pathos, low buffoonery, violent transitions from onslaughts upon particular urchins to whining appeals to "my deeyar children" and "young friends." The heavier matter of adjurations, objurgations and pious ejaculations was interspersed with clumsy jokes, with crocodile lamentations over the lost *Molly Bawn*, and asseverations to the effect that these young Berborians before him might be as wicked as the men of Nineveh. Strenuous condemnations of Jonah's cowardice were added as dressings to this salad.

A vivid and forcible description was given of the fate that overtook this backslider, and, after many excursions, the orator proceeded to sum up in this style :—

"Yes, my children, God can hear us anywhere, on the mountain top and down in the bottom of the sea. Jonah prayed, and Jonah was saved. He took the only way that was left for him to make his escape. What a fool he would have been had he tried to get out of the whale's belly all by himself. Perhaps he had no knife with him, but suppose he had, it would have been no good for him to try to cut his way out of the whale's belly. ("No, no," shouted sundry lads, noisily.) That would have been scuttling the ship, with a vengeance, eh! (A ripple of mirth.) Don't laugh, deeyar children. I forbid you to laugh. Be sad rather, and think of Jonah's helpless state. If he had hacked a hole in the whale's belly, and come forth, he would have been drowned as sure as the men in my ship, alas! And he couldn't address a remonstrance to the whale; never a bit of him. The Scriptures do not inform us that the whale, although it was the Lord's whale, could speak like Balaam's ass. No, depend on it, he did the right thing, and the only thing he could do. The whale could not have heard the voice of Jonah in its belly, even had it understood. Jonah could only cry to God, and God heard him. Oh, if he had only saved the men in my *Molly Bawn* as he saved Jonah."

"Hey, there! Really I can't stand this any longer. I'm insulted, teachers, insulted before my face, by that good for nothing young scamp, Harry Weardale, in Mr. Buncombe's class. I saw him—I most distinctly and clearly saw him—put his tongue in his cheek and wink—yes, wink, a big, long, vulgar wink—at that gawky girl—what's her name?—in Miss Belinda Cook's class. Come forth, Harry Weardale. Stand out, sir. You deserve a whipping, sir. Come up to my desk, beside this other vagabond, sir."

Harry Weardale looked foolish, but budged not. This enraged the deacon beyond bounds, and he yelled "Do—you—heeyar—me—sir? Have—I—got—to—tell—you—twice? Come here, this instant, and stand by my right hand, or else leave the school."

The boy still sat irresolute, with a frown of wrath gathering on his face, but when his teacher approached, in order to collar him and drag him out, he jumped up, pushed his way past the two or three boys between him and the end of the seat, and made his way to the door, with a sort of insolent slowness. Opening it, still moving slowly, he stole outside amid dead silence. Rebellion like that was new in Goliath Sunday School. Once sure of a free course, Weardale, a stout, rosy-cheeked, curly-haired boy of about twelve or thirteen, made no haste to disappear. Turning round in the half-open doorway, with his body well outside, and his hand on the latch, he suddenly thrust his tongue out, first at the school generally, and then at Deacon Brown in particular. The deacon made a step down from his desk, and Buncombe turned to dart at the door, but before either got near it, Harry managed to shout, with his head just visible from behind it, "Ah-yah! owd sneaks, who drownded my feyther?" Then he banged the door, and was off like an arrow.

Consternation overtook all and sundry at the spectacle of this dreadful open rebellion, and a hum of excited under-talk arose which the deacon for once found himself unable to quell. In vain did he shout " Silence there!" "For shame!" "Listen to me!" "God will punish you for this behaviour to those above you," and other phrases which he kept handy, as a stone-throwing boy does pebbles, to fling about him on emergencies. Nothing quieted the children. Many of them had seen the painful flush that gleamed over Mr. Brown's face when he heard Harry Weardale's accusing question. They had seen a black scowl of hate follow the flush as he clenched his hands nervously and shook them at the door.

A full minute elapsed before he regained command of himself, and though he shouted on mechanically, everyone could see that his mind was elsewhere. And when he had succeeded in mastering his emotions all control over the audience was gone. Perforce he had to bring his address to an abrupt conclusion without the usual peroration on repentance and the fear of the Lord. The school might have dispersed like a swarm of bees without a queen but for Mr. Buncombe. He, with ready resource, created a diversion in favour of order by giving out a hymn, which he proceeded to sing. When that exercise was ended the ordinary superintendent mumbled a few words of prayer, Mr. Brown, in a tremulous voice, pronounced the blessing, and, for that Sunday, school was over.

After the scholars had dispersed, Mr. Brown threatened all sorts of things against " that scoundrel young Weardale," and forbade Mr. Buncombe to let him come back to his class. This prohibition was unnecessary; Harry never tried to return.

CHAPTER V.

A WELL LAID SCHEME OF A DEACON AND A JEW.

So dramatic an interruption of an edifying discourse could not be without results of some sort in a community like that of Goliath Chapel. It is not, however, with these that we are specially concerned in this history. We deal with greater events than chapel tattle and chapel spites. And great events did undoubtedly flow from this startling episode. Behold, once more, "how great a matter a little fire kindleth."

Amongst the people with whom Deacon Brown did business, accusations like that launched by the boy were not altogether unknown. But they were generally considered little more than malice-seasoned, passing gossip. It was a different matter, however, among the sailors who had for some years past displayed increased reluctance to go to sea in the deacon's vessels. The average loss of Brown's ships was becoming higher and higher every year, they said ; and so great had the dread of " Brown's coffins " become in the harbour, that his skippers had latterly been forced to make up their equipment of men by stealth and duplicity. Scarcely a month antecedent to this Sunday school thunder clap, a crew thus secured had deserted, when they discovered that they were aboard one of Brown's hulks. The vessel was bound for the coast of Africa, and the men declared her to be both rotten and over-laden. So they fled, and the Christian deacon had been forced to invoke the arm of the law. With the aid of the magistrates all the truants except two were re-captured and put on board to risk their lives in their employer's service, whether they liked to or not. That was their equity in the matter.

You may, however, feel quite sure in your own mind that the deacon's tender heart was wrung with sorrow at having to coerce these men. Had the law been different he would no doubt have obeyed it, just as he might have been convinced that it was wrong to over-insure if that custom had been a legal crime.

A man's morals, you know, cannot reasonably be expected to transcend the height attained by the statutes of the Realm. Being what they were, those laws regulating the relations between employer and employed in seafaring life, Deacon Brown could do no other than accept them. Such a good man, however, a man so full of the sounds of human loving kindness could not possibly relish the measures the law allowed him to take, were it for no other reason than that the law's action insured publicity. All the world knew through the proceedings in court, that Deacon Silas Brown had to threaten a crew with jail before he could get his ship to sea, and knowledge of this kind was, to wagging tongues, like sheaves to the threshing machine. Merchants who had already acquired a bad habit of shrugging their shoulders mechanically when Brown's " enterprise and

D

success" came under their observation had, in episodes
of this sort, the means of putting two and two together.
Thus the deacon stood in danger of losing the support of
some narrow viewed men whose ruling desire was to
barter goods with other countries, not to sink them in
the sea for the sake of plundering the poor underwriters.
His general trade might not thereby suffer, but his
reputation for holiness must do so, and did.

Hitherto, I must admit, Deacon Brown had carried
himself tolerably well. No man in Berborough was
more determinedly respectable, with a fine broad-cloth
sanctification, than he. The most recent crew episode
would blow over, as many a one of a similar kind had
done before. Skippers and underwriters might doubt
him, but he lost his vessels on the whole so cleverly, and
with such a neat apportionment of untoward circumstances, that they could not bring their minds fully to believe that beneath the saint's cloak hid the rascal. A man
who rarely lost vessels in calm weather, and who had even
been known to reward officers and men for bringing
overladen and leaky vessels safe through storms that
should have sunk them, could not be a rogue much
beyond the conventional limits sanctioned by the
customs of his trade.

Still there were uncomfortable rumours attached to his
name, and here and there an unbeliever lurked. Thus, at
the very moment when that rude, ill-bred urchin, Harry
Weardale, thrust forth his tongue and asked a question,
the deacon was anxiously desirous of seeming to be, beyond
ordinary, pure. The *Molly Bawn*, in which Harry's father

was presumably drowned, was the third ship in Mr. Silas Brown's fleet of about fifteen, which had been lost within twelve months. For a place like Berborough that was a high percentage. A year of immunity from untoward accidents might be required to reassure the underwriters, and meanwhile much semblance of grief.

But could the deacon hope to play his part efficaciously now that the scandal-mongers of the chapel had become possessed of so sweet a morsel as the Weardale query? The deacon doubted and feared and hoped by turns, and wished more and more fervently that the "brethren and sisters" who came to sympathise with him in his latest sorrow and disaster, and to sting him now and then, if possible, could be put for a little under the sea. From past experience he knew only too well that, as oil alone makes the salad insipid, so life would be intolerable to these effusive people had they no opportunity to distil the vinegar of their malice behind a man's back.

Yes, he could imagine how the story went the round of the chapel, swelling in the startling character of its incidents as beautiful human ingenuity gave impulse, for he was a shrewd man, Silas Brown. Nevertheless, he hoped to escape by keeping still. In a month's time, at most, some new love affair, or a slander about the minister, any waft of new excitement from no matter what direction, might be trusted to set the chapel *commères* off to a new enjoyment.

And a most just appreciation of probabilities, too, this would have been if Mr. Silas Brown had not possessed an enemy—a real downright enemy—within the sacred walls of Goliath Chapel itself. Ordinarily the back-biters and slanderers who say all the ill they can imagine of each other do not act from motives of hate. They dissect and scarify for love or for a "mixed motive." Not so the true foe. He is silent often, biding his time, caring not to show his purpose to those who might repeat the words uttered on the first opportunity, for the foe's warning and guidance.

So it was in this instance. The deacon had a sworn enemy, and knew it not, for not so long ago this secret hater had been his friend. A deep faith in the noble qualities of Mr. Brown's head and heart had once filled the soul of Mr. David Hogg with admiration, and now all this was turned to gall and bitterness. Why? for what? Because Mr. Hogg had lost money. Money—cursed lucre—had come between the two men; base and despicable cause of heart burnings.

David Hogg was Silas's dear friend and brother, a pious chapel Christian of the solidest type. Five or six years before he had come to Berborough with his inherit-ance and had started business as an underwriter, under the guidance and patronage of Mr. Brown. At the end of this period he, though a shrewd man, had lost half his capital, and he blamed his first patron for the loss. As claim after claim wrung his cash from him, his mistrust and hatred of the deacon deepened, until at last he listened to that much tried man's expressions of sym-pathy and pain with feelings of an almost homicidal description. He had ceased to believe a word he heard the shipbroker utter, or to take a line on any of his ships, and he hoped for a day of vengeance.

Had that boy Weardale put the scorpion's whip in his hands? He meant to see. As a member of the Goliath flock he heard the whole story on the evening of that fatal Sunday when Harry's rebellion burst forth. A man stone deaf and blind was alone incapable that night of learning the facts. A teacher bestowed on Hogg a full account of them. Hogg laughed low, all to himself, but said little. Next morning, however, he found his way very early to the house of the widow Weardale, with whom he held a conference that lasted an hour or more. And on the Tuesday young Harry was taken into his employment as office menial, a post expressly created for his benefit.

This last piece of news also reached the chapel folks and added to the excitement of the gossips to whom the growing dislike of Hogg for Brown was better known than to the self-confident shipbroker himself. The deacon did not hear of it till the following Sunday, when one of his chosen acolytes of the Sunday school told it to him in due commiseratory language. "Infamous malice and spite," &c., &c., were the motives this teacher laid to Hogg's charge with the view of gratifying his leader.

But to his astonishment Deacon Brown entered not with spirit into this condemnation. Instead of the customary voluble effusiveness of chastened imprecation there came a start, a sudden pallor, a muttered "Good God," and gloomy silence. For once the cue taken by the follower had proved the wrong one, and he retired discomfited. That evening the deacon was not in his pew. It had perhaps dawned on his spirit that David Hogg had cause to hate him.

Surely no sensible man ever took a step of greater imprudence than did Brown by this absenteeism. It was a challenge to the scandalous chroniclers of the chapel to attack him, and, excited as they were by rumours, they were not slow to take it up. Why was Deacon Brown away? What was he doing that Sunday night? Where had he been? These and such like questions were started as the chosen people grouped round the doors after service, and gave rise to many surmises, whetting curiosity to a high pitch.

Soon it was discovered that instead of praying at chapel the deacon was visiting widow Weardale in his turn. This thickened the mystery. It became absolutely necessary to the peace of mind of several people, all holy folks, to interview the widow themselves. Nothing loth, she told her tale volubly to all and sundry, but it did not amount to a great deal beyond the fact that there was a mysterious letter of her husband's which she had given to Mr. Hogg, to the great wrath and discomfiture of Mr. Brown. That was all the inquisitive people could gather from the mourning widow at first, because Hogg had, for reasons of his own, desired her to hold her tongue off particulars. Threats were probably likewise uttered by Mr. Brown when he found that the letter in question was beyond his reach, and between them the woman imbibed enough fear to be a restraining force.

By and by, however, the fact was ascertained that a letter had come from the lost husband, Tom Weardale, which hinted at a design on the part of the broker and freighters to wreck the ship. Mr. Timothy Buncombe, among others, devoted much attention to the mystery, and unravelled it to his own satisfaction and ultimate profit.

The great investigator, however, was David Hogg, and to his memoranda I owe it that the reader of this history can enjoy a full, true, and particular account of the whole episode. It is the narrative of an enemy, doubtless, and therefore I do not ask any man to believe more of it than he pleases. Mr. Brown himself denied it, of course, but did not prosecute his moral assassin for slander. Still it would be wrong to treat the deacon's name and memory with too much harshness. He was a God-fearing man in his own way, and it is quite possible that he felt his God had nothing to complain of in the business. A man's chosen deity, I find, is seldom or never tyrannical. What the worshipper desires, that he obtains as a rule. He gets it how he can and when he can, and the more he succeeds the more sure is he that his Deity blesses him—until the day when the per contra account is handed in.

Brown came to grief in this instance, and therefore it is to be inferred that his God was angry or tired out, or had presented his account. It may be so. I do not care to argue the point, for it is one that does not directly affect the life of Timothy Buncombe.

The wrath or approval of Mr. Brown's Deity does not concern us, that is to say, but his lamentable misfortunes do, and this is how they were all accounted for according to the best obtainable evidence :

Among Mr. Brown's ships was one called the *Molly Bawn*, as already mentioned. She was rather old and leaky, but still classed at Lloyd's, as in some measure seaworthy. For years past Brown had employed her in trading along the coasts of northern Europe, now to one port, now to another, and as she had done so it might be presumed would she continue to do.

The Deacon had bought her from a bankrupt in Belfast, in one of the oft recurring crises to which the shipping trade is as subject as children are to measles.

She had come to him cheap enough, and after "titivating her up a bit," as he expressed it, Brown had insured her for about three times the price at which she stood in his books. That was all right and proper. The law allowed it ; the custom of the trade permitted it ; therefore it was morally right—as moral as the Song of Solomon. Mr. Brown had merely made prudent provision against untoward events, so that even they should not happen without redounding to his gain. Why should he not ?

Years elapsed, and the *Molly Bawn* attained the position of one of the least admired vessels in all the rising broker's fleet. It had become a question with him whether he should not part with her in her entirety to the small capitalist, for the underwriters had made him lower the sum for which she was insured once already, and might soon do so again. If she became a ship that did not pay him to lose, it was more profitable to him

that she should wholly belong to other people before
foundering. When the insurance was high he kept the
bulk of her shares himself, and he held them still, but
with doubt.

This was the deaconly man's state of mind when one
day a member of the Riga firm of Blumenkohle, Zurhelle
and Co. waited upon him at his office. It was a firm of
German Jews, and Herr Zurhelle, the Israelitish gentleman who waited on Mr. Brown, was its representative in
England. They had often done business together before—questionable business and other—and, like Mr.
Brown himself, Herren Blumenkohle, Zurhelle & Co.
were desirous of making money " mighty kvick," as Herr
Zurhelle often remarked.

It was not by any means an unusual thing to find
Herr Zurhelle in Mr. Brown's office, and Timothy Buncombe, did he choose to speak, could perhaps tell some
remarkable stories about what they did and said during
the years they had assisted each other to make money.
We only know the *Molly Bawn* incident, and that
through, possibly, the distorted medium of Mr. Hogg's
mind. On this occasion, then, the German Jew briefly
unfolded a bold plan whereby both parties might net a
fortune almost at a stroke. It was not a new scheme.
Money had often been made by it before and will be so
again, but hitherto Mr. Brown had never gone quite
so far.

He, therefore, recoiled when he was boldly invited to
arrange for the loss of a ship freighted with a cargo of
rubbish, which was to be fraudulently described as

valuable merchandise, in order to cheat the underwriters out of fifteen thousand pounds or more, besides the over-value of the ship. The deacon's respectability was shocked beyond measure at such a proposition, and he held out against it for a day or two until his mind became familiar with the conception, and satisfied that it could be done in secret and safety. Then he consented with sighs and groans as to a sad necessity. Ships he could lose, but fraudulent cargoes, oh, it was sad!

"Noting in dis vorlt can be easier," Herr Zurhelle assured him, "ve can do it in several ways. Ve can overload de ship and arrange a loose plank or two in her bottom, or if you can find a skipper to trust, ve can run her ashore somevere in de Baltic and save de crew. Dis plan has its dangers, but ve have lost a goot many hands lately, and it might be better to change de accident."

Brown agreed. We may assert, indeed, that this thought of saving the crew had great weight in bringing the shipbroker's mind to a state of acquiescence in Herr Zurhelle's plans. It had all along been one of the most disagreeable features connected with his business, that in order to make money "mighty kvick" he had to drown so many men every year. Nothing, therefore, could be more consoling to his tender heart than the thought that he might sweep a small fortune out of the pockets of the underwriters into his own without the loss of a man.

This point cleared up, everything else was easily adjusted. It was arranged that the *Molly Bawn* should go to Cronstadt with coals, and call on her return at

Riga for a cargo, really of chaff, chopped straw, and rotten rubbish of any kind, procurable for the clearing away, but ostensibly of linseed, isinglas, hair, and tallow. This *Molly Bawn* was of nine hundred tons burthen, and they reckoned that at least one thousand two hundred tons might be piled upon her, and that this cargo costing, perhaps, one thousand five hundred pounds all told, could be so represented as to be insurable for nearly twenty thousand pounds. Brown stipulated for two-fifths of the profit, whatever it might be, and he expected to net in addition about four thousand pounds on the insurance of the vessel. Both parties to the enterprise were to go equal shares in paying the bribe of three hundred pounds, which it was settled after some negotiation was to be given to the skipper whom Brown was to find.

CHAPTER VI.

FLY, OR FIGHT, OR FAIL?

As it was arranged, so the plan was put in execution, and but for a mistake on the part of the selected skipper, through which all hands were lost, and for Tom Weardale's letter to his wife, the arrangement might have succeeded *à merveille*. The idea had been to lose the ship in a part of the Baltic sea from which the crew might reach land either in boats or by waiting till the ice enabled them to walk ashore. But it so happened that the captain, whether from incapacity or carelessness, blundered, and ran the vessel, already leaky and much overladen, upon a sunken rock, in deep water near the Swedish coast, and she foundered with all hands.

Mr. Brown might have shed tears, and did publicly bemoan himself on this calamity; but due attention having been paid to propriety, he would have pocketed his money and gone on his way to triumphs new save for the man Weardale's letter. It was not a long letter, but it sufficed, once in the enemy's grasp, to change the entire aspect of affairs, and snatch a fortune from the deacon's extended hand.

Thomas Weardale was a steady, intelligent sort of fellow, who had been out of work owing to bad times.

He was by trade a ship carpenter, and as he had a wife and family to provide for, he soon became not over particular as to what kind of employment he accepted. When, therefore, the post of ship's carpenter on board the *Molly Bawn* came in his way, he took it thankfully enough. His wife, however, was but too well aware of the reputation enjoyed by Mr. Silas Brown, and when she failed to persuade her husband to break his contract, she made him promise to write to her from every port touched at, to help to keep her mind easy.

Weardale, like a true-hearted man, kept his promise, much though he hated the trouble and expense of letter writing. His wife heard from him when the ship reached Cronstadt, and she received two letters from Riga. It was the second of these that did all the mischief, and here it is, barring the spelling :

"On Board the Molly Bawn,

"Riga, 15th Oct., 185—.

" Dear Nan,

" I did not think to write more, but I fear all's up with us, so I write this on my knee, and will give it to the pilot to post, if I can. I would have bolted yesterday whatever come had I known what I knows now. Not but what I suspected something wrong, for the captain was so mad to have the cargo aboard, and looked after the loading himself all day long, which I thought queer. Perhaps we'll get thro', but if the ship aint wrecked with all this muck aboard it will be because the devil's against us. I went into the aft hold last night a lookin' for a tool I wanted, with a candle, and saw rotten straw sticking out of a bag loaded as hair.   That made me rip open some more, and they was all alike—a tuft or two of hair, and the rest muck.   If all the cargo is of that sort there's a game on as may send us all to the bottom. The captain, I suppose, means to wreck the ship so as he can get away, any-how, but how it will be with the rest of us, I can't tell.   So good-bye, and God bless you and the kids, Nancy, lass, for this may be the last you hears of your affectionate,—T. WEARDALE."

This was the epistle which the weeping widow, Mrs. Weardale, had handed to Mr. David Hogg, and though he, of course, lost nothing by the wreck of the *Molly Bawn*, he found it profoundly interesting.   A boat of the missing ship had been picked up bottom uppermost by one of the last steamers that came down the Baltic that season, and she had been posted as " missing " at Lloyd's the day before little Harry demanded "who drownded his feyther."   The news had its customary effect on the tempers of the underwriters, who, however, began to arrange for a settlement of claims with Mr. Brown and Messrs. Blumenkohle, Zurhelle & Co.   Before they could pay up, Mr. David Hogg intervened, armed with the letter.   After reading it, the underwriters interested unanimously resolved to wait explanations.   This decision was intimated to the Jew merchants and to the shipbroker when they called for their cheques.

Mr. Brown's anxiety to possess himself of the incriminating letter will now be understood.   So far as he personally was concerned, that was the only evidence of foul play the underwriters had.   His correspondence and books would betray nothing—all that was not destroyed being perfectly regular. Zurhelle had probably been equally careful, and as all the documents relating to the cargo were in order, Brown felt that his position would have been unassailable but for that confounded letter. He could not think how the pilot came to be such a fool as to post it, and pilot and writer and widow came in for a share in his wrath. It was a bad blow indeed, and neither he nor Zurhelle could see their way to parry it. They held several consultations together about it, and it must be admitted that the German Jew took the matter much more philosophically than the pious dissenter.

"It is damn'd awkvard, I vill say," Zurhelle summed up on the occasion of the last of these meetings; "damn'd awkvard ; and vat makes it vorse, to my mind, is dat in spite of your letter-writing carpenter, ve should have been all right if your blooming fool of a skipper hadn't lost all de crew mit de vessel."

"Nay, I'm none so sure of that," was Brown's answer. "No, hang it, it's the other way about. Weardale, you may be sure, would have told the rest of the men what he had discovered, and we should have had the whole lot peaching on us had they not gone to the bottom. Devil take it, it's just this letter, and nothing else, that has played old Harry with us."

"Vell, vell, it may be so. I don't care ein damn. Vat I see is, dat de money is not forthcoming, and I should like to know vat ve must do ?"

"Do ! Brazen it out, of course. Those underwriter idiots have no other evidence. They can't try us on that

blasted letter.   Let us turn the tables on them and
demand payment, and threaten proceedings to recover, if
they don't stump up.   Hang me if I'm to be done in this
style," shouted Brown in a passion.

"Goot, very goot, my friendt.   Nodings vood pleass me
better, but I don't feel sure on me groundt—not sure at
all.   It's all very vell to say 'fight 'em,' but de unterwriters are a powerful lot, and dey might get more
evidence in Riga.   De firm's books perhaps are not so
goot kept dere as mit me.   Peoplsh might be got at, as de
saying is, de peoplsh as made up de cargo, for instance.
In fact, if ve fight, as you calls it, dere's no end to de mess
ve might be in ; and if ve fight and looss, who vill pay
de bill, eh, my goot friendt ?"

"Oh, the bill be damned !   We must fight, man.
We can't sit down with this thing hanging over us.   It
would ruin me, I tell you—utterly ruin me in pocket and
reputation if I submitted to this blow.   They have
nothing but this beastly carpenter's letter, and before I
submit to be bowled over by that, I'll swear the whole
affair is a cursed plot and forgery of Hogg's.   Anyway,
fight I must and shall, and, as we are both in the same
boat, you had better join, and go halves."   As he said this,
the Deacon rubbed his face fiercely with his handkerchief to hide his emotion, which was so great that the
proprieties of chapel holiness were forgotten.

"Hee ! Hee !" laughed the Jew in his dry way, " not if
I know it, my tear boy, not if I know it.   I have not vat
you calls reputations to lose—nodings at all—and I don't
mean to go to jail just to please you, my goot friendt.

Dat's vat fighting means in my thinks. 'Penal servitude' you calls it. Oh no, tanks, not if I know it," and he rubbed his hands deprecatingly, the fat little man.

" Rubbish " ejaculated Brown, but his face grew deadly pale.

"Oh, but it is not rubbish dough, not at all rubbish, I tells you. You look at it in de calms, mein goot friendt. Veerdail's letter is vat you calls a clue. If you ask for de insurance money, de unterwriters follow up dis clue and get plenty evidence—loads of it. Den dey turns on us and say "conspiracy of frauds" or sometings like, and ve find ourselfs in jail. Oh, no, dat don't suit me, not at all."

"Ha-ah!" said Brown, and shivered. "What would *you* do then?"

"Nodings, my dear boy, nodings. You see if ve sits kviet and ask for no money dem fellows vill be easy, and vill not care to vaste moneys for prosecutions. Den by and by it vill all, vat you calls, blow ofer. Nobody vill know vat ve did, and ve can have anoder try. Vy, suppose ve licked de unterwriters in de law ve vould let all de vorlt know ve had been accused. Oh, no; not me; I knows better; I lets it alone. It is for me a *coup manqué*, and I satisfies myself to lose de money dis chance. As for de, vat you calls it, reputations—I have none, hee! hee! I don't care ein damn copper groschen for reputations. Venn de fools dey vill not trade mit me in dis town, I goes to anoder. I is free, and I goes vere I likes. But, begin dis fight, and ve are ruined."

E

"But, my dear sir," said Brown in a half wounded, half pleading voice, "it's all very well for you to say that; but, I tell you, for my own part, I'm ruined if those fellows don't pay up."

"Sorry to hear it, me dear friendt, sorry indeedt; but den, vy don't you do as me—go avay. You should be able to take vat you calls a 'tidy pile' in your pockets, and dem fellows den might hvistle for it, you know."

Brown sat with his head down for a short space, as if tempted to take this advice; then he looked up, and heaving a great sigh, said:

"Nonsense, nonsense. Whatever you do, I can't go away; I must stick where I am, and make the best or the worst of it. Perhaps I may have a chance here. I'm a deacon of a chapel, and an old citizen. Out of this I could have no chance at all. Go away, bolt, never! It would root my whole connection up, man."

"But look you here," exclaimed Zurhelle.

"No, I shan't, I can't, I won't," interrupted Brown feverishly. "If you won't help me to fight, let me alone to do it myself, and I wish to God I had never seen the face of you."

"Oh! all right, all right!" cried the Jew, rising in real or pretended dudgeon. "As you pleass, my friendt. I give you good advice, and you not take it. Vell, vell, you is insolent, I tink, so I shall say ta, ta! Ven you have orders, you know vere to find me in Riga." With that he pushed back his chair, and made for the door, muttering "I tink he is a fool, ein verdamt fool." "Ta, ta!" he repeated, as he opened the door. "I may be off to-night—a *coup manqué*, you know.   No good to vait, no good at all."   Bowing, with a sneer on his face, as he said this, he closed the door behind him, and Brown was left alone with his reflections.

These were not of a sweet kind.   The panoply of respectable well-clad chapel holiness beneath which the man had hidden his true self began to show terrible rents. His very conversation, as you will perceive, had degenerated, and his tender feelings of sympathy for poor sailors all evaporated before the fire of this great calamity. Should these "damned underwriter scamps" stick to it and keep his money, he kept saying to himself, his loss would be a matter of ten thousand pounds ; that is to say, he would not gain that sum, and no man could be expected to see so much money slip away from him without losing his equanimity.

What made the matter the more serious for Brown was that he had counted on this money coming to him, and had spent it in anticipation.   Only a fortnight before the catastrophe he had bought a couple of steamers from a Tyneside firm, by whom they had been built on "spec;" and he could scarcely hope now to get the small investor to take their shares freely off his hands.   With these boats he had intended to take a new departure in shipowning, having till then never traded in any but sailing vessels. Could his hopes of becoming a great steamship owner now be fulfilled?   There was room to doubt it.   For the two steamers he had agreed to pay fifty-five thousand pounds, and he considered them cheap at the money. As he could not pay this price out of his own pocket, it had been agreed that the builders should hold a mortgage on them for thirty-five thousand pounds until Brown had succeeded in placing the shares ; and now all chance of doing this, to the extent necessary in the time allotted, was probably gone. If the haul expected from the wreck of the *Molly Bawn* had been landed, Brown could have scraped twenty or five and twenty thousand pounds together, and might have devoted that in part to meet these obligations.

That hope was gone, or as good as gone ; and, to make matters worse, Brown could not now repudiate his bargain. Not only had it been concluded, but bills had been drawn for the whole of the purchase money. Part of these bills, of long date, and renewable, the builders held as collateral security for their mortgage, as blinds to hide its existence, in fact. The rest Brown had insisted on having drawn at four and six months' date, because he had felt so sure of his future. Perhaps by an effort the shortest set of these bills might be met when due, but he could not possibly meet them all. The question, therefore, which presented itself to the deacon's mind now was—Is it worth while going on ? Would it not be better, in other words, to make a smash of it right off, and so save the money he had, rather than attempt the impossible ? Times were not propitious for a struggle against adverse fortune, and, when hostile underwriters were added to lagging trade, the causes for discouragement were ample.

"I shall only be throwing good money after bad," the deacon said to himself ; and that was never a game he liked to play. But then, if times were adverse to a man fighting, could they be looked upon as favourable to a man going to make a smash? Not in one sense. Shipping was a drug in the market, as the slang phrase runs. Owners on every side, Brown himself, had vessels laid up. A good sale, whether of his steamers or his sailers, was, therefore, not to be looked for. The best that Brown could expect would be that his creditors might permit him to buy back the ships at his own valuation; and, had his name been unsmudged, that would have been an excellent speculation. Bad times would then have been a great blessing for him. His bankers might have advanced the money necessary to pay a composition of six or eight shillings in the pound, and all would have gone swimmingly, Brown's creditors and the shareholders in his vessels alone suffering. But a happy deliverance of this sort was more than he could now expect; so, if a failure had to be accomplished successfully, some other way must be discovered of making money by it.

Ruminating deeply on these knotty questions, the deacon's mind was for a week or two on the rack. All thoughts of fighting the underwriters left him. His attitude was that of a much maligned man; and to those he called his friends he spoke bitterly of conspiracies and what not, but his threats proved to be breath, poisoned breath if you like, nothing more. In the chapel, which he attended as closely as ever, his aspect was meek, as of one full of the spirit of holy resignation; but his thoughts were so far away that more than once he forgot to rise when it was necessary to do so ; and once, on one of the last Sundays of his regular and orthodox appearance *quâ* deacon in the familiar pew, he stood motionless and self-absorbed for a considerable time after all the rest of the flock had sat down to hear the minister pray.

The only place he forsook completely was the Sunday School. There the children never looked upon his Jovian countenance again. Nor did he wait willingly for the loving handshakes that used to greet him as the flock gathered round the doors after service. Moody and silent, he strode away.

Altered manners of this kind produced a strong impression upon the minds of the observant worshippers of Goliath Chapel. Those whose hands he saw not when they were thrust towards him, backed by saintly hypocritical smiles, helped each other to tear the remaining shreds of his character to bits when his ears were out of hearing. Ere three Sundays were over the general consensus of opinion was that the deacon had been hard hit, and was meditating bankruptcy. Some went further, and declared that they fully believed Brown would soon be arrested on a criminal charge ; but that view did not meet with general acceptance. The knowing ones cried, " No, no ; old Brown is far too fly for that. He may have done queer tricks in his time, but he ain't fool enough to let the law get a grip of him."

To what lengths these disputes might have gone, I will not take it upon me to say. All I feel certain of is, that, to the deacon's face, none of these assertions were made. If anything, perhaps, the cringing attitude of the crowd towards their beloved "pillar" in his afflictions was more pronounced now than before. The words that unheeded reached his ear as he passed in and out were all soft and honeyed. To hear them one would have supposed Mr. Brown to be the best-loved man in all the congregation. It was all, "How are you, dear Mr. Brown;" and, "I'm so delighted to see you, Mr. Brown;" "From what I had heard, I was afraid you were ill, Mr. Brown." "Glad to see you looking so strong, Mr. Brown;" and, "was not that a dear comforting sermon we had to day, Mr. Brown; I feel sure you enjoyed it;" *and so weite.*

This lasted for several Sundays. One evening, however, the deacon intimated to his wife that he was not going out to chapel.

"Are you ill, my dear? Shall I stay at home with you?" she exclaimed.

"No; I'm all right; you just be off to chapel, I want to think a bit, that's all;" and the deacon kept in doors. From what occurred in the course of succeeding weeks, it is probable that, on that Sunday night, Mr. Brown arranged in a general way his plans for a bankruptcy.

CHAPTER VII.

WHILE these events were passing, Mr. Timothy Buncombe had continued to plod along in his accustomed groove. Full five years had come and gone since the eventful day when he took Penelope Drabble home as his wedded wife, and he was a man now close upon thirty, endowed with two children, and an income of one hundred and twenty pounds per annum. That was the utmost he could screw out of his pious employer, whose freight clerk he still was. When he pressed for more pay, Mr. Brown always declared that his services were most highly appreciated, and that it was his wish that Mr. Buncombe should be better paid.

"I would gladly give you three hundred pounds a year, my dear sir," Mr. Brown had said quite recently, "but times are bad, as you know, and I cannot afford it. We shall see, though, what the steamers can do for us."

It was always thus. Can you wonder then, that Mr. Timothy Buncombe hated his master? His domestic name for the great deacon was "the old scuttler," and he harboured thoughts of a reputedly unchristian kind in his heart. "I'll be even with the fellow one of these days," he ventured to say to his wife now and then, and if she demanded "when,"

"When my ship comes home, Old Truepenny," he would reply, and pass it off with a laugh.

Naturally Timothy's household arrangements were of the humblest. The little cottage on the outskirts of the town which he took on his marriage had been his home ever since, and its furniture had grown shabby with wear. About a year before this his wife and he had once more revelled in the prospect of fingering Mr. Bob Cutler's cash, but the cup of bliss they dreamed of had not been tasted ; perhaps never would be now. The ship-chandler then lost his wife, and with her death Mrs. Buncombe, reasonably enough, had hoped that the one obstacle between her uncle and his money had been removed. The old rascal, as the loving pair called him, had but to die himself now, and all would go merry as lambkins in June. Meantime, perhaps, the untramelled hand of the widower might be opener.

It was not to be so ; and really I do not find it in my heart to blame Mr. Timothy for swearing round oaths over this new disappointment. No saint, ancient or modern, could have stood by meekness under the circumstances. Instead of greater generosity, the wretched old chandler displayed more stinginess. Any hint from his niece that a little money would be welcome put him in a passion. She tried twice, thinking that perhaps on the first occasion the moment had been inopportunely chosen, but the second attempt fared the worst of the two. Mr. Cutler not only swore huge mouth-filling, ear-rending oaths, he threatened as well.

"If you ever dare come here with any more of your damned beggin' again," he yelled, "devil take me if I don't kick you out, and cut you off with a shilling."

As has been already hinted, when Mr. Timothy Buncombe heard of this threat, he forgot himself, and swore in turn, mingling strong invective against his wife and all her kindred with his oaths.

Mrs. Penelope first opened her wide mouth in dumb astonishment at this terrible language, and then wept. After the tears came speech, and when her tongue got loose it clanged and clattered about a man's ears, stinging sharper than a lash of whip-cord. The irate husband was soon reduced to fuming silence, and then Mrs. Buncombe renewed the fountain of her tears.

So well did she replenish it that it kept her cheeks moist, her eyes red, and her solid lips swollen for the space of two days. That might have been endured, had it been all. But Mr. Timothy's food and clothes suffered the while. They then kept no servant ; all power was therefore in Mrs. Buncombe's hands to make or mar her husband's comfort, and she had long ere then discovered that raw or cold food, administered with persistence and judgment, soon reduced her husband to abject submission.

It was so on this occasion. The sulky attitude of the pair had to be abandoned first by the head of the house. He became calm, submissive, kind ; and, once more, there was peace. Within three days from the date of the outbreak they were so well in accord once more, that they decided to lay the blame of Mr. Cutler's misconduct, not upon his own head, but upon that of his new housekeeper.

When Mrs. Cutler forsook this lower world, Mrs. Penelope Buncombe had generously offered to go back to the ship chandler's dwelling, taking her husband and children with her; or if he preferred it, Mr. Cutler, her dear uncle, might sell his business give up his house and come and live with them. The hard hearted old man spurned both proposals; at first with sulky grunts and furious puffing at his long clay pipe, and then, when his niece persevered, with violent language.

"I'll see you blowed first," he shouted. "I aint a-goin' to have that smooth faced sneak of yours and his dirty brats eatin' me out o' 'ouse and 'ome; so you be off and leave me alone, will yer!"

"Oh, uncle, how can you be so cruel. I'm sure I was thinkin' of your comfort more than of ours," sobbed Mrs. Penelope.

"Was you, tho? I'm blest if I can see it. You wants to nobble me so as to make sure of my cash, that's wot you does. But I ain't a fool, though I'm an owd un, an' yer ain't a comin over me, I say. Clear out, d'ye hear?" and a grin spread over the wicked old man's face, making his red blotchy cheeks pucker up till his small ferret eyes almost disappeared. Mrs. Buncombe looked as if she would dearly have loved to give play to her tongue, but money-loving prudence kept the mastery, and she merely cried "Oh! uncle," and proceeded with her weeping. The hard hearted uncle looked at her for some time with evident satisfaction, and then said in a mock sympathetic tone,

"Well, then, Penny, my gell, I ain't hard hearted, you know, so you can come back an it suits yer. Bless my heart alive, if I thowt you had so much affection for your owd uncle. Come back yourself, by all means. I can put up wi' yer." And the old rogue leered as if a good joke lay in his words.

"Oh, do you really mean that, uncle," exclaimed Mrs. Penelope, brightening up at once.

"In course, I does. On'y—on'y ye must leave sanctified Tim and his warmint where they be, ye know. It would be a good riddance, I should think;" and the old sinner laughed loud and long. His joke was out.

It was too much for his niece. Rage took the place of every other feeling as she rose to depart.

"You are a nasty, wicked, old wretch," she bawled, I wonder I ever came near you, drunken sot that ye be. You'll come to a bad end, I do believe. Some trollope of a woman will get hold of you and starve you to death; see if she don't; and serve you right, too; and when you send for me on your dying bed to help you, I shan't come: there!"

"Go it, go it, an, w'en ye're blown, be off! I shan't be sorry to see the last of you; never was; and be hanged to you," roared the uncle in return. Before the words were well out of his mouth, Mrs. Buncombe had departed, carrying her fury with her.

She had spoken the truth at random. Old Cutler had already consoled himself for the loss of his wife by promoting the charwoman who cleaned for him, to the post of housekeeper. She was a buxom, coarse featured, big-boned, middle-aged female, who had already, as she was wont to boast, buried two husbands ; and who loved beer. The pair were well matched, and got on all the better together perhaps, that they were not tied to each other in "holy matrimony." They could drink together, quarrel with each other, fight at times, and make it up again, all in a style calculated to relieve life of much of its monotony.

To the Buncombes the advent of this powerful female was destruction. Forgetful of his threats, Mrs. Buncombe returned more than once to her uncle's house, but soon had to give up the contest. The charwoman might have " marked her for life," as she threatened, had she not done so.

CHAPTER VIII.

A DEACON'S DILEMMA.

ENCOMPASSED thus by sordid cares, crushed under the ashes of dead hopes, small wonder would it have been had Timothy Buncombe now lost heart and forsaken the faith that was in him. No doubt he was tempted to do so at times; but he never actually fell. The chapel still had his assiduous attentions, and his power at the office, as well as his knowledge of his master's affairs, grew and increased. Not even did he get drunk to drown his sorrows. He did not become careless in his dress, loose in his language, nor, by any outward sign, betray a doubt of his destiny. Bob Cutler's rascality was a severe trial to him; but he bore it as he bore others, if not without domestic brawls, at least without public complaint.

And surely his steadfastness was justified. Sore tried had he been. All these years heart sickness was his constant experience, but patience had its reward at last. At the very time when the world looked blackest, when, in addition to the brutal cruelty of the ship chandler and his brawny paramour, the troubles of Mr. Silas Brown threatened him with complete loss of work, the day of Timothy Buncombe's brighter future was at the dawning.

Of course he knew all about the *Molly Bawn* affair. Not only did he know, but he had possessed himself of evidence that would have been most useful to the underwriters had they chosen to prosecute. That, as Zurhelle had astutely guessed, they did not. They merely stood on the defensive, waiting for Brown to begin. If he made no push to get his money, they were, apparently, content to let the matter drop, and to treat the facts revealed to them as a warning to avoid Brown's ships in future.

In all probability this supineness added to Mr. Timothy Buncombe's disappointment. While on the one hand he feared that the deacon could no longer hold up his head in Berborough, on the other he saw a chance of notoriety, and, perhaps, advancement, slip past him. The telling evidence of an honest clerk, whose soul revolted at the deeds of his employer, was not to be given in court. His great virtue would, consequently, be hid in darkness, and work would have to be sought by him just as if he had been an ordinary clerk in want of a job, work all the more hard to get because of Mr. Brown's reputation.

That may have been Mr. Timothy's view. It would naturally be so, although other people might, perhaps, have thought that a clerk who kept copies of his employer's letters, or the letters themselves, and who made notes of conversations overheard in his master's sanctum, was not a desirable being to have at hand. That is also as it may be. The cardinal fact is that the question was never put to the test. Mr. Brown did not "fight," as he had threatened, and he was let alone. Instead of fighting, he decided to make a good failure, and by a wonderful freak of mind, settled upon his freight clerk, Mr. Timothy Buncombe, as the one man of all his staff, to aid him in that arduous undertaking. Why he should have done this, I cannot imagine; but, probably, Timothy's remarkable quiescence under his many disappointments had made the deacon misjudge his character. Meek men, sleek, menial sort of men, are often excellent tools in the hands of clever people ; and as this was the general superficial aspect Mr. Timothy Buncombe bore, Brown was to be pardoned for selecting him as the most convenient and likely agent he could get for the work in hand.

The deacon's one difficulty in becoming a bankrupt was how to make the operation profitable. A ruinous bankruptcy was not to be thought of for one moment. On looking into his affairs he found that, ravelled as they were, it might be in his power to pay a composition of ten shillings in the pound, and to continue business. Had the times been good for selling ships, he would have been worth more than twenty shillings in the pound. To get whitewashed for ten shillings, and obtain the chance of future trade improvements, might, therefore, have seemed not so bad a job. That, however, did not satisfy the deacon. "Scoundrels," as he put it, had "forced him into a corner," and he meant "to make them pay for their fun."

So after weighing the question in all its bearings, he concluded that, if he could only make himself look poor enough, two shillings-and-sixpence in the pound would be a liberal composition to offer to the creditors. He had known men, and well-to-do men, too, let off before now for one shilling in the pound, and even less, but of course the stupid creditors had not known that any wealth was concealed.

In his own case, notwithstanding his deep conviction that half-a-crown was a most handsome payment, Mr. Brown did not feel at all sure of his ground. The general impression, an impression he had done much to encourage, was that he had saved a great deal of money, and, if he must plead poverty now, his creditors would naturally ask where this money lay hid. And unless it was effectually hidden, the profitable bankruptcy would end as disastrously as the *Molly Bawn* speculation.

Mr. Brown was thus in an emergency which kept him worried for some weeks. At the end of that time, on the Sunday evening already mentioned, he made up his mind. It must have been then, for on the following Monday morning, the moment he reached the office, he summoned Mr. Buncombe.

F

CHAPTER IX.

A DEACON'S DEVICE.

WHEN, in answer to the call, the freight clerk entered the room, a look of mild curiosity on his face, Mr. Brown was seated at his desk in all his ancient dignity of deportment.

"Take a seat, Mr. Buncombe," said he, with a gracious wave of the hand towards the nearest chair; "I have somewhat of importance to say to you."

Mr. Buncombe's face fell. He thought this greeting a preliminary to an intimation of dismissal, but he merely bowed as he sat down, and did not speak. There was a moment of painful silence, and then Mr. Brown resumed.

"My dear young friend—young, though old in the service of this firm—I have wished for some days to have a little conversation with you." Here he paused, and went through part of the facial pantomine so familiar to Sunday school and chapel.

"Yes, sir," said Buncombe, and waited.

"My friend," resumed the deacon, "I have, as you well know, long watched your career with satisfaction, and, I may add, with admiration. You have been a faithful servant to me, Mr. Buncombe, all these years, and it has, as you are aware, been a source of regret to me that

I have not been able to more fully reward you ; but," and as he laid stress on the " but," Mr. Brown placed the tips of his fingers together in front of his ample stomach gently, thereby bringing into prominence a large diamond ring of great lustre, " but who knows, the time will come ; and though I may not be able so to do, for misfortunes have overtaken me, the Lord will yet reward you, Mr. Buncombe. 'Faithful over a few things,' you know ; that promise never fails."

Timothy mumbled some indistinct phrase or other, he did not know what, for his mind was too much bent on trying to guess what the "old sniveller" was driving at. But the deacon took the sound for sympathy, and went on.

" Yes, I know, my deeyar young friend ; I have never doubted it ; you have a feeling heart ; and it is because I know this—feel it here, sir," laying a large paw impressively on his bosom, "that I have resolved to confide some of my cares to you. What do you say, my friend ? May I trust in you ? Are you willing to aid me ?" With that he leant forward and fixed his large protruding eyes for a moment on the face of his clerk.

" I'm very sorry to hear that you need help, sir," answered Buncombe, rousing himself; "and if I can be of any use to you, I shall be only too delighted to give you all the aid I can."

" Just so ; I thought so. I felt sure I could count upon you. I flatter myself I am a good judge of men, Mr. Buncombe ; and I have watched your career too long not to know you by heart, as it were ; and when affliction and loss overwhelmed me, the Lord himself seemed to direct my mind towards you, Mr. Buncombe. 'There, he seemed to say, you will find a true friend;'" and the deacon rolled his great eyes and solemnly wagged his head.

Timothy again bowed in silence, more puzzled than ever.

Dropping all at once the canting whine in which he had hitherto spoken, the deacon resumed in his curtest business style.

"This is settled then; and now to business. The fact is, Mr. Buncombe, I find myself in difficulties—temporary, but still serious difficulties—all through having enemies. There are men, Mr. Buncombe, pursuing me with relentless hatred. They are trying to crush me, but they can't succeed; they can't succeed if you will only stand by me, and do as I direct. If you do this, you shall not go unrewarded. Let the storm only blow over, and I shall make you a partner in my business. I give you my word of honour, as a gentleman, and (here came the whine again) 'as a Christian.'"

Once more a pause. The deacon heaved a gentle sigh, and seemed to hesitate about coming to the point; Mr. Buncombe, therefore, judged it prudent to assist him; so he said,

"I am very much obliged to you, I am sure, Mr. Brown. What you promise I have sometimes hoped for; but what is it that you want me to do?"

The deacon's first answer was another brief, keen scrutiny of his clerk's face. The inspection appeared to satisfy him. It was an impassive face, and revealed no more than a mild look of satisfaction. Mr. Brown, therefore, drew a long breath, and resuming partially his unctuous whine, proceeded:

"You know that I am being hunted down, Mr. Buncombe? Alas! for the malice of the human heart. A ring of foes encompass me. I know not where to turn. They will take my little all from me, if I let them, just because of a forged letter, which that unchristian man Hogg has circulated about the *Molly Bawn*. No one, I declare before God, could regret the lamentable loss of that ship more than me, Mr. Buncombe; but my enemies will not hear a word in my defence. Every penny I have in this world will they take from me if they can, and cast me into the street to beg my bread. Oh, the wickedness of the human heart, Mr. Buncombe; little do you know of it yet, thank God!—thank God!"

The deacon stopped to blow his nose, overcome by his emotions.

"Really, Mr. Brown, I am awfully vexed to hear this," began Mr. Buncombe; but his master waved his handkerchief like a flag, and interposed with an eager haste,—

"I knew you would be—I knew you would be; I felt convinced of it; and that is why I have turned to you. You can help me to baffle my foes; and you will?"

"To the best of my power, I am ready, if you will only tell me how," repeated the mystified clerk; who, however, began to have a suspicion that he was to be asked to assist in some kind of fraud; his employer appeared so piously reluctant to come to the point.

"It's the simplest thing in the world, my dear sir," resumed the deacon, once more in his most matter-of-fact style. "The fact is I have been looking out for these attacks for some time, and have taken steps to defeat the designs of my enemies. Part of my hard won savings have therefore been put in what I may call a portable shape, and what I want you to do is to become the depository of these until this storm blows by. You understand?"

"Become the depository? No, I confess I do not quite follow you, Mr. Brown."

"Eh! don't you? But, my friend, nothing can be simpler," said the deacon, leaning forward and speaking fast in a confidential half whisper, " All you have to do is to take my place as owner—temporary owner—of a few securities and valuables I possess, so that these scoundrels who are hunting me cannot lay hands on them. They are bloodhounds, and will suck me dry if they can, don't you see? So if you'll be my deputy for a time, their game will be up. Don't you understand? It's a mere check-mate, you know. When you deal with ruffians, you must have the wisdom of the serpent. Eh, Mr. Buncombe?" concluded the deacon, with a nervous laugh. He was not sure how his clerk would take the proposal ; wrapped up though it was in guarded language, its villainy might shock an unsophisticated mind.

It did nothing of the kind, and the fears of the deacon on this score showed his ignorance of Mr. Buncombe's character. That gentleman now understood perfectly what was expected of him, and, like the man of genius he was, he saw in the task his long-waited for opportunity. A gleam of joy flitted across his sallow face, but it was with well-feigned reluctance that he gradually brought himself to agree to the proposal. The difficulties he raised did not concern the morality of the transaction. That he adroitly left on one side, and contented himself with making objections to the modes suggested for effecting the transfer of the property. Only when these were one by one triumphantly overcome by the deacon did he finally urge legal doubts.

"Might there not be some risk in what you propose, sir?" he suggested, with a timid air. "Couldn't the law lay hold of us if they found us out?"

"But they won't find us out, my dear friend," the deacon answered, now quite elated at the prospect of cheating his creditors. They can't, you know, if you keep quiet, and I keep quiet; besides, I am not going to become bankrupt this week or next. We shall have plenty of time to destroy all traces of everything. I shall, meantime, turn most of my securities into bonds and debentures to bearer, and then I'll defy the scoundrels to trace where the money has gone. Its disappearance can all be explained by my losses, you know."

Buncombe still affected to hesitate, although agreeing that this would be a splendid retaliation for the hatred of wicked creditors, and his final scruples were vanquished when Brown offered him a hundred and fifty pounds down for the trouble and slight risk he undertook. This was altogether irrespective of the promised partnership, and clinched the bargain so far.

CHAPTER X.

A DEACON'S DELUSION.

BUT when the confederates, as we may now call them, came to discuss details, Mr. Timothy Buncombe's cautious mind again took fright. Should the plot be found out his situation would be dangerous, and were he to remain in Mr. Brown's service while the " whitewashing " was in progress, it was at least possible that the creditors might subject him to awkward cross-examinations. A mind that harbours thoughts of self-aggrandisement at other people's expense is usually fearful.

Then, further, there was the question of Brown's resumption of business after the failure. " Do you think you can do that at once, my dear sir? " Mr. Timothy had ventured to ask.

" Why not ?" said Brown, in surprise,

" Well, you see, it is not merely the fact of your having failed that will stand in your way, but those unfortunate slanders about the *Molly Bawn*. A man down, you know, is usually a man trodden on, and your enemies will not spare you when you give them so good a chance."

" Mm! there's something in that," remarked the deacon ; " but what would you suggest ? I can't go out of business altogether, you know. I can't afford that ; not yet."

"There's not the least necessity, if you will accept a suggestion I venture to offer you," answered Buncombe in his softest tones.

"And what may that be, pray?" asked the deacon, with just a shade of suspicion in his tone.

"Oh, the simplest thing in the world ; it is agreed, you know, that afterwards I am to enter into partnership with you."

"Yes, of course," ejaculated Brown.

Without heeding the interruption, Buncombe proceeded. "Now, what I have been thinking is this : would it not be better that I should leave you before the smash came, and start business for myself. We might appear to have quarrelled, you know ; and when the whole affair was well over, we could make it up again, and you could then join me."

"Mm ! ah !" exclaimed Brown, doubtfully ; "I don't quite see, my friend, how that plan would serve us."

"Don't you, though ; just ponder over it for a little, and don't say 'no' in too great a hurry. You see, I have looked at the thing on all sides, and it struck me that, if we parted now, to all appearance as enemies, your creditors would never dream that you had made me the depository of part of your savings. Nothing in the world would look less probable."

"Ah, so, yes, good ! I never thought of that. That's not a bad idea. I see !" and, as he jerked out these phrases, the deacon rubbed his hands, his face beaming with pleasure. "You are a clever fellow, Buncombe," he continued. "Hang me, if I thought there was so much in you. Let's see, tho', when shall we quarrel? Ha, ha!"

"The sooner the better. I have my eye on a little office, a few doors up the street, and could go in there at once."

"Good: but I say, though, how will you do for money? You can't begin business on nothing, you know."

"I have thought of that too, and I think I can manage. You see I shall have the hundred and fifty you give me, and I dare say I can scrape up a few pounds of my own. My idea, in fact, is to give out that my uncle-in-law has helped me with the needful, and then——"

"Capital! First rate! Gad, you're a perfect trump!" shouted the deacon in his eagerness. "But I interrupted you—you said, 'and then——'"

"Yes, I was going to say that, of course, as your enemy I'll cut about trying to pick up the business that is falling away from you. By this means what is best of it will, perhaps, be kept together against the day when you can join me."

The delight of the pious shipbroker over this scheme was unbounded. It seemed to smooth away his last difficulties. In his joy he never gave a thought to the possibilities of failure; never dreamt that his frugal clerk might play him false if he liked.

That same afternoon the confederates contrived to get up a scene before the other clerks, which ended in Buncombe leaving the office, vowing never to return. Before another Sunday came round, all Berborough knew that Brown and Buncombe had quarreled and separated, and that the latter had commenced business on his own account.

What Berborough did not know was that Mr. Buncombe carried with him, or received within a few days of the separation, securities to the value of something like twelve thousand pounds, which Mr. Brown handed to him for safe custody. Amongst these securities were a number of shares in Brown's best ships, and the title deeds of a strip of land on the bank of Berborough's estuary, nearer the sea than the town. Mr. Brown had just bought, through a lawyer, this land as a speculation, in the belief that one of these days it would be wanted for docks, and having faith in the future, he naturally did not want to part with it. So Timothy "stood in" as the ostensible owner. Most of the property, however, that Mr. Buncombe received from his late employer was in the shape of securities to bearer, the ownership of which can so easily be made untraceable. It was by a juggle indeed that some of the shipping shares were transferred. They were not originally in Brown's own name, but were held for him by dummies. He, in his view, merely changed the dummy.

"It's rather a risky business, you know; but I think we shall be too many for them," Mr. Buncombe remarked to the deacon more than once at the secret interviews the pair held while this transfer was in progress.

Brown had no doubt at all on that score. His sanguine spirits had re-asserted themselves with all their native exuberance. He felt that he was in trim to make a first-class smash up.

In the chapel the separation of master and clerk made quite a sensation, and their behaviour to each other convinced everybody that they lived in a state of deadly hatred one with another. The general impression was that Buncombe had got money at last from his ungracious uncle-in-law, and had taken the opportunity afforded by Brown's misfortunes to break with him.

Anyhow, the hatred now existing between the two was obvious to everybody. They went out of their way to exhibit it. Brown ostentatiously scowled every time his eye lighted on his late freight clerk, and Buncombe treated him to a stare as cool as if he had never seen the deacon before in his life. It was excellent comedy, excellently played.

CHAPTER XI.

A DEACON'S DELIGHT.

LESS than three months after their little arrangement had
been completed, Mr. Silas Brown duly stopped payments,
just as everybody had expected.   At the preliminary
meeting of his creditors he laid so doleful a story of his
losses and misfortunes before them, that in spite of a few
bitter complaints, they ultimately agreed to accept a
composition of half-a-crown in the pound, rather than
throw the estate into the hands of those sharks of
bankruptcy officials.   So meekly, on the whole, was the
blow received that Mr. Brown felt disposed to regret his
generosity.

"I do believe they would have accepted eighteen-
pence," said he, the day after everything was settled.
It did not occur to the good man that his non-payment
of his debts might ruin or cripple dozens of families;
that by hiding his property he was a thief.   Nothing of the
sort.   Mr. Brown had done an excellent stroke of business.
It was much more satisfactory for him to "pay out'
his creditors in this way, as he often said to himself,
than to "pay up."   What did it matter to him if numbers
of little tradespeople who had invested their savings in
his ships lost nearly their all, and had either to fail

themselves or to battle with hunger in order to pay their own debts. All Mr. Brown's creditors were to him "enemies." He was at war with them, and in war all crimes are lawful.

So far from being ashamed of his deeds, Mr. Brown could exult over them, and thank his God for the victory. His proud humility in chapel, the Sunday after his "afflictions" were at an end, was beautiful to look upon. The gusts of his song—all out of time and tune—swept athwart the rythm of the choir with a force that nearly led the singers among the flock astray. He was bellowing forth his hymn of victory, and the light of triumph shone in his eye, even while his head was bent.

David Hogg sat there to the left of him, and a seat or two forward. He had the impudence to turn round and frown at Brown's song more than once; but what did the ex-deacon—Brown had resigned on the smash, expecting to be at once reinstated in his honours—what did the ex-deacon care for Hogg or any other underwriter? On them as on all his other foes he had had his revenge, and when he caught the underwriter's frown he returned it with interest, singing louder, more out of tune than ever.

During the sermon his head wagged solemnly at the minister's periods, and when that excellent man, bent on improving the occasion, dwelt upon the afflictions which follow men's footsteps in this sin-laden world, afflictions which even penetrated within their sacred fold, Brown leant his head on his hand and looked upward with a gaze so intent, that one might have imagined his goggle

eyes saw visions through the roof. But there was no
sadness in that look. Why should there be? Was there
not a snug little pile of securities and accrued interest
lying up there in Mr. Timothy Buncombe's little safe,
which he could now handle when he pleased? Doubtless
his mind dwelt much on this sweet thought as he stood
up to sing, his left hand playing absently with the seals
of his massive watch-chain, still there, notwithstanding
ruin, and half-a-crown in the pound.

CHAPTER XII.

A DEACON'S DESPAIR.

SHORT-SIGHTED mortals that we are. The wisest and most pious among us see no further into the future than a bat at noonday. While Mr. Silas Brown was entertaining his long harassed soul with visions of peace and abundance, an old age made respectable by wealth well hoarded, had not Mr. Timothy Buncombe equally good grounds, nay better grounds, for permitting himself the same indulgence? Might he not at that very time be solacing his weary spirit with these same thoughts?

In the interval between his departure from Mr. Brown's office and the failure, he had not been idle. All that was good in his late employer's business he had striven to draw into his hands, and already his intimacy with exporters had enabled him to load several ships in a satisfactory way. The smudge that attached to Brown's name did not touch his, and he meant to make his conduct worthy of confidence. The future, therefore, had hope for Timothy Buncombe. A better day had dawned. Fortune lay within his grasp, perhaps, if he but played his cards well.

As he thought of these things his mind gradually familiarised itself with the idea that it might be an excellent thing to keep the ex-deacon's money and securities. When he took charge of them the notion of doing so was vague. Money would be useful to him, he felt ; but not all at once could his soul rise to the height of this great conception.

That Brown should never be his partner, he, from the outset, decided ; for he saw that any association with a ship-sinking rascal would destroy his chance of success. But he had not been clear as to the money. Some of it he felt he must keep, he could not get along without it. It was not, however, till his business began to grow, and his conceptions with it, that he felt the impossibility in his heart of parting with any of this capital. To hand it over to a scoundrel like Brown would be suicidal. And did not Brown really owe him as much, or nearly as much, for unrequited past services ?

These were the thoughts that filled the restless brain of Mr. Timothy Buncombe Sunday and Saturday ; but he kept them to himself. The complacent Christian professor who had trusted him never suspected their existence, and went, when the " whitewashing " had been completed, to take back his hoard without the shadow of a doubt.

It was in March, a bleak, bitter night in March, that Mr. Silas Brown ventured to steal along on his errand of reclamation to Mr. Buncombe's little cottage. There was no moon, and the feebly-lighted streets were dark enough to hide burglars, let alone pious citizens seeking their own. Nevertheless, Mr. Brown had disguised himself to the best of his ability, in a broad brimmed wide-

awake, and a muffler of sober-hued tartan. His step
was methodical, and almost slow, for he feared to walk
fast lest he should betray himself. When, therefore, he
reached Mr. Buncombe's door, he felt cold, and it seemed
to him like a long ten minutes before the door was
opened in answer to his gentle ring. Once inside he felt
little better than before. The room into which the
maid-of-all-work ushered him, no doubt Mr. Buncombe's
best parlour, was cold and damp as the outside air—
fireless and lightless.

When the girl went to tell her master, she closed the
door behind her, and left Brown to stand and shiver in
utter darkness. Mr. Buncombe also seemed to him a
long time in coming. Brown felt for a seat, and stumbled
and nearly fell over a footstool. This put him out of
temper, and could he have seen the door he would have
opened it and shouted; but it was too dark, so he
shivered and stood still.

At length the door opened, and Mr. Timothy Buncombe entered, carrying a lighted candle. Closing it
carefully behind him, he advanced and put the candle
on the table in the middle of the room, at the end
nearest the exit.

"You've been a devilish long time, Buncombe,"
cried Mr. Brown, his teeth almost chattering in his
head. "I thought you were going to leave me here
all night."

"I beg your pardon, I'm sure," was the reply; "I'm
very sorry; but the fact is, Mrs. B. was putting the
children to bed, and, as usual, I had to help her, and to

hear them say their prayers. Family duties, you know, Mr. Brown."

"Well, well, but it's deuced cold here ; you might have had a fire, man. I'm chill to the marrow of my bones."

" Really, I'm so sorry, but you did not tell me you were coming to-night, you know. Had I known you were to honour my humble home with a call, I should have had a roaring fire for you. But we have to be economical in these times, especially when you can't tell how things will go."

" Ah, just so. Don't apologise. I must make my visit the shorter. You've got, eh, those papers in the house, I dessay, and if you'll just hand 'em over I'll be off faster than I came, I can tell you."

" Papers ! what papers ?" answered Mr. Buncombe, in a tone that was meant to affect great surprise, but which did not quite fulfil intentions.

" Eh, what ! Why, of course, those bonds and things, you know, that I entrusted to you last November. You haven't lost 'em, I suppose," exclaimed the ex-deacon, with a gaspy attempt at a laugh.

Buncombe looked at him with a cold stare, and replied, in his most measured tone, " I have nothing at all in this house belonging to you, Mr. Brown."

" The devil you haven't. Then where are my bonds and other things ? Tell me how and when I can get 'em." Brown began to feel warmer.

" I have no knowledge of the documents to which you allude," replied Mr. Buncombe in the same slow, cold accents.

"What!" almost yelled the ex-deacon. "Do you mean to tell me, Buncombe, that you've not got the property I left with you three months ago?"

"I did not say that. I know nothing about it."

"What the deuce do you mean, then? Do you think I came here to be played with? Hand those securities over at once, or it will be the worse for you. This is a pretty go, and no mistake." The last sentence Brown spoke as if to himself. Then, as Mr. Buncombe stood silent and motionless, he hissed out "Did you hear me? Confound you, you sweep, you don't mean to say that you intend to stick to my property?"

"I do not understand what you are talking about," said Buncombe, slowly; but at the same time he edged a little nearer the door.

"Oh! come now, I like that. You don't know that you have twelve or fourteen thousand pounds of mine in your hands, don't you, you innocent. That's a good 'un; but I don't quite see your game, my man. You can't hope to keep that money, surely. Good God! whatever shall I do? This is horrible. Come, I say, Buncombe, you're joking, ain't you? Drop it, man, drop it, for God's sake, and let us to business. It's too cold here for larks."

The poor ex-deacon was beside himself with rage, fear, disappointment, and the last lingerings of hope, and looked now anything but cold. Heavy balls of sweat were gathering on his forehead, and began to trickle unheeded down his flushed face. He gasped, he puffed his cheeks, and blew his breath out like a man in desperate need of more air, and Mr. Timothy Buncombe stood and looked at him impassive as a figure in stone.

Receiving no answer to his threats and cries, the ex-deacon, after a short pause, burst forth on a new tack.

"Oh! I see what it is; you ain't pleased with what I gave you for the job, eh? Well, my dear boy,"—here the poor wretch tried to grin, and held out his hand, " What was it, one hundred and fifty pounds, two hundred pounds? Well, make it five hundred pounds, and say it's a bargain. You know I'm not mean with a friend. Take five hundred pounds and give me my papers, I want to get home soon. I've an appointment at nine."

Buncombe did not speak, but shook his head.

" Eh, what—damnation! You want more, do you. Well, speak up, can't you! Tell us what you do want, and be done with it. I can't stand here playing the fool all night."

" I have told you," said Mr. Buncombe, "that I know nothing at all of what you are talking about."

"Oh, damn it, no, you can't mean that, Buncombe. Heavens, no! Say you are joking, and give me my papers, and let me go. Buncombe, Buncombe, my boy, don't be hard on me. Take a thousand pounds and let us be done with it. Say it's a bargain and I'll give you half the business. Oh! Buncombe, you wouldn't swindle a poor devil, would you, now? I have been your master, you know, for more than twelve years. Buncombe, I say, speak up, man. Don't look so black as that. Say it's a joke; pay up, even if you take two thousand pounds, and the interest you have in hand. Give me the rest and let me go home in peace." And Brown fairly broke down. Tumbling back on the ricketty couch near him, he covered his face with his hands and sobbed like a child.

Mr. Buncombe stood without moving a muscle of his face, and did not attempt to speak until the paroxysm of angry sobbing had partially subsided. Then in the cold indifferent tone he had thus far maintained, he said :

"It's not the least use, Brown. What I have, I keep, so the sooner you give up your attempts to extort money from me the better."

"Extort money from you, you thief, you scoundrel, you miserable sneak, you hang-dog looking blackguard!" yelled Brown, starting to his feet and clenching his hands as if to dash upon his enemy : "Never, never while breath is in my body! you black-hearted villain! Give up, must I? It's attempts to extort money, is it? Urrrh! By God, I'll kill you first." As he uttered this threat he stepped convulsively forward and shook his fist in Mr. Timothy Buncombe's face. For the first time that gentleman quailed. The coward rose in him, and with blanched lips and trembling limbs he involuntarily sought the door. But the ex-deacon anticipated him. With a dash he swept past, and planting his back against the door, yelled :

"Now, you fiend incarnate, out of this you don't budge till I have my money. I swear I'll choke the life out of you, if need be ; but I'll have it."

Buncombe's answer was to spring to the window, open it, and call "police! police!" not very loudly though.

In an instant all fighting humour left Brown. His hands fell by his side, he trembled from head to foot, and crept to the nearest chair.

"Don't, for God's sake, don't, Buncombe," he pleaded. "Surely we can settle our little business without the police. Close the window, man, and come and sit down and talk it over quietly. You put me in a passion just now by your little jokes, and I didn't know what I said. But I wouldn't hurt you, Buncombe, really I wouldn't. Don't call the police, there's a good soul." As he spoke he rose again, crept up to the window, and laid his hand pleadingly on Buncombe's arm. The latter, who had drawn in his head, answered—

"I must call the police if you refuse to leave my house quietly."

"Don't, Buncombe, my boy. Don't be hard on a poor old fellow," whined the ex-deacon.

"I tell you, once for all," said Mr. Buncombe, speaking low and slowly, but with some show of heat, "I tell you, once for all, that I know nothing about money of yours. I have not got any, and though you plead here till doomsday, never a penny shall you have from me."

"Don't, Buncombe, my boy; shut the window, do, and be reasonable. You're having a little game with me, ain't you? You wouldn't see a poor old fellow like me ruined now, would you? Why should you keep all my money? I've never done you no harm. I've been your friend all these years. Don't take all my money, Buncombe; give me half of it, and I'll be satisfied."

"Haven't you done me harm, just," was Buncombe's reply, catching on purpose at one phrase in his late employer's incoherent pleading; "who but you has kept me a slave and a drudge from my earliest boyhood? I've worked for you year in and out, early and late, coining money for you, and seldom got even thanks for my pains. You just gave me enough money to exist upon, and, for bonus, snivelling cant and bushels of good wishes for the next world. I might have died in a ditch for all you cared. No, no, Brown, you'll get nothing out of me. It's my turn now. All I have got will no more than make up for your past robberies. I consider it due to me, and I mean to pay myself now I have the chance. If you don't like it, then—then, by Jove, *you* can go for the police; but it's not the least good your stopping here."

Gradually, as Brown listened to this bitter speech, all force seemed to leave his body. His limbs grew limp, his jaw fell, his head dropped on his breast, and his dull eye became fixed. Even by the light of one candle it could be seen that his face was ashy white. As one stunned by a mortal blow, he stood there rooted to the spot, gazing vacantly towards his late clerk.

"Yes, yes!" he gasped out at last. "I'm done, then; fool that I was, I might have known. But I'll go for the police, yes I will," he added, in a more determined tone. "I'll go rather than you should keep my money, Buncombe: curse you, yes, curse you for a hell-hound. My curse will go with that money; the curse of a ruined man. It will blast you yet; see if it doesn't. Eh! penal

servitude, say you ?   Who'll get penal servitude, I'd like
to know, if not the thief that steals my money ?"   This
query was in answer to a hint quietly dropped by
Buncombe.

"There is such a thing as cheating one's creditors,
you know, Mr. Brown," was the cold rejoinder.

Brown's jaw fell again, and he turned and made for
the door.   With his hand on its knob, he stopped, and
once more tried to strike a bargain with Timothy.

"Look here, Buncombe," he cried, in his old wheedling
tone, "let's divide the money ; give me five thousand
pounds of it.   Hang me, that's more than fair.   Don't
be hard, now ; say you'll do it."

"You have got all the answer you'll get from me, I
tell you.   You may plead till doomsday, if you like, but
it won't procure you a penny."

"Then, by God, I shall lodge a criminal information
against you," cried Brown, once more flushing up
feverishly.

"As you please, sir ; only if you do I'll take precious
good care that the money goes to your creditors."

"You can't do that."

"Can't I, though !   Before you can let the law loose
on me I shall be in communication with your creditors.
They shall know all, and you'll be the sufferer, I guess,
not I."

"Buncombe, you are a devil incarnate," exclaimed the
poor beset ex-deacon, and he pulled out his handkerchief
and wiped his flushed face, like a man at his wit's
end.

Buncombe took no notice whatever of this observation, except to fold his hands across his breast, and gaze fixedly at his dupe.

"Mark my words," Brown resumed, "you may triumph now, I'm beaten; yes, and I'm a fool, but I'll have my revenge on you yet, you fiend, or my name isn't Silas Brown. As sure as God made me, I'll pull you down. I'll dog your steps, I'll expose your black-hearted villainy. The town shall know it. I'll proclaim it to the Church; you shall not get off. Urrrh! you scoundrel, I could slay you where you stand."

As the ex-deacon said this he caught up a chair and rushed at his enemy. But Mr. Buncombe knew his man now, and instead of recoiling, merely caught the chair by the legs and wrenched it out of Brown's hands. It fell on the floor between them, and they stood and glared at each other in the dim candle light.

How the scene would have ended had the pair been longer left to themselves, I cannot say. In a fight, not improbably, a fight wherein I am not sure that the younger man would have had the best of it. At this juncture, however, Mrs. Buncombe created a diversion by opening the door and looking in. The noise the two men made had excited her curiosity to a point that rendered it impossible for her to refrain longer from trying to discover what was going on.

"My goodness, gracious me," she cried, before she was half inside the room, "whatever are you two a-doing in here, argufying in the cold? If you hadn't made such a row, I'd a thought you were gone out."

Mr. Buncombe first scowled at this interruption, and then smiled, as if congratulating himself at the chance of deliverance his wife's inquisitiveness afforded. Mr. Brown shivered involuntarily, drew a long breath, and thrust his hand through his grizzly stubble as if to collect his thoughts. Neither, however, spoke, but that in no wise abashed Mrs. Buncombe.

" My goodness me," she resumed, " you look like a couple of hicicles. Won't you come into the back parlour, Mr. Brown, and finish your talk there? There's a fire in it, and the children are all abed. You'll get your death of cold if you stay here, I'm sure. What were you thinking on, Tim, to keep Mr. Brown in this damp room. There ain't been no fire in it since last Sunday week, for you was up at Grimsby last Sunday, and I kept the children in the back parlour. Won't you come in, Mr. Brown, and get yourself warmed up a bit? Sorry we havn't a grander place to invite you to, but, you see, we're poor yet, though, if all Tim hints is true, we ain't a-going to be for long. Do come along, Mr. Brown."

" Ah, n—no, no thank you, my good w—Mrs. Buncombe ; no, thanks, not to-night. I must be going, I think ; yes, I must be going. I shall see you again, Mr. Buncombe. We have not finished with each other yet," he added significantly, and without lifting his eyes, or offering to shake hands, Mr. Brown pushed past Mrs. Buncombe in rude haste, out into the passage, caught up his hat and stick, fumbled at the door latch for a moment, and then opened it and disappeared into the night.

"What a funny man," cried Mrs. Buncombe, ere the door had banged behind him ; "whatever have you two been up to? You looked like fightin' when I popped my head in. Is the old skinflint cut up because we've begun business for ourselves ? "

" Just that, my dear," answered her husband, "and I'm very glad you came in when you did ; though," he quickly added, " I trust you will not make a practice of it, my dear. It mightn't be always so convenient."

"Oh, of course, you think women in the way, I know. Just like you men ; nobody is any good but yourselves," sniffed Mrs. Buncombe.

"All right, my dear ; be satisfied that you did me a good turn this time, and you shall have a new gown to show you that I'm not ungrateful."

"Oh ! laws ! will it be silk, pappy? Do make it silk, a nice black silk, with lots of flounces."

" All right, my dear. Have your own way this time ; I think I can afford a little extravagance," agreed her husband, as the ghost of a smile flitted across his pale face. The struggle he had gone through had put a strain on his nervous system.

CHAPTER XIII.

A DISAPPEARANCE AND A DEATH.

IN this way Mrs. Buncombe's thoughts were diverted from Mr. Silas Brown and his affairs. She asked no more questions, possibly thought no more about it. As for Mr. Buncombe, he doubtless considered his boast a pretty safe one. He had placed Brown on the horns of a dilemma, and felt sure that there the man would stick. The least movement he made to denounce his spoiler could only procure his own destruction.

Silas Brown knew this as well as Mr. Timothy Buncombe, but he did not therefore desist in his attempt to get back part, at least, of his money. To get hold of that money, in fact, became his fixed idea. Early and late, at all times and seasons, when it was possible to catch Mr. Buncombe alone, Brown begged for that money, threatened and wept by turns, and all in vain. His persistent hunt after the lost treasure, was, indeed, the means of completing his ruin. To follow that quest he neglected what little was left of his business, and allowed his rivals, including Mr. Buncombe, to take it out of his hands. Most of it, in fact, went to that fortunate and rising young man.

Poor Brown had raved of vengeance, but surely the vengeance was falling on himself. A few weeks of this agony sufficed to make him look years older; a few months of neglect of business reduced him to penury. And as he sank in purse the once resplendent Christian professor became looser in morals. There was no object now in being respectable, the wretched fellow seemed to think. He had never been reinstated in his forfeited deaconship, and by degrees he ceased to attend public worship. The sanctified world-subduing air with which he formerly walked the streets gave place to a hurried slouch, ending all too often in a dive into a drinking bar.

With the loss of the garment of pietism, all was lost. From being a back-slider in the eyes of the holy, he became a reprobate—an outcast from the sanctuary. All too clearly did the world now see the true character of Silas Brown. Pietism had been with him what it is with most talkers about religion—a trick. By means of it he had hoped to conceal his true character, so that he might cheat his fellow men with the greater impunity. His money lost without hope of recovery, the motive for sustaining this mockery disappeared, and before many months were over Silas Brown became a loafer, a man who drank hard and swore hard, more ready to weep over his wrongs among loose companions in drinking dens than he had ever been to shed tears for his sins in the meeting place of the godly.

Revenge! Were not the men and women whom Brown's misdoings had made hungry, the children whom his rotten overladen ships had rendered fatherless, now being revenged upon the human mawworm who had done them evil? Yes, if retribution be revenge; if not, no.

Unknown to himself there was one man, however, upon whom he was perhaps more effectually reaping a harvest of gratified vengeance by his sottishness than he could have done by any other known means. That man was Mr. Timothy Buncombe. Cool, scornful, collected, defiant he had been towards his former employer as long as that unhappy being kept his wits; when he got drunk it was quite another affair. In his cups he might tell secrets to Mr. Buncombe's hurt. A man with nothing to lose, in whom hope is as good as dead, often becomes reckless. No fate, no human punishment can add to his degradation and misery. He may therefore take vengeance upon an enemy merely to force that enemy to share his own degradation.

Astute Mr. Timothy Buncombe saw this contingency, and became afraid to an extent that caused him to begin to hand to Silas small sums of money when that fallen star came in his way. There was in sober truth little ground for the fear which prompted this "generosity." If Brown dreaded one thing more than death itself it was the jail. The last rag of respectability to which he clung, was, not to be a jail bird. That had restrained him from openly attacking Mr. Timothy Buncombe when first he found himself overreached, and it held him in its grasp in the worst hours of his degradation. When drunk he talked loudly and oft about his misfortunes, and about certain mysterious wrongs from which he had suffered, but never did he condescend to particulars ; a dread of consequences always held him back. The terror of the law was upon him when his eye was bleared, his voice thick, and his legs erratic, more perhaps than when he was possessed of his usual faculties.

I was about to say, happily for him, Mr. Buncombe was unaware of this, but I am not sure that it was happily. The money which the rising ship broker doled out in his conscience-troubled way to his old master did no good. It was given from no good motive, and degraded both giver and receiver. It helped to augment the speed with which Silas Brown made for the gutter and the pauper's grave. A year, or little more, saw the last chance of making a living at his old occupation in Berborough gone from him for ever. Before two years had expired his house was broken up. His wife had died of a broken heart within eighteen months of her husband's bankruptcy. Shame and grief killed her. Two unmarried daughters, the last of the ex-deacon's family, had departed to try to make their living as governesses, or something of that sort, for their father could no longer keep a home for them. Alone in the world, forsaken, despised, a besodden wreck of his former purse-holy self, it had been better had Silas died then, too. But he lived on, and periodically debauched himself with Mr. Buncombe's hush money. Several people gave him odd clerking jobs to do, but he stuck to nothing, drifting ever downwards.

At last, in the winter of 186— Brown disappeared from Berborough altogether ; where he went, or what became of him, none knew for long after, and few cared. Mr. Timothy Buncombe thought it was the best thing he could have done to take himself off. To him, at least, the disappearance was a relief, and had that been possible, he would, doubtless, have gone about his daily business with a straighter back in consequence. A lighter heart he assuredly had, delivered as he was from his fear of the drunken tattlings of a ruined man. The star of Buncombe was in the ascendant.

About this time, too, the rising shipowner was blessed by what he would still have deigned to describe as another God's mercy. Mr. Bob Cutler died. Hale he was, and strong looking ; but, nevertheless, he too disappeared, and, unlike Brown, without danger of returning. A "stroke" carried him off somewhere about the age of seventy. "It was 'baccy as did it," his paramour declared. "I allays said as 'baccy would be the death on 'im." Perhaps so ; anyhow, dead he was, and, what was better still, from the point of view of the Buncombe family, he died intestate, baulking thus the hopes of the charwoman, who, after a few brief years of ease, had to take to her drudgery again. He left much less money than had been expected, a matter of four thousand pounds only, and Mrs. Penelope Buncombe was unable to secure the whole of that modest sum. Other relatives started up as claimants, of whom she had never heard, and, rather than throw the estate into Chancery, a compromise was agreed upon. The estate, when subdivided, yielded Mrs. Buncombe about eight hundred pounds. Small as this sum was, her husband accepted it as a kind of solatium.   His marriage had, after all, not been absolutely barren of good.   " Providence," he confessed to his " dear Penny," was declaring itself on their side, and the " wicked " were obtaining their deserts.

CHAPTER XIV.

AN INTERVAL.

WERE I a German annalist, the dozen years of Mr. Timothy Buncombe's life which followed the epoch brought to a satisfactory conclusion in the last chapter would be detailed with proper minuteness. I might tell when the great man bought his gold watch, when he made his first move upwards in the matter of dwelling-place, when he became a chapel deacon and assumed a modest lordship over that part of God's heritage represented by Goliath chapel, when Mrs. Buncombe first tried to mend her grammar and took to wearing silk dresses at breakfast, how her husband made money and lost it, all his ambitious hopes, disappointments, chagrins, what was the progress of his business, and the degrees of his ascent in popular favour. It might be possible to make this chronicle interesting to one person in a million or two, for there are still people living who find delight in the speeches of peers, temporal and spiritual ; and I met a man not long ago who had read "Blair's sermons;" so, at least, he said. But I cannot bring my hand to the execution of so arduous a labour; no, not even to gratify one man in half a million. I should prefer, only that it suits not a maker of books, the scriptural style—

"After that he lived so many years, and begat sons and daughters."

That is all the record most men's lives require; but excellent though this summary is in a general way, it does not quite apply to Mr. Buncombe. His success in the multiplication of his species was small. At the end of twenty years of married life he had only five children; one son and four daughters.

The formula, therefore, of the old Jewish chroniclers would probably have to be modified, in any case, before it could be applied to the successful individual whose deeds, and thoughts, and words it is my pleasant task to chronicle.

He made money, for example, in these years; and, as I have hinted, lost it, too. A ship or two did sink in spite of his utmost care, and in one case where this untoward accident happened, he might have suffered in the estimation of his enemies but that he nobly took the bulk of the loss on himself.

Not only did Mr. Buncombe make money, on the whole, but he spent money. There was nothing of the niggard about him, nor yet did he sink quite to the level of the purse-swollen brewer, or parvenu stock gambler, or corn dealer, and become a slave to gold chains, diamond studs, and champagne cup.

Mr. Buncombe cultivated, to better purpose, the art of gentility, and deserves the more praise that he did so under difficulties. His wife wished to second him, without doubt, but unfortunately only brought her vulgarity into the greater prominence by her attempts. Worse still, the children took after their mother, until Mr. Buncombe packed them off to expensive boarding schools, there to acquire the arts and graces esteemed proper to "good society."

This was an excellent arrangement in more ways than one, and, not least so, because it permitted both Mr. and Mrs. Buncombe to enjoy life without the cares of rearing a family. If I must be particular, and go so far as to tell a little about these years, I may, indeed, admit that Mr. Buncombe was not at all a family man, and did not effusively love children. To him it was no overpowering joy to be a father.

In this respect he bore great resemblance to a wizened, carroty-headed little creature I once knew, who laboured under the delusion that he was born to be a statesman, and to "rule the Senate." This droll fragment of a man issued an ukase forbidding his children to appear in his presence until they had reached their teens, lest their senseless chatter and infantine absurdities should distract his mighty mind from the contemplation of his own advancing greatness.

Mr. Timothy Buncombe was not on quite so lofty a pinnacle of parental indifference as that, but he came near it, and was glad when his offspring were out of the house. While holidays lasted he was more or less miserable. There was no sympathy between him and his children. They chafed at the discipline he tried to maintain in lieu of sympathy, and he in return drew the reins the tighter the more they rebelled.

Twice every Sunday, when at home, these youngsters had to appear in the family pew at Goliath chapel, and every evening of the week they were obliged to attend family prayers. Frivolous amusements were frowned down. Mr. Buncombe was a pharisee of the strictest sect in those days, and the more gloomy he made life to his children the more satisfied was he that he excellently fulfilled the duties incident to fatherhood.

What more could he do, indeed? Money they had, good clothes, abundant food, excellent tuition, advantages all of which he had never known, as he constantly told his boy.

All this they had, and still the household was not a harmonious one. Disobedience was common, truth not always present, ingratitude obvious. Preach as the father might, he could not bring these brats, as he called them at times, to see that they ought to be always melting in gratitude for what they enjoyed beyond their father's youthful portion.

At times possibly Mr. Timothy Buncombe may have thought that this ingratitude and these indications of rebellion were his punishment. He may have so thought; I cannot say that he did. Evidence of his feeling on this subject does not exist, and if I were to evolve a conjecture from my inward experience, I should say that he was much more likely to think himself a man wronged and misjudged.

But what does all this lead to? Where is the laudable resolution with which this chapter opened? Ask not the question. I never made any resolution, or, if I did, I abandoned it as soon as made, which is the fate of all resolutions. They are the most cruelly treated products of the human mind, and I do not boast of better behaviour towards them than my neighbours—far from it.

CHAPTER XV.

A "MERCURY."

THE fact of the matter is that I knew all the while of one event which happened within the period, I, in a sort of way, resolved to slur over, which could not possibly be left unnoticed. It has nearly—not quite—as much to do with the riper career of Mr. Buncombe as the fall and exit of Mr. Silas Brown had to do with the rawer. This event was nothing less than the untoward and disobedient marriage of his eldest daughter with that good-for-nothing fellow Henry Weardale.

"How on earth could that happen?" you exclaim; "Meetings and mixings of that kind never occur except in sensational novels."

Well, of course, it was odd; I do not deny that for a moment. Not odd that the girl should have married without leave, but odd that she should have selected Harry Weardale. It looks so, at least; but just as my carefully-executed disquisition on the moral economy of the Buncombe family must have prepared you for any ridiculous proceeding on the part of the younger branches thereof, so will the narrative I am now about to unfold convince every sensible mind that the marriage of these two persons was not merely the most natural event in the world, but the only event that could have happened in the circumstances.

When last we saw Harry Weardale he had just performed the vulgar, low bred feat of thrusting out his tongue at a great pillar of the Church worshipping in Goliath chapel. That was quite a dozen years before his introduction to the Buncombe family, and he had grown since then. The raw, common-place boy has become a man, not unpleasant to look upon, and the office messenger of Mr. David Hogg has developed into the sub-editor of the *Berborough Mercury*, and the writer of much doggerel verse, mercifully long since forgotten.

If you ask me how this happened, I can only reply— in the way such things always do happen. The boy Weardale was thrown early on his own resources, and necessity sharpened his naturally strong wits. A literary faculty, of a kind, dawned in him, and he "drifted into journalism." From being a volunteer contributor of doggerel and essays to the *Mercury*, he rose to be its sub-editor, and so on.

The *Mercury* was a paper of Liberal politics, on strictly orthodox party lines, and leaned towards Dissent in matters religious. It affected, also, to be the leading commercial organ of the town, and as such brought its staff into contact with most of the merchants and ship-owners.

Henry Weardale therefore knew Mr. Timothy Buncombe on his mercantile side as a mere matter of ordinary business, but he likewise knew him as a man taking a prominent part in the politics of the borough.

Mr. Buncombe might be mayor some day, and would certainly be one of the aldermen whenever he chose to put himself forward. He was a man who often spoke on public occasions, and more than once had noticed with pleasure how well reported he had been by the *Mercury*.

This led to enquiries, and he found that Henry Weardale was the reporter who had taken the "note" of these speeches. "A man like this may be useful to me," Mr. Buncombe concluded, and forthwith told his wife to invite "the young scribbler" now and then to her *omnium gatherum* sort of parties.

All that followed upon this imprudent laxity on Mr. Buncombe's part was just as natural as the fusion of two drops of water in juxtaposition. First of all the sub-editor, with true masculine cunning, secured himself in the good graces of Mrs. Buncombe, who, worthy woman, with all her desire to come up to her husband's standard, never could recognise with promptitude the grading it was necessary to give her associates. All who came to her house were put on the same level of familiarity by her. She never could understand the distinction between friendliness and social policy. To deck herself out in re-splendent garments, with as many rings on her fingers, and brooches and bracelets and chains of gold about her person as she could come by, and then to blaze forth in smirks and handshakes on all and sundry with an even measure of underbred effusiveness, was Mrs. Buncombe's *summum bonum* of human happiness in giving parties. And when she returned from other people's houses all glittering in silk and gold, her cook was generally the confidant to whom she recounted all she had seen and felt and heard, whether at a mayor's reception or a " Dorcas meeting."

To a lady of this character there was nothing out of the way in an intimate association with a newspaper reporter. Henry was good looking, a tall, bright-faced, brown eyed, curly headed young man of three-and-twenty, with a lively rattling tongue and the capacity to sing a good song. Mrs. Buncombe could not possibly resist such a fellow as that. In a sense, she fell in love with him herself; opened her house and heart to him as if he had been of her own flesh and blood. That shows you what I mean; nothing scandalous, in the least. The rising shipowner's wife was too homely, too commonplace and unintelligent ever to be capable of making scandals. She left that for the great.

No; Henry Weardale simply brought a glimpse of sunshine with him into that sombre dwelling. When he was there mirth was there, the girls played the piano, or, at any rate, Beatrice, the eldest, did, for her education was " finished;" Harry sang, cracked jokes, flattered the mother, and left a blank when he departed.

This intimate intercourse went on for many months unnoticed by the head of the house; a proof that family affairs had little interest for Mr. Buncombe. That gentleman may, indeed, have felt so fully convinced of his own excellence as a father as to be justified in taking liberties with his family. At all events he spent most of his evenings abroad, either in the Union Club, where traders congregated, or in the houses of his friends.

And it cannot be denied that this conduct gave, on the
whole, much more pleasure to his household than his
supervising presence would have done.   There was
laughter in his absence, which his approaching step on
the gravel walk sufficed to hush.   Unless a " party " was
on foot, Weardale never stayed when the " master " happened to be at home ; never a sound of his voice was
heard.

Happiness of this furtive kind could not last for ever.
Better grounded happiness often does not.   Mr. Buncombe
stumbled at length upon the horrifying fact that "the
young scribbler " had dared to fall in love with his eldest
daughter.   His wife let the secret out in the innocence
or stupidity of her heart.   A scene followed, black clouds
lowered over the path of the lovers, clouds to which the
mother's secret sympathy formed but a thin, uncertain
silver lining.   In language of contempt and scorn, Henry
Weardale was forbidden to set foot again in Pimpernel
Villa, Mr. Timothy Buncombe's abode, and the luckless
girl was commanded to abandon, on the instant, all intercourse with her presumptuous swain.

CHAPTER XVI.

THIS was all, you will perceive, quite in the orthodox style of father and children. The incensed parent lost his reason in wrath, and played tyrant so effectually that he produced rebellion. Henry Weardale rebelled, Beatrice rebelled, and finally Mrs. Buncombe, overcome by her daughter's sobs and by the lover's importunities, connived at rebellion. So it is always. A passion that, left alone, might soon have cooled down is fanned into unextinguishable flame. Lovers who, neglected, might have tired of each other in six months, rise to a height of longing which makes them deem life worthless apart. An affection, a penchant which trembled and hid itself from all eyes in its modest infancy, blazes up before the world, and so heats its victims that they defy authority, cast prudence and propriety to the winds, and dash headlong into matrimony.

For two months did the torture of Henry Weardale and his sweetheart endure. Sobs, vows, sulks, tear-bedewed cheeks had no more influence upon the obdurate father than summer rain on a brick wall. Tempests burst often in that household in the course of these eight or nine weeks, and when they were over the stern parent stood erect, harder of heart than ever. This could not go on. The courage of Beatrice rose to the sticking place, and, with the secret furtherance of her mother, she ran away with her sweetheart, whose heroic soul had long ago prompted that course. A magical priest or parson tied an unloosable knot in consideration of handsome payment, and the pair were made one.

Great was the rage of Mr. Timothy Buncombe when this disobedience of a girl of eighteen came to his knowledge. Never in her life had dumpy Penelope Drabble, the wife of his bosom, seen her lord in so wild a rage. A scum gathered at the edges of his mouth as he stormed and swore over it. Threats and curses tumbled out of his overcharged heart in a half articulate medley. When the fury was at its height, he swore that he would separate himself from the whole lot from that day forth.

"You're a drag and a disgrace to me," he shouted. " Get-out of my sight. Take your brats, and begone. Marry them to thieves and tinkers, if you like ; I don't care. They are none of mine ; I hate 'em all. You're my bane. After all the money I've spent on their education, that one of them should marry a vagrant, loafing, lick-spittle penny-a-liner. It's abominable! But what could I expect with such a mother to guide them. Out of my sight, I say. Go to the devil, and take your brood with you."

Unhappy Penelope wept, grovelled, bent low before this storm of wrath, and when it had well-nigh spent itself, took up her defence. She, you may remember, possessed a sharp tongue of her own, and on this occasion did not spare her lord. In fact, and his outburst notwithstanding, it must be admitted that in the end the victory lay with her. The burden of her discourse was the low origin of no less a person than "T. B." himself, as she contemptuously styled her husband.

"You set yourself up for this and that, do you! You would look down on me, would you! I like your cheek. A pie-wife's son as nobody owned. You were no better nor a tinker yourself when I took pity on you. Lord, but our memories are short! We are a great man, now, we are, and we can look down on the wife as we once thought too good for us. She can go away, she can, and take her brats with her. Very well, 'T. B.,' I'll go; I don't want to stay where I'm not welcome. A nice Christian you'll look when I'm gone, won't you; but if you don't care for the exposure, I'm sure I don't. Why should I? I haven't done nothing. Break up your 'ome, do, by all means, and welcome; I'm sure it has never been much of a 'ome to me. You're too cold for my taste, 'T. B.,' snivelling owd humbug that you be; and you've something on your mind, I know. I don't lie awake a-hearin' you talk in your sleep for nothing."

"Eh! what the devil!" exclaimed her husband, startled out of himself at these words.

"Oh! you're touched, are you; I knew that 'ud make you squirm. But you don't do it now—oh dear, no! we have forgotten the past, we have, and Silas Brown's money, and all that. We are a great man, we are; but I know you, 'T. B.,' and if I go I ain't a-goin' empty-handed, you may depend."

"Woman, what do you mean?" cried Mr. Timothy Buncombe, starting forward, and catching hold of his wife's arm. This "row" took place in the dining room after the servants had gone to bed.

"What's that to you?" she returned, jerking her arm sharply out of his grasp. "I'm to go, you know; you've got no more use for a wife, you haven't. She's a drag on our greatness, she is. All right, 'T. B.,' I knows my thoughts, but I ain't got to tell 'em to you."

"Look here, my dear, let us drop this nonsense," said Mr. Buncombe, in a softened voice. "I have been very angry, I will admit, and not without cause, surely, but you know as well as I do that I did not mean half what I said; so don't let us rave at each other longer. What's done cannot be undone. Beatrice has disgraced herself, but we need not quarrel over her now; she has left her home, and found another; let her stay there, and drop her out of our thoughts. Come, now, make friends," and he bent to kiss her, but Mrs. Penelope was not so swiftly mollified.

"Oh no, you don't," she exclaimed, jumping up and facing him. "You'd soft sawder me now, would you; you think I knows a little too much, but I ain't to be gammoned like that. Hard words ain't nothing to you; you've no heart to wound, but I have, 'T. B.;' and I'm not a-goin' to have mine broke by your cruel tongue any more. You said go, and I'm a-goin', so you leave me alone, will you." With that Mrs. Buncombe threw herself down on the rug, and broke into hysterical weeping.

But a woman who weeps is a woman melted, and Mr.
Buncombe had experience enough to see that a little
perseverance in what his wife called "soft sawder" would
restore harmony. Much coaxing, and a considerable
space of time was required to bring her round, but she
did yield, at last, so far as to dry her eyes and sit up.
But the battle was not quite won yet, and when, by
about midnight, she at last consented to be friends, it
was only on condition that her intercourse with Beatrice
should be at least connived at.

"Please yourself, my dear," Mr. Buncombe had at
length said; "I'll have nothing more to do with her or
with that scoundrel she has married, and they are not to
come here; but you can do as you like about going to
see them."

That being all he could be brought to concede, Mrs.
Buncombe, in her turn, was slow to explain what she
meant by her hints about Silas Brown's money. At last,
however, her husband wormed all she knew from her,
and found that his alarm had been, in large measure,
groundless. All that his wife had heard had been
broken sentences, uttered by her husband in his sleep.
"You shan't have the money, I tell you, Brown; I have
nothing of yours; nothing—nothing; the money's mine,"
and grunts and exclamations less articulate. These had
ceased altogether after Brown's disappearance from Berborough, and had long been forgotten by Mrs. Buncombe,
upon whom they made no very deep impression, until,
in the extremity of her rage, the memory of the incident
flashed across her when she flung the hints at her

I

husband, without knowing whether they would produce any effect on him or not.

His sudden calming down was, therefore, like the revealing of a secret to her, and when Mr. Buncombe discovered this to be the case he cursed himself for a fool. Thanks to his precipitancy, his wife now suspected a great deal more than she had ever done before, and to the height of her suspicion had him in her power. Such a weapon in her hands forced him to be circumspect.

Unable to put out upon the wife of his bosom the chagrin which this discovery produced, Mr. Buncombe became increasingly bitter in his attitude towards his daughter Beatrice and her husband, and swore he would make the town too hot for the pair of them.

CHAPTER XVII.

NEMESIS IN A NEWSPAPER.

HE was in a fair way to make that intention good when Weardale, in turn, gave him a terrible fright. It was done partly out of pure mischievousness, partly to show Mr. Buncombe that he, Henry Weardale, had the power to be troublesome if he liked.

Weardale and his wife, with that strange "luck" of which the world is full, stumbled across a daughter of Silas Brown's when honeymooning. She was an invalid, a poor schoolmistress, over-working herself into her grave, and had come, for a week's rest she could ill afford, to the inland watering place where the runaways took shelter. Hearing that the young couple came from Berborough, Miss Brown talked to them of the old place, and soon the whole story of her father's failure and flight came back to Weardale's recollection.

The remarks and hints which had floated about in Berborough regarding Mr. Buncombe's connexion with Brown rose in his memory as these conversations went on, and made him put questions that led to half revelations of what looked like a crime, but not until afterwards did it occur to him to utilise this half knowledge, for it was no more, against his father-in-law; only when that great man proved not merely obdurate but contumelious did Weardale resolve within himself to play the fellow a trick.

From Miss Brown he learnt that her father had died only a few months previously as an inmate of a London workhouse. Poor woman! She had heard that before he was taken into the workhouse infirmary to die, he had picked up a precarious living by attending to horses at a public-house door. Thus far had drink and the loss of hope in life dragged him down.

Absorbed though he was in his happy love, these confidences sank into Henry Weardale's mind, and mingled with the revived recollections of old tales of fraud which had floated about Berborough after the deacon's fall. Miss Brown had moreover asserted that her belief was some one had robbed her father, for it was not till a little while after the failure that he broke down and went to the bad with drink, or blasphemed against some unknown individual whom he called a " black-hearted villain."

A kind of suspicion arose unbidden in the young man's mind that his father-in-law must be this villain. There was no direct evidence that it was so, but the rise of Timothy Buncombe had, he well remembered, for it was the talk of Hogg's office, and of all the town, coincided with Brown's collapse, and that coincidence alone awoke suspicions.

Not, however, until he became exasperated by Buncombe's scornful treatment of his wife and himself, did these uneasy presentiments crystalise, as it were, into a sort of half conviction. Buncombe's brutality forced him to assume a retaliatory attitude, and one day it struck him that it might be a good thing to try whether some allusion to Silas Brown would not make the tyrant change his attitude.

The irate father-in-law had gone so far as to try to get Weardale discharged from the *Mercury* office, and when that wickedness, as he naturally considered it, came to Harry's knowledge, he was angry enough to believe Buncombe capable of any iniquity. It was faith, therefore, rather than knowledge, which decided Weardale to try an experiment—a random shot like that fired, unknown to him, by his mother-in-law.

Without a hint, then, to Beatrice, such are husbands, or to anybody, the young scribbler, in mood to make mischief, penned the following paragraph, which duly appeared in the "notes and news" column of the *Berborough Mercury*, from which Buncombe had not yet succeeded in removing him :

"Strange, indeed, are the ups and downs of fortune. Fifteen years ago who was there in this town more respected, more prosperous, more looked up to than Mr. Silas Brown, the well-known ship broker ? Everybody thought of him as one of our merchant princes, and looked to see him grow from greatness to greatness. But life is a lottery. A series of misfortunes came upon the great shipowner, not the least of which, it was vaguely reported at the time, was the faithlessness of one of his employés, by whom he was defrauded in some way never yet cleared up. From being fortunate and prosperous, he became a man familiar with adversity. The blow proved too much for him ; he sank down, down until drink obtained the mastery of him. Then, when his business had disappeared, when even the charitable feelings of such a generous man as his old freight clerk, Mr. Timothy Buncombe, now so prosperous and an orna- ment to the town, were pumped dry by importunity, Brown disappeared, invoking the vengeance of God on some man who, he declared, had robbed him.   Nothing more was heard of him in Berborough.   Whether he was dead or alive none knew or cared.   Yet some there are, perhaps, who still remember his portly form, and to whom the news, learned by us in a manner, accidentally, that he died about six months ago in Camberwell work- house infirmary, London, will come with a certain shock.   Poor Brown, mayhap he was more sinned against than sinning."

For brilliancy of style this paragraph would not be hard to excel, but for effectiveness in the quarter its writer intended, it was unsurpassable. Mr. Timothy Buncombe, like his neighbours, read it on the Saturday morning, and was momentarily "*boned*" by it, as the fishwives would say. His first impulse, on becoming conscious that his bones were still there, was to rush off in quest of Weardale, and demand explanations.

"Find out how much the fellow knows," a voice whispered within him, but a moment's reflection satisfied him this would not do. Yet, what was he to do?   All that day and all Sunday he brooded over the question. The guilty conscience of the man woke up and spoke out, giving him no rest. Now, when too late, he remembered that Weardale, whose history he knew well enough, might be aware of a great deal more than most men through his connexion with David Hogg. And this was the man he had suffered to enter his house and carry away his daughter, the man he had been doing his best to convert into an open foe. Uneasy were his slumbers between Saturday and Monday, nor were the fears about his own danger the only ones that haunted him. He could not help shivering before the thought that, on his head lay the guilt of Silas Brown's ruin. "Through me that old man died a miserable drink-besotted pauper," he felt, and the thought made him writhe again.

Mr. Timothy Buncombe, however, was not the man to rest long under terrors of this kind. He was too strong willed for that, and by Monday morning his mind was made up. Whether Weardale knew much or little was a point he could not stoop to clear up, but it was necessary, it would be prudent, to alter, in some degree, his attitude towards that fellow. Instead of hounding him from Berborough, it would be better to help him to move away.

Acting on this view of the case, Mr. Buncombe not only ceased hostilities against his son-in-law, but actually intimated to his wife that he had had enough of revenge. "You can invite Beatty and her husband to come and see you, my dear," he told Mrs. Buncombe on the Monday morning, and Mrs. Buncombe's eyes opened wide at the intimation.

"My goodness, gracious," she exclaimed, "What's up now. Has young Weardale come into a fortune?"

"No, my dear, not that I know of, but I can't always go against my own flesh and blood, you see. I'm not equal to the strain."

"I'm glad to hear it, I'm sure," struck in Mrs. Buncombe; "but I wish you had thought of that a bit sooner; it 'ud ha' saved me and my daughter, too, many bitter hours. I've allays said, what's the good of crying over spilt milk. What's done can't be undone, noways, and I've never seed where the benefit was a-makin' my child a beggar."

"Excuse me, Mrs. Buncombe, but you go too far in saying that."

"Do I, though? not a bit of it, Mr. B." Penelope always said "Mr." when not in a passion. "I know you, I'd be a pretty fool an' I didn't by this time, I reckon. You've been a-tryin' all you know to turn Weardale out of his place, and if he hadn't had a good master the lad 'ud ha' been without the means to get his livin' by now. I can't see no sense in that sort of behaviour—never could. It 'ud better become you to give him a lift."

"Well, well, don't run on so fast; what a tongue you have, woman."

"Woman, indeed!" sniffed Mrs. Buncombe, "of course I'm a woman, and I must be put upon; but I know what's what, for all that; never you fear, 'T. B.'" Penelope was waxing hot.

"Listen to me," cried her husband, impatiently, "you might save yourself much waste of breath, if you would but control yourself, and hold your tongue at times. Let me explain, can't you."

"Ay, ay, soft sawder's cheap," and Mrs. B. pouted and tried to look a poor, ill-used creature without much success. She was too stout and comfortable-like for the part, for all her nagging temper.

"What I was about to say," Mr. Buncombe went on, in a sharp tone, "was just this, that I think we have had enough of wrath, and, inasmuch as I find Weardale to be a steady, well-behaved young man, I have made up my mind to give him a lift, if I can. I think he should go to London; he might get along there; there are more chances for a clever fellow there than here."

"Oh, that's it, is it," exclaimed the suspicious wife of his bosom; "you can't manage to drive Weardale out of the town, so you mean to coax him to go, do you, and you want me to help you, of course. I know; I can see through you; but I ain't a fool, Mr. B.; let me tell you that."

"Nonsense! Bosh!" ejaculated her husband hotly; "you ask the couple here, and don't be so cantankerous. I tell you I mean to do something to help the young man; is not that enough. I'm not likely to chuck him on the parish, am I? Recollect that I am a father, and have a father's feelings towards my child, at any rate."

"Oh, have you," answered his wife, with a subdued yet spiteful air; "you ain't been guilty of givin' way to 'em much lately, I'm thinking. But I know how it is; it's all along of what I read in the *Mercury* yesterday; I know. You think Harry knows of Brown's money, and might blab. Oh, I know you, T. B., I ain't a fool."

"Hush, woman, for God's sake, don't babble in this way of things you know nothing about. Brown's money, as you call it, has nothing to do with it, nothing in the world."

Mr. Buncombe said this nervously, and with an anxious look towards the breakfast-room door, which was half open. His face became a shade paler than usual in spite of his great self control.

"Oh no, of course not; there ain't nothing on your mind about Brown, never was. But I know——"

"You know nothing at all, I tell you; so hold your peace this instant. I will not tolerate anyone speaking to me in this way; least of all you."

" Ay, ay, get in a passion, do, Mr. B. But I ain't——"

" I'm not in a passion," again interrupted her husband, rising from the table as he spoke, and going up to his wife; "I'm not in a passion, Mrs. Buncombe, but," bending over her, and speaking almost in a hiss, "mark my words; if you do not desist from language of this kind, I will not tolerate you here. I would rather leave the place and the country for good than submit to it; so take care."

Mrs. Buncombe quailed before the gaze of her enraged lord, and hung her head, unable to find a ready retort.

" Now mind," added her husband, as he straightened himself, and turned to leave the room, " If you disobey me in this, or anything else I choose to order you to do, it will be the worse for you."

Mrs. Buncombe cast a look of impotent fury at him, and cried, "you're a wretch." Then, flinging her arms on the table, and her head upon them, she commenced a good noisy fit of crying, which her husband did not wait to witness.

None of the children were present at this scene, for the very good reason that none were at home. Mr. Buncombe believed most thoroughly in the system which delegates the anxieties and duties of rearing the young mind to the masters and mistresses of public boarding schools, and packed his off as soon as it was possible to get them admitted. Perhaps both parents might have restrained their tongues oftener than they did had their offspring been around them, so that the system of ostrich nurture prevalent in England, under which the members of a family grow up strangers to each other, has its disadvantages. But an occasional brush with his wife was a small affair in the eyes of Timothy Buncombe compared with the nuisance of having a lot of noisy, squalling "brats" always about the house.

CHAPTER XVIII.

CREEDS AND AN AMBITION.

MR. BUNCOMBE'S tactics succeeded to admiration. At first the much suffering son-in-law held aloof from the blandishment of his mysteriously softened relative, vaguely suspecting the cause of the change, but his wife soon brought him round. Beatrice was a good girl at heart, a better girl than might have been expected under the circumstances. Her husband, too, received her before she had had time to be ruined by her home surroundings. The pride of wealth and high status as the daughter of a man of plutocratic renown had not come upon her, and her contact with Weardale's strong, sunny nature brought her best qualities of head and heart to the surface, and made them expand in time.

It was, therefore, with a brave loyal heart that this young wife seconded her father's interested anxiety for her husband's advancement. Bravely too did she stand by her husband's side when, yielding to Mr. Buncombe's representations, they settled in London there to begin the world anew. Her father soon talked Weardale over, to see as he wished him to see, for Weardale was ambitious. A prolonged residence in a quiet place like Berborough had no attractions for him. Newspaper editing and reporting there were not a pursuit of literature, he was fond of saying, while in London, that great maelstrom of humanity, where the strong swimmer rose to the surface and found sure foothold on the rock of fame and fortune, all things were possible. To the man so thinking the prospect of settling in London was not long to be resisted.

It was little though that Mr. Buncombe could do to help him there, beyond presenting the pair with a couple of hundred pounds, and a few letters of introduction when they went away.

Nor was it altogether Buncombe's fault that he could not do more. The world of journalism in London, as in all great centres of newspaper enterprises, is a thing by itself. It has its privileged classes, its hall-marked university men, who stand by each other, praise each other's work, form coteries apart, and, aided either by fellowships, or by the powerful interest of their strictly limited university trades unions, contrive to obtain a majority of the great prizes of the profession.

But outside this privileged caste with its snobbery, its shibboleths, and its intimate relationship with the bureaucracy,—which also, orders to the contrary notwithstanding, poaches in the field of newspaper literature,—there lies a great journalistic democracy. In that introductions avail little, interest has practically no power. The career is open to the talents, and if after due trial a man approves himself capable, he may go far. The jealousy and hatred of the high castes may help to carry him far. It is a rough world, though, this world of

democratic journalism, and the proofs a man has to
undergo are hard and bitter.

Kindly withal, open hearted and open handed, ready
always to help a fellow craftsman in distress, as these slaves
of the printer's devil are, there is yet a stern uncom-
promisingness among them, which takes nothing for
granted. Testimonials will not lift a man into an easy
way of living ; favour will rarely retain the fool where a
wise man ought to be, and no new comer can count upon
earning his bread until he has been tested again and
again. The question asked of such is not " Who are
you?" but "What can you do?" and woe betide the
man who can do little, who is careless, whose hand is
uncertain, whose talents are not, on one side at least, of
the hodman order. Either he is driven out of the ranks
altogether, or he becomes a waif and a menial therein, be
he the best born, most influentially backed son of Adam
alive.

Needless to say it was in the ranks of the democracy
of journalists that Weardale had to enroll himself. His
apprenticeship was rough, his struggle prolonged, but the
battle did him good, and it did his wife good. When the
worst was over, and they could pause to look back thankfully, to look forward in hope, they felt that they were
the better for the years of anxiety and privation. Their
love for each other was deeper, truer, at the end than at
the beginning, and their moral tone was higher. Once on
a time they had been disposed to repine and to think ill
of the man who had condemned them to fight for their
lives instead of making them sharers of his wealth ; but

that day was long gone by, and both Henry Weardale and his wife were glad ere many years were over that they had never made but one appeal to Mr. Buncombe for help after coming to London, and that he had left his daughter's letter containing it unanswered.

Nearly ten years passed away before Mr. Buncombe and his son-in-law came in contact with each other again, and when they did it was Mr. Buncombe who made the advance. In those years the shipowner had continued to prosper, and as his business grew so did his ambition. His only son had finished his education at Cambridge, where he perfected himself in the art of smoking a short briar pipe, and acquired indifferent skill as an oarsman. In other respects his education had been neglected. He was ignorant of business and of letters ; but he made a most excellent wealth waster. No aristocrat of long descent could have spent money more handsomely, or got into debt with an easier conscience.

Mr. Buncombe's eldest remaining daughter had made what he and all the world considered at the time a brilliant marriage with the son of a reputedly wealthy corn merchant and seed crusher in Lincolnshire, named Foster ; and the third girl, Penelope, had been carried off by a high church parson, who intoned prayers and otherwise buffooned before the Deity in gorgeously embroidered vestments. This holy man had a private income of one thousand five hundred pounds a year in ground rents, and a living worth two hundred and fifty pounds, or about as many pounds as there were souls in the parish. The youngest daughter, Evangeline, aged about seventeen was still unwed, and reserved for high destinies.

These facts will lead the student to infer that as his wealth grew and his refinement of feeling, Mr. Buncombe's chapel zeal grew cold. It was so. His deaconship had been laid aside long ago, and was only a memory that made him blush. No more devout, or rather no "higher" churchman was now to be found in all Berborough than Mr. Buncombe.

A ritualistic parson had captured the whole family with his religious travesties and his sensuous music. This parson belonged to that party in the church which believes the hope of the future to lie in an escape from the trammels of State control—but an escape with all the plunder. Ritualism was in this shape so far consonant with Mr. Buncombe's prejudices against a State Church, as to make it easy for him to become reconciled to the change of religion. "I am all for disestablishment," the parson said, "and therefore on that point at one with the dissenters."

Disendowment, though, was wholly another affair. "The property of the church belongs to God, and no man has the right to take it away," was the axiom upon this question. Liberationists were thus at the opposite pole in reality from this school, but Mr. Buncombe did not enquire deeply. It was a step upward in "society" he desired far more than theological consistency. What after all could it matter to him whether the sect he decided to join contemplated a robbery of the nation or not. His end was gained.

But for another ambition which dawned in his mind soon after his secession from chapel, Mr. Buncombe would probably never have given a thought to the question of how far the ritualist's ideas and his old prejudices coincided on the question of Church and State. He had, however, for some time nourished a desire to enter Parliament. It did not seem to him that his prosperous career could be crowned and rounded off without this warranty of success. And, being a shrewd man always, Mr. Buncombe had early in the days of this desire recognised that it would be easier and less expensive for him to enter Parliament as a Liberal than as a Tory, whatever he might afterwards become.

That this is not the case to-day may be true, but the reader will please bear in mind that I am writing of yesterday, or, rather, of the day before yesterday, when Tories still claimed to be gentlemen. At present this venerable party—but never mind it ; we have nothing to do with it. Mr. Buncombe did not profess Toryism, and that is enough. Selecting Liberalism, as he had done, it was necessary for him to maintain the semblance of consistency in religion, at all events until he found a constituency. After that—well, all would depend upon the constituency.

Another consideration had weight with him, and that was his complete ignorance, or, at least, his complete unfamiliarity with the " true inwardness " of Toryism. He did not even know whether it had any inwardness, but his mind had been familiar from his youth with the catchwords, as well as with the professed aims of the

K

"party of progress," as the Liberals described themselves. For these and other reasons Mr. Buncombe deemed it a sensible course to pose as a " Liberal" in politics.   That offered, he thought, the best chance of getting M.P. stuck to his name.

Even as a Liberal Mr. Buncombe found himself in perplexity when the time came for him to woo a constituency.   Local politics he knew, but the catch words of Imperial politics were less ready at his tongue end. A man whose life has been taken up by freights, charter parties, and the general arduousness of money getting, cannot be expected to keep abreast of political creeds, ever changing as they are.   He may assent to the doctrines formulated for him by his party, but be quite unable to give a reason for that assent when called upon by the electors to expound the faith that is in him.

This was just what Mr. Buncombe felt, and in his trouble his mind reverted to his journalist son-in-law.   " There's a fellow, now, who might be useful to me as a coach," he said, and almost immediately he decided to enlist Weardale, if possible, in that capacity.   Was he not ashamed to think of such a step?   Not a bit of it ; why should he be?   It was a condescension on his part to notice the fellow at all.   Mr. Buncombe had too profound a belief in his own excellencies to doubt for one moment that Weardale would be delighted to assist him when called upon as far as lay in his power.

So when a general election seemed to be looming in the near future, the great Berborough shipbroker took a run up to town and called on his son-in-law.   That gentleman was now the editor of an influential weekly paper, and had made himself known by writings outside the immediate circle of journalism, so that he was comfortably off, and in "a good position," as the world measures such. "Society" knew little of him. He refused to be trotted around like a pet St. Bernard or a performing ape by the professed savage tamers of the West End, but his life was all the more comfortable for that.

CHAPTER XIX.

WANTED A "COACH."

In a meagre fashion Mr. Buncombe knew that his son-in-law had prospered beyond the average of "newspaper fellows," but he was not prepared for the degree of comfort, not to say wealth, which was disclosed to his eyes when he reached Weardale's house at Highgate on the afternoon of the Monday he arrived in town. Not finding Weardale at his office, he had obtained his address, and, without the least hesitation, went to his house in quest of him.

I cannot say that Weardale's reception of his father-in-law was cordial, but neither was it awkward or embarrassed. Mrs. Weardale was much more put out at the unexpected sight of her father. Old memories rose in her mind, bringing tears with them, and awkwardness and coldness of speech and looks. But Mr. Buncombe was an effusive talker, and laughed and made a fuss with the children on their return from school, and strove, with a fine effrontery, to make himself and every one else feel at home.

As for Weardale, he kept wondering what in the name of fortune had brought this relation of his there, and the inward discussion of this problem made him absent-minded. He talked vaguely, answered the sallies of Mr. Buncombe in monosyllables, and otherwise conducted himself in a stupid manner all the time the family party took tea. Only when it was over, and the children had gone away to lesson-learning or to play, did the shipowner descend to his own affairs.

"Can I have a talk with you on business, my dear boy," he said in his most cordial tone.

"Certainly, by all means," replied Weardale, with a slow, half-bewildered air. "Will you be good enough to follow me to my den. We shall be quieter there." And as he rose to lead the way he wondered if Buncombe had come to tell him he was going to fail. Nothing but a smash up seemed to him to furnish a strong enough motive to bring his father-in-law to his house.

"All right, my boy, I shan't keep you long, you know," was Mr. Buncombe's answer, as the two men entered a little room at the back of the house, the walls of which were lined, and much of the floor littered with books and papers.

Weardale mechanically took his accustomed seat, and motioned his visitor to a chair near him. A strange contrast they presented, these two men, as they sat together, the glow of an autumn evening on their faces. Weardale was stout and comfortable looking : Buncombe thin as he had ever been. Weardale's hair, though streaked with grey, still curled thickly round his broad square forehead. Buncombe had only a thin line of lanky hair round the back and sides of his head. The journalist had a bushy beard ; the shipbroker had not a hair on his face. That face, instead of being full and healthy, like his son-in-law's, was pale and in some degree shrivelled ; a grey face with deep lines of crow's feet gathered round the small, keen, greyish blue, ferret-like eyes, that never rested on any one's face for more than a moment. But for the hardness displayed by the thin-lipped, sharp cut mouth, this mobility of the eyes might have been set down to nervousness, but the whole aspect of the face made that supposition untenable. It was a hard face without human sympathy in it, selfish, calculating and cold ; a face to which the restless eyes gave the stamp of cunning and insincerity.

Great indeed was the contrast between this man and Weardale, whose broad well-filled figure and quiet good humoured look bespoke a man at peace with his kind, devoid of malevolence, open hearted and generous. Little more than thirty-six, he yet looked in spite of his grey hairs, young for his years, whereas Buncombe's wizened face and bald pate made him look aged. He was in fact barely fifteen years older than his son-in-law.

The two men sat in embarrassed silence for a few seconds, and then the restless shipowner jumped to his feet, as his manner was, and strode to the fire-place. He never could sit still. When the room was not large enough to be paced with irregular jerky strides, Mr. Buncombe was wont to relieve the monotony of con-versation by frequent alternations of sitting and standing.

" Can you guess what I came here for," he suddenly exclaimed.

" No, that I cannot," answered Weardale; "I was never more surprised in my life than at the sight of you here."

" Ah ! just so, but wonders will never cease, you know. You'll soon get over your surprise. The fact is I want to get into Parliament, Weardale, my boy, and it occurred to me to—— "

" Oh, you do, do you," exclaimed Weardale in a tone of mingled relief and astonishment.

"Yes, of course, what on earth did you think had brought me here—a visit of ceremony, eh? Let by-gones be by-gones, forgive and forget, and all that sort of thing eh? No, no, my dear boy ; I came on business."

" Indeed ! but I don't quite follow you, though," struck in the journalist, in a cold tone which Buncombe caught the ring of.

" Of course, you know," he resumed in a wheedling tone, and jumping back to his seat. "Of course, you know, I'm deuced glad to see you again, and so forth. No doubt about that at all. It was a mistake on my part to chuck you over. I admit it. I apologise for it, and we need say no more about it. We all make mistakes, you know, and how could I tell then that you were going to turn out such a devilish clever fellow, eh? Besides, I did give you a leg up at the start, you remember," and he sprang to his feet again, gathering up the tails of his coat mechanically as he turned his back to the fireplace where no fire was.

Weardale smiled a quaint amused smile as he answered " All right, all right ; I am sure *we* have no desire in the least to rake up the past, or to reproach you; nothing could be further from Beatrice's thoughts or mine."

"Good!" said Buncombe, and he thrust his hands down to the bottom of his trousers pockets and kicked out with his feet jerkily. "Good! Then, these preliminaries over, let us to business. As I was saying, I want to get into parliament, you know, and I want your help."

"My help; how do you mean?"

"Well, the fact is, you see, I'm not very well up in politics. They're not quite in my line, you know; and I'm a bit at sea when I get talking to the people; so I want you to tell me what's the game now. Give me the points, you know; I can easily lick 'em into shape, once I have the cue, eh? You understand, don't you? It's all as plain as A. B. C. to you, ain't it?" and Mr. Buncombe again flopped down on his chair, casting a sharp rapid glance at his son-in-law's face.

"Yes; I understand," answered Weardale slowly, "but, ah,—have you decided which party you will join?"

"Eh, what! well, that is a good 'un. Do you mean to say I can pick and choose my party as I could a coat; as if, with my antecedents, I could be anything but a Liberal?" Mr. Buncombe rose to his feet once more as he said this, drawing himself up with dignity as if to repel a vile insinuation.

"All right; there is no necessity to get excited about it. I did not know your politics, of course, and I only wanted to ascertain before giving you an answer. After all, so far as the country is concerned, it does not much matter, I guess; but you personally are wise, no doubt.

It will be on the whole easier to get in as a Liberal than as a Tory, especially just now when the whim of the electing classes runs that way."

"Eh, what do you mean? Isn't the country always Liberal?"

"Bits of it, no doubt, but not London and the southern counties. They come and go with one side or the other, leaning on the whole to the party which spends most money. We like wars here, because they conduce to good living for our official classes, our usurers, and our flunkeys. Provided we are gratified in this respect, principles may go to Jericho."

CHAPTER XX.

A COACH THAT WENT TOO FAST.

"Oh, I see, you are a Radical, I suppose," exclaimed Mr. Buncombe, with something of a sneer, taking a good stare at his son-in-law's waistcoat. "You don't think anybody can be sincere in politics except yourselves, eh? Much obliged to you, I'm sure."

"Pardon me, it's not a question of sincerity at all. You may be a fanatic in sincerity if you like. That matters little so far as the actual ruling of the nation goes."

"Oh, doesn't it, though?"

"No, certainly not. Politicians of all shades are in the same box. Once let them into office and they have to obey a power, superior, nineteen times out of twenty, to anything the tongue alone can call into existence."

"Oh, I see. The press, of course; I might have guessed that. Nothing like leather, eh? You chaps govern the country."

"No, not the press, either. It is not in the running; on the contrary, its influence seems to me on the decline. I meant the bureaucracy, the Horse Guards, the fetish of German royalties with all their corrupt surroundings and tax-consuming swarms of toadeaters. These are the powers that rule England."

"Bosh," exclaimed Mr. Buncombe, in an excited tone, and dancing round the room as fast as the small space and the encumbered floor would let him. "Do you mean to tell me that the great Liberal party have done nothing in the past to extend the liberties of the people, eh? answer me that!" and the speaker paused dramatically in front of Weardale's desk for a reply.

"My dear sir, I beg you not to get excited; all this is beside the question. The 'measures of reform' that politicians chatter so much about are mostly humbug and delusion. They mean not more freedom as a rule, but more chains; a bigger load on the backs of the people; greater power to the bureaucrats. You are, if you will allow me to say so, too unsophisticated; and, if you mean to enter Parliament, must knock lots of these wild ideas out of your head."

"But"—interjected Buncombe—

"Nay, let me finish; I shan't detain you long. You are going into Parliament, you say. Well and good. Then the first thing you have to learn is that it does not matter two straws what reforms you promise the constituency you make love to. Delude the people to the uttermost; you are perfectly safe, because none of your promises have the least chance of being fulfilled. Promise economy; promise a policy of peace; promise local government; promise church disestablishment, if that will catch more votes than it will take away; promise greater freedom everywhere; do and say anything you please to win votes, and never fear the result. Nobody expects you seriously to keep your promises, because you could not if you tried."

"God bless my soul," cried the shipowner, fairly taken aback. "That is the funniest thing ever I heard in all my born days. And you, a Radical, and a Free Trader, and God knows what; you tell me this! I never—God bless my soul and body!"

For once in his life the shipbroker was non-plussed.

"We were not discussing honesty, or anything of that sort, you know," Weardale proceeded, hardly noticing the exclamations and looks of his father-in-law—"nothing except facts. I say it does not matter what you profess or promise before the electorate, because you can do nothing, and the proof of this is that the party in office habitually disregards the essence of its pledges. It cannot do otherwise. This country, I must repeat, is not governed by the men whom the deluded voter supports at the polls. The poor fool of a voter is as helpless to-day as he was in the days of Sir Horace Walpole or of Pitt, as helpless, but far more puffed up. The English electoral system is, under what we are pleased to call our Constitution, neither more nor less than a device to hide the bureaucracy, by whom we are really ruled. Do our soldiers want a little war or two? They have it, no matter what the chosen of the people say, and the people are only good to pay the bill. Is there a departmental job to be perpetrated, involving perhaps the waste of millions of money? It is done without hesitation by the bureaucrats and their allies, courtly and *new*-courtly. Money by millions upon millions is flung away like chaff every year, and your great party leaders stand by as helpless as oxen in a slaughter-house. One *vox populi* Premier goes and another comes, and still the nation jogs along with its soft head in the air towards universal bankruptcy and the devil."

"God bless my soul and body," ejaculated Mr. Buncombe once more. "You are mad, surely ; clean mad. I've come to the wrong shop, I see."

"Ha ! ha !" laughed Weardale, in high good humour at the effect he had produced. "Not a bit of it. I shall be delighted to help you if I can. It's always such good fun to see your voters marching to the polling booths penetrated by the conviction that this time at all events they are going to make an end of bad government. Their faith is touching, as well as droll. Nothing teaches these ' dim, common populations.' After each batch of talking puppets has ignominiously failed to lessen their woes, they solemnly, and with imperturbable conviction, pin their faith to a fresh supply, rush to record their votes, and go home, saying to themselves, ' now we have settled it ; now the world will go as we wish.' It is sublime, Mr. Buncombe, touchingly sublime, and would be the greatest fun under heaven, were it not so sad withal. Nothing teaches them, these yokel millions. They see, as the result of their stout-hearted voting, mobs of gilded and jewelled aristocrats change places before the throne. Lord Longodds succeeds Baron Grousemoor as Governor of the Queen's dogs ; Her Grace of Barsinister displaces the Duchess of Rackrent as chief dresser ; Earl Fitzdotterel condescends to replace the

Marquis of Spawnroyal as head flunkey, and His Grace the Duke of Groundgame ousts some other peer as upper stable boy. It is the old, old story; the people play the game, and high croupiers divide the stakes."

"Bosh," interjected the ship broker. "What has all that court flummery got to do with politics and reforms? What the nation looks to is the Ministry. It doesn't care a hang who gets the court places."

"Just so; nevertheless the court mob decides the fate of ministries often. There is no political intriguer in the world equal to your courtly woman and your lick-spittle peer. And after all, how much better is the ministerial reshuffle? The scramble after place is just the same, the results of the stakes' division just as negative. One wonder-working silver tongue, on whose lips a nation has hung rapturously, displaces another, bringing his train of placemen—all of more or less skill in tongue fence—along with him, and the people shout for joy. But they are puppets all, and after a year or two the silly voter awakes to the fact that he is not one whit the better for the change. Taxes increase just as before, because bureaucrats breed and require more and evermore to live upon. Wars are waged by the party of 'peace, retrenchment and reform,' just as recklessly as by the truculent Jew-controlled Tory gangs who rave of England's mission to rule the world; and your silver-tongued orator, divine *vox populi* premier, exhausts his ingenuity in finding excuses for crimes, lapses and exactions, so as to avert the gathering storm. By and by the popular fury breaks upon his head; he flies ignominiously from 'office;' the polling booths are thronged again; a new squad of puppets come to the fore, and the game is begun anew with a triumphant self-satisfied electorate doing its duty. It is sublime."

"I—I—really, Weardale, my boy, I don't understand you. You seem to me raving mad. Do you imagine that I can go before a constituency and utter rank nonsense like that. I'd rather not, if it's all the same to you."

"How you do fly off at a tangent, Mr. Buncombe," laughed the journalist. "Don't you see that I have merely been putting you through a preliminary elucidation ?"

"Oh, just so, of course; I understand, quite well," answered the ship-owner, in an offended tone. "You won't do for me, I can see that, anyway. I had hopes you might have helped me with your advice when I entered on my electioneering campaign, but I now find I was mistaken."

"Nay, nay, not so fast. Tell me the views you desire to put before the electors, and I'll lick them into shape for you, with pleasure, if that is what you want. It's all the same to me, you know," and again Weardale laughed softly.

CHAPTER XXI.

AN UNSTEADY COACH.

"THAT'S not what I want at all, man," Buncombe asserted afresh. "God bless my soul, if I had only wanted ideas shaped I could have done that myself, surely. I'm not such a green-horn at public speaking as all that. What I wanted was the correct tips, you know, and after what I have heard you must excuse me for saying that I should be afraid to trust you for anything of the sort. Why, you laugh at the Reform Bill, the ballot, and everything. It's dreadful; positively dreadful."

"Ha, ha, all right, Mr. Buncombe. I'm sure it makes no difference to me ; but I really did not think the views I have just expressed were so horrifying. Most journalists of experience hold them, you know. They see too much of the way the miracle is performed to have deep faith in its efficacy."

"Do they, by Jove ! Then all I can say is they must be a bad lot."

"Not so very bad either. They speak merely of what they see and know. To them at any rate it is patent enough that parliamentary government is more of a delusion than an efficient factor in making men comfortable and happy. They see your great ministers led by the nose one after the other by a corrupt bureaucracy. What can they do, therefore, but laugh your platform heroes, your demi-gods of the tongue, to scorn with a certain bitterness. Why—"

How far the journalist might have ridden his hobby it would be hard to guess, and Mr. Buncombe had evidently no mind to let the experiment be tried. Nervously kicking his legs about and looking at his watch he interrupted Weardale at this point with——

"Well, well, my friend, I'll hear you another time. I must be off now, I promised to meet Holmes, of Grimsby, at eight, and it's past seven now."

"Nonsense; won't you wait and have supper with us. We dine in the middle of the day and sup about nine: you will be most welcome to a share of what's going. Beatrice, I am sure, counts upon you."

"No, thank you, I can't really. You must excuse me now," cried Mr. Buncombe, getting up to go. "Sorry we could not hit it off, you know," he added.

"Well, but stop a moment," exclaimed Weardale, "you need not lose all your trouble in coming out here, because I am not to your taste. Though you can't trust me to coach you, you may accept my advice as to who can. I know lots of fellows who would be only too delighted—for a consideration."

"Eh, well, well, that's not a bad idea;" and Mr. Buncombe immediately plumped into a seat again, totally oblivious of his haste to keep an engagement.

"In fact," continued Weardale, "I think I know the very man for you. The only drawback is that he takes

L

spells of drinking. But if you can compel him to be sober—and he keeps the pledge on occasion for months at a time—he is the best electioneering wire puller alive."

"Hum! Rather awkward though if the fellow got tight at a critical moment."

"Oh, but you must not depend on him to hunt up your voters on the polling day! He's a chap to send spouting around among them as a sort of free lance ; a man also to whom you yourself can apply for information as to the attitude, wants, and wishes of the electors. His hints would help you immensely to a knowledge of what to say, and when to say it. His being drunk now and then does not in the least weaken his value for such objects. It lowers his market price merely. In fact, I would be of no use to you at all in a thousand ways where he would be invaluable."

"Hum! You seem to have a great admiration for this drunkard," remarked Mr. Buncombe, with a suspicious glance from his ferret-like eyes. "Is he a particular friend of yours?"

"On the contrary, he hates me like the devil, I believe, and even were it otherwise I fail to see what interest of mine would be served by misleading you," answered Weardale drily.

"No, no, of course not," the shipowner effusively cried, desirous of effacing a bad impression. "I believe you are quite right ; but, if this fellow hates you, how am I to get to know him?"

"I will introduce you."

"God bless my soul! how's that?"

"Because he hates me it does not follow that we are not superficially the best friends in the world ; nor yet does it follow that my introduction will not carry some weight with him—especially if you are prepared to stump up. He is a politic fellow, Edward Lister."

"Hum ! God bless my soul and body," was all that Mr. Buncombe felt equal to ejaculating as he sprang to his feet and backed to the fireplace.

Weardale laughed. "Let me see," he resumed, "you will probably find him in the lobby of the House of Commons somewhere. I rather fancy in the centre lobby, for I have been told he gets drunk too often, and kicks up too many rows to be trusted inside. But everyone knows him there. Suppose I give you a note, and you hunt him up."

"All right, I can but try, you know. Shall I find him to-night ? " Mr. Buncombe had apparently forgotten all about his engagement with Mr. Holmes, of Grimsby.

"Sure to, I should think. He writes descriptions of scenes in the House for a syndicate of country newspapers, and is always hanging about the lobby, drunk or sober. But what's your hurry ; can't you stay to supper? My wife will be disappointed if you bolt in this fashion."

"No, thank you. Very sorry, you know ; should have liked very much to stay, but I can't. I must be back at Berborough by to-morrow night. But tell Beatty never to mind ; she will see enough of me if I get into Parliament."

"Ah! that reminds me," said Weardale, accepting the reiterated refusal of the invitation to supper with much equanimity. "Have you found a constituency yet?"

"Yes; at least, I'm not sure. I've had my eye on Oldhills for some time; but the fact is I'm not sure it isn't too radical."

"Oh, don't let that stand in your way whatever you do. It's a capital place, I should say—quite beyond the range of the London ooze of tax consumers, courtiers, money-lenders, stock-jobbers, and toadies. Just the very thing. It will have a modicum of honest men, and a ruck easy to buy. You have spent money on the place, I suppose?"

"Y—yes; I've nursed it a bit."

"Then stick to it, and swallow all formulas; never fear. I shouldn't lose my invested capital, if I were you."

"There you are again; I never saw such a fellow. 'Pon my soul and body; I believe you are a—an—an anarchy man," cried Mr. Buncombe, jerking out the last phrase as if he had made a discovery, but did not know quite how to define it.

"Perhaps," was the quiet rejoinder, "but, here's your note." Weardale had been writing between his sentences. "You go and find Ted Lister. He will talk as wildly as any man; but you are quite safe with him. He knows the party ropes, and, by the way, he knows most of the party leaders too. If I were you I'd get him to introduce me a bit, just for a start. A new man must not be too particular how he makes his way."

Mr. Buncombe took the note from his son-in-law's hand promptly, and as promptly said good bye. He was almost too impatient to wait until Mrs. Weardale came to say good bye also, in answer to her husband's call. Effusively, with regrets, excuses, promises to come again soon, all as it were jumbled together, Mr. Buncombe made his farewell and posted off to the House of Commons.

"Have you offended him, my dear?" said Beatrice to her husband, when the door closed behind her father.

Weardale smiled, "No, not exactly," he said. "He wanted me to coach him for Parliament, but my ideas did not please him; so I have given him a note to Ted Lister."

"What, that disagreeable, drinking fellow, who came here once and stayed till four o'clock in the morning, and told us the State ought to bring up his family."

"The same; but he is a first rate canvasser, you know. That's in his line, not mine, eh, wife?"

"I should think so," said Mrs. Weardale proudly. "All the same, I believe my father will be dreadfully shocked when he discovers the kind of man you have sent him to. But what in the world does he want to go into Parliament for?"

"My dear, he has made money, it seems," replied Henry Weardale, and to his shrewd wife that appeared to be reason sufficient.

CHAPTER XXII.

RED NOSE AND RIGHT HONOURABLE.

Mr. Buncombe went straight to the House of Commons from his son-in-law's house in Highgate. A certain amount of impatience possessed that soul of his he so often asked God to bless. So far as his son-in-law was concerned, he felt that the journey he had made to town was wasted, and he was not without nervousness regarding the fruits of that letter of introduction he carried in his pocket. To make a man given to drink his guide, philosopher, and *âme damnée* in the forthcoming electioneering campaign seemed much like providing for failure beforehand.

It was therefore with no very confident feeling that the shipowner made his way to the outer lobby of the two Houses of Parliament, and asked a policeman to direct him where to find Mr. Lister.

The policeman took him familiarly by the arm and led him a step or two into the House of Commons corridor. "There he be," said he, pointing to a stoutish little creature with a red nose and an excited air, who was seated on a bench, talking with great volubility and insistence to a tall, dark, cock-sure looking man who held a bundle of papers in his hand.

" He's a-talkin' to a hex-cabinet minister," whispered the policeman, " p'raps you'd better wait," and he pointed to a vacant bench on the opposite side of the passage.

" Ho, ho!" thought Mr. Buncombe to himself, as he sat down. " Weardale was not so far out after all then. This fellow, Lister, is somebody ;" and he gazed with interest at the couple opposite.

A greater contrast could hardly have been imagined than these two men presented. The tall man, "hex-cabinet minister," as the policeman explained, and the Right Honourable Launcelot Orchidion, M.P., for Smutty-ton, and former Vice-President of the Aristocrat's Out-door Relief Office, as we may explain, was elegantly dressed—neat and dapperly dressed as a tailor's perambulating advertisement. His linen was faultless, his wristbands resplendent, and on his fingers flashed jewels. His interlocutor had been a handsome man too, was in a sense handsome still ; but was shorter of stature, with a well knit frame and a powerful looking head. Years of hard living and drink, however, had left their mark on him, and now he seemed more or less a wreck. His linen was dirty ; so were his hands, to which frowsy edged wristbands of three or four days' wear formed fit offset. A towsy shirt front equally well became the rough, soiled, ill-made clothes which covered his back. " That man surely is a waif," the casual observer would have said.

He was no waif though, judging by the suave, almost humble attention which the beautifully tailored politician paid to what the little fellow said. Lister appeared to be

half seas over. His eye rolled wildly, and his face was
flushed. He spoke with an excited feverish sort of voice,
doggedly too, and fiercely at times, as if determined to
force Mr. Orchidion to take his view of the point in dispute,
whether he would or not. And always the sweetly per-
fumed political demi-god smiled, and looked delighted
and cordial, and wagged his head and seemed to weigh
with deep earnestness every word the journalist
spoke.

Sitting opposite them, Mr. Buncombe necessarily
caught a good many of the phrases; fag ends of
sentences reached him through the gaps left by the
stream of men passing to and fro. For the life of him
though he could not find Lister's language so fraught
with wisdom as to make it worth absorption thus earnestly
by one of the nation's leading lights.

"Oh! but you must, b'God!" was a phrase which
more than once caught his ear. "You must, or else the
country will cast you out, root and branch." * * *
"The times are ripe for revolution, I tell you, and b'God
no man knows that better than I do." * * * "I tell
you it's no good shilly-shallying; there's no help in the
Lord for you if you do that. You'll have to apply to the
other party, and, damn it, he won't." * * * "I'm
in relation, in intimate relation I may say, with every
Radical association in the three kingdoms, and as sure
as the Lord's salvation, I tell you that if you are not
prepared to pretty well hang every damned landlord you
can lay hands on, you may as well throw up the
sponge."

"But, my friend,——" the ex-cabinet minister ventured to say, in a bland tone.

"'But,' there's no but about it, b'God ;" interrupted Lister in tones loud enough to smother every other sound. "But me no buts in the matter. Here's the road, and you have got to follow it or land in the ditch. Heh, heh! The way of salvation was always hard, you know, and, like it or not, b'God, you must abolish the landlords, strip the parsons of their stolen property, and give the poor a chance all round. Heh, heh, heh !"

"Well, Mr. Lister, I'm sure I'm delighted to know your views, and I assure you they lose nothing from the forcible way you put them. They require much thought. * * * Interests are against——"

"Interests be damned !" yelled Lister, growing more and more excited ; but the Party leader probably thought he had now done enough for propitiation's sake. So he rose abruptly and held out his hand, with an "Excuse me, Mr. Lister, I must go now, for I have to speak presently ; but depend upon it I'll not forget what you have said," and without waiting for an answer he hurried away.

Lister looked after him, as Mr. Buncombe rose to introduce himself, and said loud enough for those around to hear—an indescribable look of drunken hate and scorn spreading over his face——

"Yes ; you'll think of it, no doubt, and be damned to you. No good will ever be done till you, and the like of you, are hung. Blasted fawning hypocrite."

As he hissed these words out, he glanced furtively in the direction of the policeman at the Commons' end of the corridor, and finding the man's back turned, darted with stealthly swiftness into the member's lobby. Mr. Buncombe was about to follow, but the policeman caught sight of him, and turned him back as a stranger.

CHAPTER XXIII.

A COMEDY AND A COMPACT.

As the shipowner emerged upon the outer lobby the policeman stationed there observed that he was alone, and at
once looked round for Lister. Seeing nothing of him, he
approached Mr. Buncombe, and asked whether he (Buncombe) had seen him go inside.

"Yes, I did," said Mr. Buncombe. "He was off before
I could speak to him, confound it."

"Do you know him, sir?" said the officer anxiously,
"because if you do you might 'elp to get me out of a
mess. I shall get into trouble if that fellow is caught in
there by my chiefs. We 'ave strict horders to keep 'im
out of the lobby," he went on to explain.

"No, my man, I do not know him. I have simply a
letter to him," Mr. Buncombe replied, beginning to feel a
little ashamed of his position.

"That would do, p'raps. Or, I say, mister, do you
'appen to know a member."

"Of course I do, several. I come from Berborough.
Mr. Elicott, the member for that town, is an intimate
friend of mine." As he said this, which was not exactly
true, Mr. Buncombe felt his sense of dignity returning.

"Then gi' me your card, sir if you please. I know 'e's

in the 'Ouse, I seed him go by not 'alf an hour ago.   I'll
'ave 'im called, and 'e can take you in to Lister.
P'raps your business will 'elp us to get 'im out."

Mr. Buncombe complied with this request, and presently
Mr. Elicott appeared, and, without ceremony, led him
into the inner lobby.

"Do you want to get into the House, Mr. Buncombe?"
he asked.   "It's a dull night to-night.   Navy estimates.
No fun.   No one knows anything about them, you know.
" Ha, ha! and the First Lord is a poor speaker."

"No, I don't.   The fact is I came on rather a wild
goose chase.   My son—ch—a relation of mine, gave me
a note of introduction to a fellow named Lister, and I
came down in quest of him."

"And there he is, by the Lord Harry," exclaimed
Elicott, in a tone of amazement.   "How the deuce has he
got here, I wonder," and as he spoke he looked round for
the door keeper.

Two policemen were there, hovering near the dangerous
intruder, but afraid to speak to him, lest doing so should
produce a scene.   One of them accosted several passers by,
pointing to Lister, and evidently begging them to interfere.
The man was met by refusals in every case, until at last
an elderly gentleman, obviously from the provinces, went
up and began to talk to the inebriate, who all the while
stood leaning against the wall, with a defiant scowl on
his face.   The result of the liberty thus taken was a
torrent of strong language, uttered in tones loud enough
to attract the notice of everybody near.   The benevolent
provincial retired discomfited, and, as he did so, the

Right Hon. Launcelot Orchidion slipped softly in, passed round the opposite side of the lobby without turning his eyes in the direction of the man with whom he had so lately held sweet converse, and gained the House.

Fear and perplexity were depicted on the faces of the attendants and the policeman, whose lack of eyes in the back of his head had permitted Lister to dodge past him, redoubled his efforts to find somebody able to get the journalist quietly out again.

Presently a tall burly looking man who had been watching the comedy with an amused look, while he conversed with his friends, stepped forward, and without ceremony caught Lister by the back of the neck.

" Now then, Ted," he exclaimed " you clear out of this, we don't want any of your nonsense here, my boy," and suiting the action to the word he wheeled the tipsy man round and pushed him unresistingly along the corridor forth into the outer lobby.

" There," he added, releasing his prisoner " Don't you try any of these tricks again, Ted, or it'll be the worse for you."

While this scene was passing, Mr. Buncombe told the member for Berborough why he wanted to see the redoubtable journalist—hesitatingly and with a kind of blush on his cheeks.

To his astonishment Elicott cordially endorsed the recommendation of Weardale.

" The very man for you," he cried.

" But he seems an ill-tempered, sour-hearted vagabond," objected Mr. Buncombe.

"Ah, that's only when he is drunk. When Lister is sober he is the jolliest chap imaginable. Egotistical and all that, but full of humour and device. Secure him by all means. He'll run you in if any man can."

Mr. Buncombe seemed still to doubt, and the member for Berborough went on : " Besides, it is worth a good deal to have that fellow on one's side as a member. I would buy him up were it for no reason but that. The scamp wields a deuced sharp pen, and he prods and scarifies those he hates in a style that makes them writhe again at times, I can tell you. They read those corrosive articles of his down in the country, and don't know Lister from a great man. The devil has such cheek and assurance. You have him on your side ; pay him a good fee, and it will be worth years of plodding work in the House to you. When Lister talks of the admirable good sense and patriotism of his friend, Mr. Buncombe, your voters will think themselves wise men."

" Ah ! then that accounts for it !" exclaimed the ship-broker.

" Accounts for what ?"

" Why, for seeing such a swell as Mr. Orchidion chumming with the fellow a few minutes ago."

" Oh, damn it, no, you don't mean that ! Was that so ? Gad, that's a good joke ; " and Mr. Elicott laughed heartily.

" But, Orchidion was quite right, though," he added, " perfectly right. It would never do for him to have that serpent's fangs in him when a big election fight is coming on. Oh, he's a downy chap, our knight errant, and knows his little game as well as any man. I shouldn't wonder if he meditates engaging Ted Lister for the campaign himself, just to keep the rascal quiet. So you had better look sharp, Mr. Buncombe, if you mean to be first in the field."

"All right," said Mr. Buncombe, "I'll take your advice, but I must say the present moment does not seem propitious to begin negotiations. The fellow looks fit to stick a knife in you."

"Well, perhaps, but, ha, ha! the difficulty is to know what time would be propitious, when the man is on the booze. I have seen Lister dead drunk at ten o'clock in the day. After all, too, if you are in a hurry, I'm not sure that the present moment is not as good as any. Lister has most likely been more fully. drunk early in the day than he is now. He must now be sobering down to be fit to write his spiteful trash by and bye, and has quite sense enough, you'll find, to know how to strike a bargain."

Stimulated thus, Mr. Buncombe bade the M.P.'good-bye, and went outside to seek his man. With some difficulty he found him, sobering himself at a side bar with another drink, and presented his letter, which Lister tore open roughly and glanced at. .

"Ah, Mister Weardale," he muttered, laying a sarcastic stress on the mister. "He's a great gun now, Mister Weardale—damned snob. What has he got to do with fine stamped note-paper, and a monogram, too. All your blasted, time-serving newspaper drivellers ape the aristocrat the moment they get enough to buy a second shirt to let the first go to the wash."

"So you want to put M.P. to your name, do you," he added, after glancing through the note, and looking up at Mr. Buncombe with his heavy blood-shot eyes. "Much good that will do you or the country either, for that matter. A plutocrat, no doubt; pockets full of money. Are ye prepared to scuttle the ship, b'God?"

"Pardon me, sir, I do not follow you," said the ship-owner, in his dryest, high dignified tone, thinking probably that the question reflected somehow on his occupation.

"Oh, no, none of you swell plutocrats ever do. But we mean to make you see daylight through a brick wall one of these fine days. You call yourself a Liberal, I see—and think yourself a Radical, perhaps. I know the cut of your coat. Because of you and the like of you the country is going straight to hell, sir. But we true Radicals mean to scuttle the ship and drown the lot of you first, and then when we have got a good riddance we'll raise the old vessel and dry dock her, and scrape the barnacles off her. Don't you know, sir, that it is two hundred years at least since the ship of the state has been docked and cleaned?"

"Eh, do you mean a revolution, Mr. Lister, may I ask?" ventured Mr. Buncombe.

"What else should I mean? B'God, Mr. Buncombe, I tell you, we'll show you money-bags what's what before we've done with you. I'm the leader of a great army, sir—one of the leaders, at least. Tens of thousands are prepared to rise at my nod and make a clean sweep of corruption. M.P.'s, indeed! What are M.P.'s but blasted self-seekers who sell the country every day in the week for pelf. I might have been an M.P. myself dozens of times. Constituencies have gone on their knees to me, sir, offering to run me in at the top of the poll, and pay me like a lord for my services. But no, I would have nothing to do with the crew of perdition. The mark of the beast is upon them, and, b'God, I shall stand aloof and see them perish. An M.P., good lord, any flunkey can be that," and so forth. The process of becoming sober was evidently not a sweet one for Mr. Lister and those near him while it was in operation.

However, the mere act of blowing off vicious self-conceit in this fashion seemed to cool the fellow down, and after about half-an-hour's disjointed raving he condescended on business, and before eleven o'clock that night had graciously agreed to become Mr. Buncombe's spouting double at the coming general election in consideration of the sum of twenty pounds down and eighty more when the election was over. That compact made, Mr. Buncombe returned to his hotel.

Next day he went back to Berborough but half satisfied with the result of his journey. Soon after he announced to the Liberals of the borough of Oldhills that he was ready to be their chosen candidate if it so pleased them, and his previous nursing, together with a speech from himself, and two or three harangues from his " sworn-sobriety" political devil Lister procured him the all but unanimous vote of the knot of local wire-pullers called the " Liberal committee."

M

CHAPTER XXIV.

A COMPETITION IN PLEDGE TAKING.

DURING the three months that elapsed between Mr. Buncombe's formal acceptance as the chosen of the Liberals, and the election, that great man lived at fever heat. He had commenced canvassing early because he was a new man, and as he proceeded his mental jumblement grew ever more alarming.

At the start the shipowner was a prim Liberal of the least aggressive order, anxious to win, of course, but by no means kindly disposed to the process of " swallowing formulas." But the moment he had fairly launched on the sea of politics, he became like a rudderless, sailless boat. Hither and thither the factions of the town tossed him until he knew not whether he was a Liberal or a Radical, or a red-hot Tory, or a Socialist, or a Churchman, or a Dissenter.

Talk of boggling at pledges, Mr. Buncombe found himself bolting them wholesale. He took so many, publicly and privately, that the overgorging brought on a violent fit of moral indigestion. That disease is curable, and it is possible that Mr. Buncombe's strong stomach might have worked its way through all the phases of the complaint without much loss of sleep, had his promiscuous absorption not at last put his chance of election in danger.

Pledges! Mr. Buncombe, in his new-born zeal for parliamentary honours, pledged himself to find employment for the three stalwart sons of the local Liberal editor; to procure places for dozens of girls in Her Majesty's post office ; to get an organist's post for the rector's lame boy—"so fond of music you know"—with heaps of the same kind. In his anxiety to please everybody, he held out a hand to the publicans, and coquetted at the same time with fanatical, local option teetotalers, whose paid secretary, he confessed with sadness of heart, it was impossible to convince of the folly of his ways.

Anti-vaccinationists approached him and received words of encouragement ; church people who desired to increase the power of the clergy over education, found his ear open to their pleadings; and Dissenters who talked of disestablishment and disendowment, were not sent empty away, if words meant more than a conjuror's miracle.

In vain did Lister curse and swear, and, when sober, discourse shrewd electioneering axioms. Mr. Buncombe had become mad to win, and in his greenness thought the surest way of doing so was to copy exactly what he conceived to be the model set up by St. Paul.

And soon he found his mistake. Alas! the electorate of Oldhills was not gullible to the extent that the ship-owner had supposed. Taunts began to be flung at him. The disappointed editor, who looked for instant fulfilment of pledges given, took to sneering ; and churchites, full of pride, and chapelites smitten with envy, became equally doubtful about the true faith of the chosen Liberal candidate. The wrangle grew loud and more furious, until, about three weeks before the date of the election, sundry wire pullers began to hint to Mr. Buncombe that, after all, perhaps he had better retire in time.

To add to his troubles, most of which might have disappeared before gold, and the excitement of a fight, who should appear in the town at this juncture, but a wandering baronet, blessed with many rents, and a zeal for water drinking. This noble philanthropist, who eagerly desired to cut off from the Exchequer its income from drink, but whose zeal did not lead him to set an example in making compensation by surrendering half his rent roll for the relief of taxation, made a great stir in the town. His limping wit stimulated the teetotalers to a tremendous pitch of enthusiasm, so wonderful was it for a man with a handle to his name to be able to crack a joke and tell a story just like Joe, of the "Wild Boar," or thirsty Parson White, of Nettlefield,— jolly chaps they knew—and to make these jokes on nothing but water too—wonderful! most wonderful!

Stimulated by this great man's eloquence and enthusiastic desire to bless all beggars with half-crowns from his neighbour's pockets, the anti-liquorites grew pestiferous in their demand. " Either vote for our views," they yelled, " or lose the election." And their threats did not seem so empty, for the presence of a baronet who condescended to "take the teetotal pledge," had put water in fashion. The trick of pledge-signing was not merely respectable, it had become aristocratic, and as the muster roll of the temporary water lovers swelled, the hopes of the pledge-bound, gagged, self-immolated Liberal candidate sank within him. It was worse than heresy on the tithe question.

In vain did he appeal in his emergency to the wisdom of Lister. Lister only swore, and when driven into a corner rushed off to the drinking bars, there to strengthen the invective of the water-intoxicated crowd, by furnishing them with a striking example.

" I have made a mistake after all in taking that sot,' Mr. Buncombe frequently said, and the more he leant to this view the more his mind reverted to Weardale in anger.

" That blockhead of a son-in-law of yours has got me into this mess," he told Mrs. Buncombe as they sat at breakfast in the hotel, one morning. " Had it not been for him I would not have been in this trouble with the teetotalers. Confound that fellow Lister, he was brought back to the hotel last night by a watchman, too drunk to stand."

" Well, my dear, if Harry has got you into a mess why don't you go and tell him, and ask him to get you out again. He's bound to see you through an' it be his fault I reckon, and it's no good sitting damning away here, and making me and everybody miserable. I'm sure after you've spent so much money and all, I'd not give in, not if all the town busted itself with water."

Mr. Buncombe did not at first incline to this advice. Soon, however, he was driven to catch at any straw, for the Tories, keen to see the weakness of their enemy, cunningly started, in addition to their own aristocrat, a red hot revolutionary and teetotal candidate, as a means of dividing the Liberal vote. Their own man was a youth named Viscount Callow, son and heir of the Earl of Powderhorn. He was but twenty-three years of age, and knew as much of politics as of Hebrew. Some skill at cricket, acquired at Oxford or Rugby, he had, and his appearance was attractive. Of jovial manners and ready courtesy, Viscount Callow was just the sort of stripling to turn the heads of the women folk, and Buncombe had found him a formidable canvasser. He went about among the people chatting of things in general, promising all he was asked, kissing the babies, and chucking comely wenches under the chin; altogether a great contrast to the prim, eager, restless shipowner.

For all his personal popularity, the aristocratic fledgling had little or no chance of triumphing unless Mr. Buncombe made a complete mess of it, or unless the Liberal vote could be split. Individually, Viscount Callow had no interest in the town, and his family had but little. His father, the Earl of Powderhorn, a man nominally the owner of large estates in the neighbourhood, was as poor as a rat, scrambling along he best knew how, under settlement and mortgages, and his only claim upon Oldhills consisted in his holding the influential office of chairman of a large railway locomotive building company, whose works were just outside the town. Through this position it was calculated that a goodly number of working men voters could be constrained to support the Viscount, whose entry into Parliament was considered to be necessary to "family interests." Jobbery, personal and collective, would be furthered thereby.

A candidature of this description is always formidable to a plebeian opponent.   Mr. Buncombe felt it to be so before John Stringer, Radical working man and teetotal candidate, came upon the scene.   After that the excellent Berborough patriot began to consider his chances as good as gone.   Gloom settled on his spirits, and appeared in his looks, a gloom that neither Lister's cocksure assertions nor the flatteries of the busybodies who fingered his money, could dispel.

But the man was dogged too, and before finally making up his mind whether he would withdraw or go to the poll, he ultimately decided to take his wife's advice and consult Weardale.   To save time he ran up to town on a Sunday morning for that purpose.

CHAPTER XXV.

MIXED PICKLES.

THE Weardale family welcomed their relation in their accustomed quiet, unpretending fashion, and it was just as well they did so, for the mind of the Parliamentary candidate was too much on the rack to leave him energy for the display of family affection. Before he had been five minutes in the house he did as he had done on his previous visit, demanded a few minutes' conversation with his son-in-law, and the pair forthwith adjourned to "the den." There Mr. Buncombe at once opened his heart and told his story.

"And now tell me," he wound up, "what's your opinion. Shall I go on and waste my money, or chuck the game up at once?"

"How much have you spent already?" asked Weardale.

"Well, that's rather a delicate question, you know," replied the candidate, with an awkward grin; "but I daresay you won't peach on me. The fact is I've had to bribe a little—in a quiet way, you know—hiring lots of wretches I didn't want, for one thing; and what with donations and subscriptions and subsidies here and there for the last two years, I can't have spent much under four thousand."

"And how much more will it cost you to go on to the end?"

"Perhaps another thousand, perhaps not so much. I must pay my agent, I suppose, whether I go to the poll or not."

"Of course. It seems to me, therefore, that it is useless for you to hesitate. You must fight it out. You may establish almost as good a claim on the party for a share in the cake by getting beaten as by winning, you know."

"But I don't want to be beaten; I hate the idea of being beaten," cried Mr. Buncombe, jumping up in his usual excited, restless fashion.

"Well, then, win. I cannot for the life of me see what is to hinder you."

"Eh, God bless my soul and body, haven't I told you that the teetotalers and the beer interests are nearly equally against me, and that the third man, confound him, is just as likely as not to carry off enough votes to throw me in a minority at the poll, and that I have offended some of the Church people as well as the Baptists. Good Lord, man, how am I to get over all that?"

"Yes, yes, I have heard the whole story, and think you frightened at straws. What's Lister about, that he cannot choke this Stringer scamp off?"

"Lister! humph! confound the fellow, he's mostly drunk now, and I believe in spite of all his bluster that he thinks the game up more than I do. Lister's a nuisance, in fact."

" But that won't do at all, my dear sir. When you return you must tell him that either he pulls himself together and sticks to his work, or you dismiss him on the instant without a penny. Getting drunk was not in the bargain, and you must stand no nonsense with a fellow like him. He is a cowardly devil at bottom, and, if you take him by the throat and threaten to shake the life out of him, he'll work like a nigger."

" Well, and suppose he does, what good will I get of that at this time of day."

" Just this : Lister is the man to run Stringer down Ten to one but he knows all about that Tory red herring, or if he does not now he can soon learn, for he is profound in his knowledge of the seamy side of politics. Tell him to expose Stringer ; to turn him inside out, so that the people of Oldhills may see him as he is, and when that is done buy him off."

" Buy him off, eh ! That's all very good, but as I've just told you my expenses have been heavy already—deuced heavy, and I don't quite relish new claims."

" Better spend an extra hundred or even a hundred and fifty than lose the election."

" Do you mean to tell me that Stringer will disappear for a sum like that. The Tories must have given him more to come there."

" I doubt that. Tories have grown economical. But at any rate, if Lister does his work well the fellow will soon be glad to leave the place. I have heard of the scamp— a mere sot and low hireling. I should certainly offer him no more than a hundred at first. You can spring a little, you know, if the blackguard proves obstinate."

"Hum! Ha! That's not such a bad idea, now," said Mr. Buncombe, lighting up. "Yes, that's worth trying, anyhow. Good, good. But, eh! I say, Stringer is only half the battle. What am I to do with the teetotalers and the low church party, and the deceased wife's sister party, and the anti-vaccinationists, and the outcry against big royal dowries and against pensions, and what about disestablishment? I'm in a regular pickle all round, in fact. What pleases one turns another against me."

"Ha, ha! The lot of all candidates, Mr. Buncombe, under our glorious democracy. Yet fellows get elected, somehow, and I don't see why you should not. Why not go in for some big 'cry' of your own? Can't you hit the whim of the hour somewhere?"

"I wish to God you'd tell me how."

"That's not so easy, perhaps. I fancy, though, that the more you can generalise on small questions the better. Play upon 'principles' and 'expediency;' dodge behind your party leaders—plead that this and the other fad or crying injustice are not yet within the range of practical politics—that's the correct phrase. Take the teetotalers for example. You can quite well tell them that you have the deepest sympathy with their aims, and that nothing would delight you more than to see a whole nation sober. But, you can add—and lay stress on the buts always— the question of local option is mixed up with two other questions of the highest importance. One is local government, and the other the reform of the imperial revenue. Before the temperance programme can be carried out we must have local representative bodies capable of administering the law, and before such bodies could be allowed to lay their hands at option on one of the most prolific sources of national income, the nation must have made up its mind about the source from which it may fill the gap.   Ask your water-daft baronet friend what amount of land tax he is ready to stand."

"Good, good.   'Pon my soul, Weardale, you are a clever fellow, and I wish you had been down there with me instead of that sodden brute, Lister.   He has said things to the same effect more than once, now I recollect, but he mixed 'em up so much with abuse of the land-lords, whose property he always proposed to take away without compensation, or raved so on 'payment of members,' 'direct taxation,' and the abolition of the hereditary principle, that I couldn't possibly trust him. There's the church question, now," Buncombe proceeded, " Why, God bless my soul and body, if that fellow didn't want me to run full tilt against all the interests of the clergy, and promise to vote for ' complete stripping,' as he called it."

"Did he though! That would have been a great tactical blunder, Mr. Buncombe. I suppose you didn't yield ?"

" Well, no, not altogether ; but I rather went against church corruption, you know—fat livings, lazy chapters, and rich bishops and all that sort of thing, and promised reform, consequently the clergy and their followers look askance at me."

"That's not surprising at all. The church sect leaves out the 'not' in its reading of that passage where Christ sets forth the nature of his kingdom. You may do anything, say anything, almost, but church property is sacred—came straight down from heaven into the hands of each particular parson, for whose benefits it has become a vested interest. But that line must have helped you with the Dissenters."

"It did, only I didn't go far enough for lots of them. They are luke-warm all round, in fact."

"That's a pity, but I don't think it matters much, so long as you have not definitely pronounced for or against disendowment. It is a difficulty which may be got over."

"Eh, no, you don't say so! God bless my soul, how?"

"By putting on a little more outward show of piety. That would please the simple hearted of all sects to whom righteousness is still more than creed, and a pure heart a sweet possession. Humour these people, and if need be promise a few more subscriptions to good causes, without partiality of sect."

"Hum! more and more money. Well, I suppose it can't be helped ; in for a penny in for a pound. But I say, Weardale, I do wish you'd come down and steer for me. Do come down for a week, there's a good fellow."

"I cannot possibly do that, Mr. Buncombe," answered his son-in-law. "My work does not admit of being left in other hands at present ; but you are always welcome to the best advice I can give you, you know."

"Thank you, I wish you could have come down, though. I can't trust Lister."

"Oh, you do as I tell you, and Lister will be all right. He needs a firm hand and strong will. You've been, if I may say so, far too timid with the poor devil, and have suffered him to think he was the master. Change your attitude, bluster a bit, and you will see his gas will soon evaporate."

"Well, I trust it will be so, and I'll take your advice. By the bye, what was that you were saying about going in for a line of my own. I wish you could put me up to a wrinkle of that sort, as a means of drowning the din of these faddists, as you call 'em."

"Ha, ha! That remark of mine was by the way, and I'm afraid you would not thank me for the advice I might give you on that head. I'm called a political faddist myself, you know."

"No, eh! Is that possible? God bless my soul, and what might your fad be? I thought. you despised all politics."

"Oh no, I don't. My fad is civil service corruption."

CHAPTER XXVI.

A NEW HERESY.

"WHEW!" whistled Mr. Buncombe, jerking himself round "the den," in his spasmodic fashion. "I forgot you said something to me about that before, didn't you?"

"I may have done so; I probably did so, in fact, for my friends declare I can talk of nothing else. It would be a capital tack to go on, though, with a lot of unruly electors, and couldn't do any harm. That's the beauty of it."

"Excuse me, I don't follow you there," struck in the candidate.

"What I meant was that a few good tirades against the corruption, impotence and waste of millions of money wrung from the hands of the poor, by the so-called Public Services would be something new to the electors, and would therefore stamp a candidate as a man not in the common ruck. The man who took that line would rather gain than lose by it, I feel sure."

"How's that? It seems to me just as with the Church, he'd make no end of enemies, if what you say be true."

"Enemies, no doubt, but enemies in and around London, not in Oldhills, and enemies who are cowards because criminals, consciously or unconsciously, and who would therefore much prefer buying a man's silence to an open fight. They can't summon the Deity to their help, you see, so the attack is safe, and might be profitable."

"What, eh? You don't mean to insinuate, do you, that I'm a man to be bought; 'pon my soul that's an insult, sir. I—really, Mr. Weardale; I—you must excuse me, sir, but you have gone a little too far. Do you take me for another Stringer?"

Weardale smiled a dry, quaint smile as he watched his father-in-law jump about, and fume and flourish his handkerchief.

"Nothing so vulgar," he answered, as Mr. Buncombe, overcome by the shock his feelings had received, dropped heavily into a chair, and began to blow his nose with demonstrative loudness. "Nothing so vulgar. At the same time you cannot reasonably expect me, Mr. Buncombe, to believe that you have no personal motive whatever in trying to enter Parliament. That is the talk indulged in before the simple, stupid democracy, but you and I both know better."

"God bless my soul," ejaculated the shipowner again; "I may have some ambition to shine before my fellow men, of course. Who hasn't; but I don't see what that has got to do with taking bribes to hold one's tongue, eh?"

"Nay, you run too fast there; it was never a question in my mind of vulgar bribes at all. What crossed my mind, more as an after thought than anything else, was that there are honours in the path of M.P.'s—titles and what not, and these I think are fully as likely to fall to the lot of a man who makes himself disagreeable to the ever swelling multitude of 'tax eaters,' as old Cobbett called them, as to that of their smirking, truckling, turn-coat tools."

"Humph!" grunted the shipowner, not yet mollified, but beginning to see business.

"Not only so," Weardale proceeded, with a look of what might be called serene impudence on his face, "Not only so, but I have no doubt at all in my own mind, that if a man like you were to take up, say the jobbery and waste of the leading spending departments, and make a hit with it, it might both pay for the pains and effect a public reform at the same time. Take the navy, for instance. I believe that the nation does not get value for what it spends to the extent of seven shillings and sixpence in the pound. The rest of the money is stolen, or flung away by sheer roguery, or what is practically as bad, by blockheadism, and the sacred stupidity of routine. That is a subject you could handle with much effect, I should think. You know the value of a ship, and by making some of your clerks go through the navy estimates for a few years, comparing the cost of all the vessels the nation builds and mends, or buys, with what you pay for similar articles yourself, you might make a most telling story that would lift you clean out of the crowd, and induce the electors of Oldhills to think they had tumbled on a man of mark. For the rest, I'd lay ten to one any day that next time the fighting departments get up a little war for the sake of peerages and pensions, and want to

N

charter ships, Mr. Buncombe's claims will not be overlooked."

As he said this, Weardale chuckled quietly, and looked straight at the shipowner, who tried in vain to assume an aspect that might be taken to represent shocked virtue. Failing in that, Mr. Buncombe considered it best to laugh too, but he was not quite happy at the turn the conversation had taken.

"I think we had better drop that side of the subject," he said in his nervous way. "The immediate question is, how to win Oldhills, and I'm not sure that your last idea would help me much to that"

"Oh! but I'm sure it would," said Weardale, more eagerly than usual for him. "Don't you see, it's a new tack which is always much in a competition of this kind. Candidates who have been officials, may know the detail of official corruption better than you, but they dare not dwell on it, or hint at it even, because they know the departments would make life unbearable to them, when the luck of the ballot box chucked them back into what they are pleased to call office. As a rule the rank and file sing chorus to their leaders, and the public is left in its fool's paradise. That gives the new man his chances."

"Yes, I see ; but do you really think now, Weardale, that the permanent departments are corrupt in this country. I have always thought and heard the contrary. Our services are held up to admiration as the purest in the world."

"That is part of the trick," laughed Weardale, "just as with holy mother Church. They are all of a piece."

" But surely if corruption prevails it can be discovered and stopped without public agitation, by the ministers themselves."

" No ; that is just the beauty of the thing, and why I tell you to go ahead.   The corruption of the public services of England is bound up with her institutions, is as old as the parliamentary monarchy at least, and many men of personal character and honesty uphold it.   They have been brought up in it, and live in it all their days as unsuspicious that it is corruption as a horse born and reared in a mine suspects that the darkness he sees is not the best light in the world."

" God bless my soul, I can't understand that at all."

" It would take long to explain, but it is true, and these very men, like the honest, upright Church parson in his line, often help to screen the grossest, most criminal robberies ever perpetrated upon any nation. But, apart from that, there is no cure for this state of things, or none short of the loss of empire.   The all-swallowing maw of the services has grown with the ill-gotten wealth of that empire, and finds its most striking illustration in the India office, than which nothing in Russia, nothing in old Byzantium, or older Rome exceeds or exceeded the turpitude and rottenness, and with the death of empire alone will it die.   Voters may rave and dash to the ballot boxes, orators may storm and curse, statesmen, or bipeds labelled as such, may scheme, and pose, and asseverate and invent, but serene above them all the permanent services stand and grow, deep rooted in the past, nourished by every selfish passion, every warrior's ambition, every thief's greed, every reformer's craze. Only when this weary heart-wasted old empire topples in the dust will these corruptions shrivel and disappear."

"God bless my soul and body! You take my breath away," exclaimed Mr. Buncombe. "I wish I could talk like that though, by gad, I would have all Oldhills at my heels, and that chit Callow might go and hang himself."

"Well, sir, there is, believe me, nothing to hinder you talking like that ; all you have to do is to get up a few figures and facts as illustrations, and fire away. Tell them of fellows who take the salary of government officials as a means of support while they study for, and push their way on at, the bar, or who use their posts to make a large income on the press. I remember one barrister chap who justified his conduct by saying that he could not find it in his heart to do any office work, because his industry would take away the means of subsistence from some poor devil of a writer at tenpence an hour."

"He, He! You don't mean that—is that true, though?"

"True as gospel, I assure you, and what is more, a capital illustration of the way all government office work is done. Not one man in a score among the upper branches of the service does two good days' work in a week, and that is not by any means the worst form of official corruption either. You have to go to the great spending departments for that."

"But it's most extraordinary. Why can't Parliament stop these misdeeds, if they are so notorious ? "

"Pardon me; there you show your ignorance of the uses of Parliament. It is the great screen, the never-failing scapegoat. When our fighting services take a header into infamy by making war on helpless savages somewhere, in order to grab millions and titles and honours, God save them! it is Parliament that bears the blame. We rave at ministers, poor wretches, and kick out one lot of palaverers to make room for another. True guilt is never punished under our sublime system. Why——but here comes my wife to stop my prosing, and invite us to tea."

"Yes;" said that lady, who had opened the door and looked in as her husband was about to start on some new disquisition. "Yes, we have waited half-an-hour for you already. Don't you know it is nearly six o'clock;" and turning to her father, she added—"You are not going to run away this time without breaking bread with us, I hope."

"Eh, no, no, my dear; delighted to stay, I'm sure," answered that gentleman, with a slightly embarrassed air.

"Come along then, for the children are hungry," and with that she led the way into the dining room, her father and husband following at her heels.

Had Mr. Buncombe been an impressionable man, his heart would have warmed at the sight of that happy family. Beatrice had developed a true motherhood. She was loving and true to her children, and was repaid by their love. In appearance she, to some extent, resembled her father, and yet the expression of her face was altogether different. Large heartedness shone in

every line of it, and the tones of her voice were full and
sweet. A gracious woman in the best sense of the
word was Mrs. Weardale,—such a woman as helps
to keep alive a man's faith in the high destinies of
humanity more than all the creeds ; but it is doubtful
whether her father saw aught of her sweetness. His
mind was too wrapped up in his own affairs, and he
talked electioneering twaddle at the tea table, as in the
study, scarcely noticing the children.

When the meal was over, Weardale and he retired
once more to " the den," and stayed there so long that
perforce Mr. Buncombe had to accept the offer of supper
and a bed. For the first time in his life, and thus far at
any rate, for the last, he slept under the same roof with
his despised son-in-law and his discarded daughter.
After breakfast on the Monday morning he hurried off to
return to Oldhills and renew the campaign.

CHAPTER XXVII.

GOD WITH A SMALL "G."

ALL the programme which Henry Weardale laid down for his guidance, Mr. Buncombe did not carry out Beyond a few vague sentences, he let the corruption of the services alone. It was not a congenial subject. Lister, however, he attacked and brought to reason. The fellow stormed and scowled at first, but when he found that his employer was determined to turn him adrift if he did not cease drinking and exert himself, he became as sober as a judge, and from the day of his drubbing till the polling day, kept at his work with wonderful assiduity. A strong will always above him might even yet have made him a man.

Thanks to his help, John Stringer, revolutionist and labour candidate, was exposed in his true colours, and duly bought off—not directly by Mr. Buncombe, of course, nor with immediate cash, but after a manner that satisfied him. Then, the field being clear, Mr. Buncombe and his henchman speechified and canvassed early and late. On burning questions that tended to divide the party, Mr. Buncombe was vague, and oraculor, but upon local fads, on such mites of questions as the perpetual pension list, on all that he could be definite upon, without danger to his election or to his future freedom, Mr. Buncombe pledged himself heroically. His motto was not exactly new—" peace, retrenchment, and reform," but he shouted it so often and so vigorously, that the people once more took it to mean something, and wagged their wooden heads after the manner of men wise in statecraft, saying, " This is the man for our money." " Buncombe for ever," in short, grew more and more the cry, as the strife neared its end, and increased in heat, and creed and other differences subsided for the time beneath the passions of a good stand-up party fight.

One mistake only did Lister make, and as it occurred the very day before the nomination it gave rise to some manifestation of feeling that frightened the now sanguine Liberal candidate into a mood for the most reckless " swallowing of formulas " ever witnessed in all that period of strained moral gastronomy.

He himself was in a sense the cause of the blunder. Since Lister had seriously tackled his work, Mr. Buncombe had repeatedly desired him to use his boasted influence with one or other of the leading word-jugglers of the party to come to his assistance. It was always " Couldn't you manage to bring Lord Windmill here, Lister," or "What's to hinder us from laying hold of the Right Honourable Edward Trimmer for a speech," and above all he demanded daily and oft times a day why Lister could not " draw " his friend the Right Honourable Launcelot Orchidion, the most popular prophet of officialdom in the three kingdoms, and a dashing reformer to boot.

In obedience to these demands Lister did apply to the great democratic orators, one after another, and from one and all received a polite refusal. " They were very sorry," " cordially wished the candidate every success," " other pressing engagements," &c., &c. Had they told the truth they would have said—" We know nothing of your Buncombe, and can't waste our wind in helping to waft a new man into the serene heaven of Parliamentary glory," but it was entirely unnecessary to be frank. Mr. Buncombe understood what the refusal meant quite well, and inveighed against the heartless selfishness of the favourites of fortune. Ted Lister also understood, and almost used up his stock of bad language. He did something else, he fastened upon Mr. Orchidion, and did not leave that sweet-speaking political chapman alone till he extracted a promise that if he, Orchidion, himself, could not run down for an hour to Oldhills, he would send his dear friend and, at that time, other self, the cultured and enlightened James Conduit, *littérateur* and eclectic sentimentalist, with whose assistance Mr. Orchidion dragged the country into a ruinous war some years before.

Mr. Conduit came and made a great speech, for he was a great man, and had behind him a large literary *claque*, which went into apoplectic bursts of enthusiasm when he opened his mouth. Mighty, indeed, was the flow of his oratory. No Cheap Jack of a country fair could have praised his wares more strenuously than Mr. Conduit glorified that peculiar put-me-to-bed-and-tuck-me-in-mother form of state socialism which was the true and only gospel of the mend-all school of politicians. "Great is the State, my friends, all powerful, all grasping, ubiquitous. Therefore, fall down with me and worship the glorious, dry-hearted, wooden-headed, many-handed, *deep-pocketed* bureaucracy, for in it only lies salvation from every human sorrow. Behold thy God, oh! toil-smitten, jolter-headed, blind, common herd, and admire me, the humble prophet thereof." That, freely rendered, was the burden of Mr. Conduit's harangue, and it carried the audience away, thoughtless, guileless, bovine-souled audience that it was. And the *claque* echoed its cheers throughout the land next morning, fit-shaken *claque* that it was.

Ted Lister was not in that *claque*. On the contrary he hated Conduit with the same impartial hate which he bestowed upon all successful men. To him, therefore, Mr. Conduit's great speech was as gall, and he prophesied evil from it. "The damned cad has no heart," he kept on repeating, "and no religion, b'God. His heart was forgotten when the Lord made him, and he gets up his gushing sentiments like a proposition in Euclid. All his ideas are stolen. He is the best brain sucker out of Hades," and so on.

Against all these assertions Mr. Buncombe protested in his strongest manner. He had seen no lack of feeling in Mr. Conduit. The hard-grating tones of the orator's voice never smote his ear uncongenially, and he was angry with Lister, so angry that he threatened him again with dismissal if he did not immediately drop his hostility. Lister once more obeyed, fuming, but he was right in a sense, and the mischief was nevertheless done. Whether from Ted's hints, or as the mere result of that prying effort to find a last chance somewhere, begotten of a failing hope, the Tories occupied themselves with Mr. Conduit's history, and on the morning succeeding the speech, the very day of the nomination, the hoardings and Tory windows of Oldhills were placarded with bills declaring that Mr. Buncombe had allied himself with infidels. In proof of this assertion a passage was quoted from one of Mr. Conduit's many books wherein he spoke in very disrespectful terms of the Deity, and showed his contempt by spelling God with a small " g."

The storm thus raised was terrific. Party spirit quailed before it. All sections of religionists rose in wrath, and pronounced solemn anathema on Mr. Buncombe's brilliant ally, and they were within two days of the poll. Hootings greeted the favourite at the hustings.

" I told you how it would be," sneered Ted Lister.

" Confound you," shrieked Mr. Buncombe, " I really believe your malicious tongue is at the bottom of this dirty trick."

" Of course, of course ; go it, go it ; abuse the helpless, gratify your spite on the innocent. That'll win you the election, won't it ?" was the rejoinder.

" Win the election ! God bless my soul, do you think there's any doubt on that score," said the candidate, his rage at once making way for fear.

" None at all, b'God. If you play the madman as you are doing now, you'll not get within sight of winning it."

"Eh, no, confound it. What's to be done, then? Don't stand there, man, cursing and jeering at me. Exert yourself. Put this cursed blunder right. God bless my soul and body! Lose the election at this time of day. It would be infamous." And Mr. Buncombe, in his excitement, spun round the private room adjoining the committee room for all the world like a clown in a circus.

"All very well to say, 'put it right,' but I can't do that alone, can I? You must do your part, I take it," said Lister, sulkily.

"Yes, yes ; of course, of course ; but, my friend, what? Eh ! tell me, man, what I'm to do !"

"Sit down, then, and don't squirm around like a hungry rat in a trap. Damn it, the nation won't founder if you do lose the election, nor the monarchy either, I guess."

Mr. Buncombe flopped down on the nearest chair, and grasped his head in his hands convulsively, Lister eyeing him the while with a look of cold contempt.

"I say, Lister," he exclaimed, after a brief silence, "for God's sake, man, tell me what we must do. Confound it all. I would not have offended the pious electors for five thousand pounds, and to think that fellow Conduit should have let us into such a hole. Why the devil did Orchidion send him here? What are we to do ?"

"I don't see anything for it, Mr. Buncombe, but that you should, to begin with, attend a prayer meeting, two if possible. It goes against the grain, I know, but you had better do it. Go as ostentatiously as you can, and to the biggest you can find. This is Wednesday, there's sure to be lots about, and if you can snivel aloud for ten minutes or so we may be saved yet."

"Is that all. I'll do that gladly, Lister. Find out where I'm to go, there's a good fellow, and drop a hint of what I'm to be up to. Have we many meetings to-night?"

"Three; but I can spare you for half-an-hour, and improve the occasion by denouncing the calumniators in your absence. Heh! heh! heh!" laughed Lister, with a hot glare of gratified malice in his eye.

"And is that all we have to do, think you," repeated Mr. Buncombe, but half assured.

"Well, no; I think we had better bill the town at once with a strong denial. We can repudiate all knowledge of Conduit's heresies, and lay the blame on Orchidion, if you like."

"All right, all right; I'm quite agreeable. You draw up the posters, my boy, and be quick about it; get the bills out before three o'clock, if possible—paper the town with them. Good heavens! lose the election after all I've spent and done! not for all the Conduits in the kingdom, and all the Orchidions too, for that matter." As he said this Mr. Buncombe rushed away to the committee-room to talk and explain and deny and apologise there, with his usual random feverishness.

The programme thus arranged between the would-be knight of the tongue and his squire, was carried out with promptitude and success. All babble of angry sects was hushed, if not all doubts removed, and the Party ranks closed up for the struggle.

Indeed, this atheistical squabble was but an episode in the heat of the strife at the most. As the polling day drew near, high politics fell more and more into the background, and in their place came party spirit—the same thing in essence as the spirit of horseracing. Opposing crowds backed their man as they would have backed a horse. The fight degenerated into a welter of personalities, tricks, lies, bribery, and chicane. Everything was forgotten in the eagerness to win. Women unsexed themselves—on the Tory side especially, for Mrs. Buncombe was of little use in electioneering—and vindicated their claims to the franchise by bullying and cajoling reluctant voters, by prying into the affairs of the poor, and by emitting slanders, at the foulness of which, let us hope they, in their calmer moments, would blush for shame. Parsons raved, and thundered, and bargained; artizans fought, sometimes with a manly independence, hopeful for the English race, sometimes with a baseness and corruption which filled the minds of calm onlookers with despair. With traders it was matter of self-interest, class interest, and above all, purse. The publicans backed the side that swilled most beer. Throughout the town passions raged and collided till the place was like a little hell. A leaven of better things was doubtless there. Good men and true fought for principle and right to the last; but they were overwhelmed by the Caliban of democracy on the day of the poll.

That was a day of raging tempest, a triumph of the baser human passions, and it ended in riots, and broken heads and windows. Thus did the mad multitude vindicate its rights. For the ever-ascending shipbroker, however, it was a day of never-to-be-forgotten glory. Victorious over all his foes, male and female, high and low, Mr. Buncombe came in at the head of the poll by a majority of more than five hundred over his opponent, Viscount Callow. The defeated Tories raged and threatened a petition, so that even the hour of the shipowner's triumph was dashed with anxious thoughts ; but the threats died away in less than a week. Lord Callow gave them no encouragement, knowing, perhaps, that his own candidature could not bear scrutiny, and certain at any rate that a petition would cost money, which his father could not find.

It is impossible, therefore, for me to say whether the charges of bribery and corruption, levelled against Mr. Buncombe, were true or not. He "nursed" the borough, we know on his own authority ; but more we do not know, except that his electioneering expenses were returned under one thousand two hundred pounds. If that was all he spent, Timothy Buncombe, Esquire, was M.P. for Oldhills at a very low price. From what he said, however, to his son-in-law, it may be thought that in making this return, the new guardian of a nation's liberties displayed too much modesty, if not a disposition to play with truth.

But the whole question of what is bribery is now involved in a labyrinth of legal checks and counter checks, which makes any discussion of Mr. Buncombe's guilt or innocence superfluous. Thanks to successive Acts of Parliament, bribery at elections has been raised to the dignity of a fine art.

Be his morals what they might, Mr. Buncombe was now an M.P., at any rate. Thus far had he travelled on the road to distinction ; a prosperous citizen, favoured of fortune, and penetrated by an ever deepening conviction that the " career is open to the talents." A proud man was he that night the poll was declared ; strongly did the glow of patriotic love for his country swell in his narrow bosom ; effusive were the words he used in returning thanks to his supporters, " for the great honour they had done him." All the way home to Berborough the next day he was like a man in a trance. The pie wife's son, indeed ! Mr. Buncombe felt now, with a strength which amounted to a resolution, that he ought to claim a grander origin. It was time to think about a crest and armorial bearings. The day-dream of an ancient lineage flitted across his spirit.

CHAPTER XXVIII.

A MOST INCORRUPTIBLE MEMBER.

FOR a time Mr. Buncombe attended to his parliamentary
duties with praiseworthy assiduity, voting with his party
leaders like a machine. These leaders had won at the
ballot boxes, and enjoyed the spoils of victory.

To a man like Mr. Buncombe that fact was less
exhilarating perhaps than the frosty air of opposition
would have been. It gave him less to hope for. None
of the rewards of victory could be bestowed upon a new,
and, as yet, obscure person like himself, and the perpetual duty of saying ditto to his commanders for nothing
made life humdrum. Had he been in opposition he
might have attacked something, but to do so in the then
position of his party would have been to play marplot,
and Mr. Buncombe, you may be quite sure, was incapable
of that at the start.

So, gradually, the provincial shipowner's interest in
public affairs slackened, and he began to cast about for
ways and means whereby to turn the advantages of his
position to personal and private account. For the first
session he refrained from taking a house in town, and
was rather glad that he did so. A feeling more than
ever possessed his mind that Mrs. Penelope Buncombe,

his beloved wife, was not exactly calculated to shine in London drawing rooms. It was sweeter, therefore, to live *en garçon*, varying the monotony of life in a Jermyn Street lodging by frequent visits to Berborough on the Sundays to keep his family in countenance, and his working junior partners, of whom he now had two, up to the mark.

Sweeter also was it to give little dinners at his club, and to wander about alone among the crowds which thronged the "receptions" by which the sublime upper crust, political or plutocratic, stoops to enter into morganatic union with upstarts from the nether multitude, tickling their vanity with the illusion that they also have become members of the glittering mob of land devourers, titled or other ; archpriests of the poor's tithe-eating sect, glorifying their God in liveried uniform, guaranteed holy by the tailor; millionaire city sheep-shearers, marvellously clean looking ; foreign adventurers, many hued; blacklegs of refined manners; fat company leeches ; swindling contractors ; retired pirates ; honourable and right honourable black mailers ; ex-brigands of a subdued fierceness ; world enslaving Jews, intent upon title buying, and padded with mortgages on human labour; ex-camp sutlers of well greased manners and gridiron fame ; sublimated pawnbrokers, over jewelled ; professional directors, high fed and fee'd ; literary quidnuncs, touts, exquisites, triflers, and slaverers ; sham heroes, much-medalled and ordered, glorious in their victories over silly women ; boudoir guardsmen of many *liaisons ;* bureaucrats full of the wisdom and munificence of the

Jew who not merely lends but gives ; together with a court-classified fringe of nondescript publicans and sinners, which, with its due complement of females, proper and improper, fat and lean, handsome and hideous, scheming and simple, vain and vacuous, political and play-acting, "blue" and bovine, mild and malicious, greedy and generous, sly and sarcastic, pious and prurient, "fast" and fatuous, inane and insolent, calls itself "Society," lives apart, and, except when elections draw near, scorns to look upon the honest, weary shouldered, toil haggard millions whom it treads beneath its feet.

Yet though he made his way into the throng of these clean and unclean parasites of a decaying civilization, on sufferance, and by a diligent cultivation of club hospitality, Mr. Buncombe did not much enjoy his new life. Nothing substantial appeared to be behind this lavish expenditure of money and time. It was an investment of capital which brought no return. Grandees, fashionable *gobe-mouches*, often out at elbows, overgrown plutocrats, circumcised and uncircumcised pagans, promiscuously accepted his invitations to dinner, and dawdled through many evenings in his company. In return he dined with such, or formed one in the crush at their "receptions," but in the end this assiduous eating and drinking, gossiping and swarming, biting and being bitten, was as nothing to the ship broker. He was nobody still.

Another portion of Mr. Buncombe's labours was for a time almost equally unprofitable in his eyes. Like all new men he was at first zealously anxious to do his duty on committees, and permitted himself to be nominated upon them right and left. But it was slavish work, and for nearly the whole of his first session he did slave, in the dark, totally unable to discover how the labour could be made to pay.

Of what possible interest was it to him that Muddlebury complained of its drains, and wanted powers to borrow large sums of money in order to get rid of bad smells, and enrich the members of its corporation? How could he feel interest in the dispute which arose over Tippleholme's Police Act, or Cinderham's water works? Still less could he find either profit or amusement in the endless wrangles and check mates, plots, overreaching contractors' jobs, and money wasting devices of rival railway directors. None of the gains they and their lawyers and contractors appeared to receive by the fighting and spending came into his pocket. Before he had been a twelvemonth member of Parliament his soul became weary within him, and he felt inclined to accord an angry assent to the common faith in the wisdom of Solomon.

But by the middle of his second year this mood also changed, and for two very good reasons. One was the discovery he made that committee work did after all pay. Not by bribery, of course. No member of the English House of Commons is ever so vulgar, so forgetful of proprieties as stupidly to pocket bank notes or promoters' cheques. Such a low American-backwoods sort of proceeding is never so much as hinted at. Parliamentary Committees pay in England because they are conducted on the reciprocity principle.

Should any powerful interest be attacked, and the attack get referred to a private committee, such interest is careful to have that committee packed with its friends, and the attack is decently smothered and put out of sight. If certain borough members in their desire to keep their seats sure " back a bill " whose unacknowledged but genuine purpose is to open the way for free-handed pocket filling by the wire pullers and officials situated in that borough, they get other members to aid them in passing that " measure," and expect a *quid pro quo*. This expectation is seldom disappointed, and by these happy-family arrangements members often do excellent strokes of local bribery without paying a penny out of their own pockets. Money saved is thus money gained.

Mr. Buncombe's cogitations had for some time led him towards this view of the committee traffic, but being a new man and unknown, it was at first only by drawing uncertain inferences that he could come to any conclusion. His second session brought him actual experience, and that through a private bill promoted by the company of which his hustings' opponent's father, Lord Powderhorn, was chairman.

The bill sprang out of a railway squabble, and incidentally became a burning question in the borough of Oldhills. Up to that time this flourishing place had been served by one railway only, and the managers thereof made it pay for this exclusive privilege. But another railway ran past the town, about ten miles to the west, and after years of rebellious submission, Lord Powderhorn's company set to work to promote a branch line to join their works, and, of course, the town also, with this rival trunk road.

The scheme was taken up with enthusiasm. All the Oldhills industries joined Lord Powderhorn's company in backing it. It received the cordial support of the corporation, and thanks to his lordship's skilful guidance, it safely passed the Lords.   But the monopolist railway which held Oldhills in its grasp, fought hard, and so powerful was it that the promoters feared the result in the Commons, especially as they were mostly pronounced Tories, and who had looked on the borough member as an impudent upstart interloper.   What they most dreaded was, that three directors of the company in possession, who were members of Parliament, should be put on the committee.   This danger, however, they succeeded in averting, so far, at any rate, that but one of the objectionable men was nominated, and he was effectually neutralised by a deadly enemy in the traffic stealing sense.   There remained the political danger which prompt action and brilliant strategy might at least mitigate, if not destroy, and when these were in question, the Earl of Powderhorn was not the man to let grass grow under his feet.

Mr. Buncombe was, as a matter of course, nominated upon the committee appointed to decide this important dispute, and Mr. Buncombe and Lord Powderhorn soon came to an understanding.   From being sworn foes they, in a day, became equally sworn friends, and the basis of their friendship consisted in a pledge, on his lordship's part, that there should be no Tory opposition to the shipowner's return at the next election, if Buncombe secured the passing of this little bill. It was a compact eminently satisfactory to Mr. Buncombe in every way, and he fulfilled his part of it with energy and success. Lord Powderhorn and his friends got their Act, and Mr. Buncombe saved at least a couple of thousand pounds. Henceforth he understood the uses of committees. Taken discreetly and in moderate doses, they were good for a member's banking account.

CHAPTER XXIX.

A RAID: BOOTY AND BREAKERS AHEAD.

THE second reason for Mr. Buncombe's altered attitude towards parliamentary life was equally potent and equally personal. When a man's mind is soured by disappointment it often happens that there is bred in him a desire to attack something. He will assert himself, were it for nothing else than to show that after all he is a man and not a marionette, jerked hither and thither by the controlling threads of fate. This was Mr. Buncombe's humour in the early part of the second year of his parliamentary life, and when it was strong upon his mind he remembered his son-in-law's discourses regarding official corruption.

"Ah! there's my chance," thought he, and off he posted to Weardale once more. Since his election they had seldom met. At first he had asked the journalist occasionally to his little club dinners, but the spirits of the two men were not congenial, and, as Mr. Buncombe soon ceased to visit Weardale's house in Highgate, the dinner invitations were soon evaded, intercourse dwindled to casual "how d'y' dos" in the street, or a few minutes' chat *pro forma* in the club smoking room, where Weardale sometimes appeared on Saturday evenings.

But when the shipowner's aspiring soul felt that it must burst forth somewhere, or, psalmistly speaking, perish within him, he experienced not the least scruple in applying to the neglected son-in-law for assistance. As good him as another—better him than Lister, the ever drunk and disorderly, for instance—but to whom, even drunk, Mr. Buncombe had to don his suavest manners under penalty of relentless scarification.

To Weardale, then, he went, and more perhaps to be rid of a bore than from any higher feeling, that shrewd man "coached" him for an attack on the expenditure of the Navy. Thanks to this coaching, and to his own knowledge of the management and cost of ships, it proved to be a damaging attack. The leaders of his party did not like it, because the duty was laid upon them of defending the wholesale traditional stealing of the Admiralty permanent officials, and that led to more lying than some of them relished ; but the sacred bats and owls of the Admiralty liked it still less. They were alarmed by it, in fact, and said to each other " this fellow knows something. Hang it, he may find out something. We must shut his mouth."

And they did. That one speech of Mr. Buncombe's in Parliament paid him better than any single piece of work he ever did, save and except his performance during his brief career as a receiver of stolen goods, when just starting in life—an episode no friend would dwell upon. No sooner had the permanent officials arrived at the conclusion that Mr. Buncombe was a man to be attended to, then his ships began to be in demand for Government

freights. Hints were given to him in a quiet way, that
if he tendered for the conveyance of troops or stores, for
one of the petty wars this glorious, most Christian, and
bishop-blessed empire is always engaged in, his chances
of success were great. Accepting these hints in the
friendly spirit which prompted them, Mr. Buncombe did
tender, and at prices which left him most agreeable
profits, after all commissions and backsheesh allowances
were deducted. Money came to him fast and easy, and
the whole attitude of his mind towards Parliamentary life
was henceforth completely changed. It had become a
life that paid.

With larger, surer revenues, came fresh hopes, more
vaulting ambitions, a wider view of life. Some of these
ambitions had to be postponed to a more convenient
season; but one dream Mr. Buncombe could at once
gratify. Already he was the third largest shipowner in
Berborough, and he determined to be forthwith the
greatest, not in that town only, but in all north-
eastern England. With money, as he always had
thoroughly believed, a man could move not merely
mountains, but mankind; and now money flowed in
upon him easily, swiftly, like a full running tide. With
this money he bought new steamers, fitted like floating
palaces, and organised a great passenger and trading line
to the East. His name and fame were in all men's
mouths; and envy and malice snarled feebly behind him,
like yapping curs well in a bloodhound's rear.

But—woe's me that there should be any "buts" in this
most clean-handed shipbroker's biography; and if one

could only romance well, and deal with the forms of life, not its substances, there need be none. Truth, fell tyrant that she is, drives me to admit that a shadow came o'er this scene, all splendid in gold and polished brass. In sober prose Mr. Buncombe o'erreached himself. Fast as his wealth grew, it could not keep pace with his ambition. Was it Nemesis, or did his history merely run in the grooves laid down for all human flesh? It is not for me to decide; but at this point in his career it must be admitted that he successfully repeated the blunder of his former master, Mr. Silas Brown, of mottled memory. The only difference between them was, that whereas Mr. Brown had spent money on the bare prospect of receiving it at a future day, Mr. Buncombe was stimulated by the money in hand to anticipate the revenues of the future.

And was there no other differences between the situation of the two men? None that I can see. "What?" cries the angry casuist, "do you mean to insinuate that Mr. Buncombe came by his wealth in the same way that Brown had hoped to come by his?" I insinuate nothing. Moralists and casuists are at perfect liberty to see all the difference that comforts them, between the man who drowned and robbed in order to be rich, and the man who sold his knowledge, and his soul, and his borough, for handfuls of gold wrenched by the tax collectors, out of the thin, horny hands of the poor. Both men were equally grand if you like, or both equally short-sighted.

Stay, though, I am going too fast. It will probably be denied by few that Silas Brown might have been wiser had he not drowned a ship's company in order to make money out of the thick-woolled underwriters, but no one can for a moment say that Mr. Timothy Buncombe made a mistake in pocketing what share of the taxes his abilities could secure. Quite the contrary, that prudent and therefore laudable proceeding had a sensible and lasting effect in strengthening his claims to be considered great. Judged by results the two men stand at opposite poles. The younger was a wise man ; the older was a fool.

For Mr. Buncombe did not give way and tumble to pieces when he found he owed a matter of two hundred thousand pounds more than he could pay. Nay, his far-seeing eye beheld the storm approaching, and he got ready to weather it like the smart broker he was. Through two petty wars did gold flow into his treasury, and, by virtue of the fears his speech on the navy produced, he had been granted a fat little Colonial mail contract. But times changed, and men ; and one day, to Mr. Buncombe's surprise and disgust, what should happen but the defeat of his party, the resignation of its chief, and the rush of a hungry opposition upon the abandoned spoils. This was indeed an unexpected blow to the great shipowner of Berborough, comparable only to the foundering of the " *Molly Bawn* ;" but comparable as great things may be to small. Just when Mr. Buncombe wanted money most he saw large sources of supply either dried up or threatened with extinction. Other men would be more favoured in the next division of the plunders incident to church-blessed murder and rapine ;

and his mail contract would close within a twelvemonth, without hopes of renewal, if the new horde held office so long. He had had his "thirty pieces" in short, and was no longer dangerous to permanent officialdom, so it could afford to make new men happy. It must be confessed that when Mr. Timothy Buncombe cast his eye over this prospect the heart within him became less adamantine, and no doubt his cheek would have blanched as cheeks are popularly supposed to do, but that they were white enough already. His heart quailed just the least bit, truth forces me to admit, but his brain never softened, nor did his nerves unbrace. No one seeing him in the lobby of the House, in his office at Berborough, at society's masques and moralities, and now and then "only for a little relief, you know," behind the scenes at the Comic Opera, would have for one moment supposed that Mr. Buncombe had anything on his mind except a dozen chances of converting two pounds into five for eight hours a day, six days a week; with the prospect, agreeable to all pious bankers and money-lenders, of good interest on his surplus during the seventh. Mr. Buncombe succumb to adversity ! Perish the thought !

So far from displaying the least indication of affliction or apprehension, this wise and sensible gilt hero took immediate steps to prove to the world that his prosperity was destined to increase. Hardly had the political tongue fencers whose lead he accepted cooled down after their scamper from office, when Mr. Buncombe determined for the first time to take a house in town. For the three odd years of his career as a public servant and

benefactor which had already passed away, he had contented himself either with a modest lodging or with a
small furnished house in the outskirts of the fashionable
world, taken for three months in the height of the season,
to pacify his wife's tongue and allow his son and
unmarried daughter to see something of the habits of
the high.   This modesty he now felt to be entirely out of
place, so he determined to take all risks incident to the
possession of a common-place wife without further parley.
Finding the lease of a house in Prince of Wales' Terrace,
Kensington, for sale, he instantly bought it, gave a
wholesale order for furnishing it, and removed to it, with
his family, in time for the forthcoming season.   In all
my wide experience of human affairs and the men who
ravel them, I never knew a course of action more worthy
of respectful admiration.

CHAPTER XXX.

A MODERN INVENTION GOOD FOR LEAN PURSES.

NOT only did Mr. Buncombe take a house in town, he set up a carriage and pair. Daily this brand new equipage drove in the park either with Mr. Buncombe himself seated in the place of honour beside his wife, or with the wife and daughter by themselves. Another prosperous man of the people, in short, had bought or sold his way to the glories of Rotten Row, and might rub wheels with princes of the blood, peers, cabinet ministers, court soldiers, turfites, game preservers, Jews, Greeks, Parsees, and bishops. It was glorious. How could a man able to hold his own amid such a far shining crowd be in difficulties?

You may well ask the question. Mr. Buncombe, however, was, if not in difficulties, at least approaching that interesting condition of life, and all the time his energies seemed engrossed by the labours incident to the assumption of a " footing " in " Society," his mind was brooding over the future. To him the great question was not at all the same as had once so futilely occupied the mind of Mr. Silas Brown. The world had moved since those days. " Limited liability " had come into fashion, and constituted itself the great medium for converting the debts of the few into the losses of the many. Thanks to this great invention, a man who had outrun the constable in a splendid or artistic manner, was no longer forced to bow his head as a pauper, and compound with his creditors. Fools and groundlings alone did that now-a-days. The wise man increased his expenditure the nearer he came to impecuniosity, and so contrived to magnify his reputation for wealth as to be able to sell his decaying or insolvent business, with all its load of debts, to a limited liability company at a handsome profit.

The great shipowner of Berborough was fully alive to the advantages of this modern system of permitting others to bear your burden. It had been in his mind when he took his town house and allowed his abounding wealth to come into flower, as it were, before the eyes of a world given to gossip. "Prosperous man," "devilish clever fellow, I hear;" "made pots of money out of Government contracts;" "some of the finest steamers afloat in that fellow's fleet." Thus did idle tongues cackle forth his fame as one result of his shrewd exhibition of the gifts of good fortune, and prove how wise he had been.

That his business should forthwith become the property of a limited company Mr. Buncombe had fully determined. Nevertheless his mind was perplexed. It was all very well, he felt, to sell his business, but what was he to do afterwards? An active man like him could not be idle. And even if it had been possible for him to settle down peacefully into a pensionary of Dame Fortune, he did not see how he could afford it.

Turn the matter how he would he failed to discover a way to make a sum of money adequate to maintain in retirement the dignified full-pursed style of living adapted to his tastes. The question accordingly ultimately resolved itself into this. " Can I sell my business to a company in such a manner as to retain the surest part of the profits thereof for my own use—the company taking all risks ? "

Here was indeed a knotty matter, and until he saw his way through it, the spirit of Mr. Buncombe was clouded. But Mr. Buncombe was a man of genius, and the more the difficulties seemed to multiply, the more did his courage rise to face them.

After all, too, it was not a plan he required so much as the assurance that his plan would succeed. The business of ship owning yields itself with extreme facility to an arrangement whereby one set of people shall bear the losses, and another much smaller set pocket the gains. All that is necessary is that the ownership of the ships shall be separated from the duty of finding profitable or un-profitable cargoes for them. Ownership in other words must be vested in one class, and the business of broker in another, and the thing is done. This very arrangement, in fact, exists in all great shipping businesses. Thanks to the liberty afforded by law, and by the customs of the trade, shipbrokers seldom entirely own their own ships. Should trade be good and profitable they may be large shareholders in their best vessels ; but at other times, or when the vessels are old and unseaworthy, so as to be uninsurable to a profitable extent, the brokers who

P

"run" them, rarely or ever stand to lose as proprietors.
Their concern then is to make their brokerages sure,
come of the mere shareholders what may. Shareholders
are merely creatures of the nature of milch kine.

The means, therefore, of carrying out his purpose, Mr.
Buncombe had under his hand. He had but to sell his
vessels, out-and-out, to a joint stock company, with
limited liability, retaining the managership of them—
the brokerage business—in his own hands, and at once
the losses would fall on other shoulders, while his income
would be wondrous sure. Why then did he hesitate?
Principally because he was ignorant. Never having
formed a company before, Mr. Buncombe was in the
dark upon the great question: How much falsehood
will the public swallow? This distressing position left
him long in doubt whether it would be possible to
attract the greedy goslings in sufficient numbers to make
the transmogrification of his business a profitable affair.

And his doubts were augmented upon this point by
the diminishing success which had of late attended his
efforts to place the sixty-fourths of his new ships among
his private *clientelle*. Had you been in the secret of Mr.
Buncombe's banking account at this time you would
have found that, as a consequence of his inability to sell
shares privately, large amounts of long dated shipbuilders' bills were lying in pledge for advances. Had
you pried further still, and seen the private ledgers of the
mighty builders of the Tyne and Clyde, you would have
discovered that they held secret mortgages upon some of
the most gorgeous ships in Mr. Buncombe's great

"Excelsior" fleet of "mail" steamers, so that they were in reality pawned twice over. Could he hope to sell in such circumstances to a confiding public of widows, half-pay officers, sharp tradesmen, tithed parsons, greedy of twenty per cent. interest, and fortune hunters of the share market in general, at such a figure as would pay all these creditors, and leave him some hundreds of thousands to the good? Mr. Buncombe doubted.

CHAPTER XXXI.

THE SPIDER AND HIS WEB.

UNABLE to resolve his doubts himself, Mr. Buncombe obtained, through one of his brother members of Parliament, who filled the proud position of chairman in seven companies, and submitted to be a common-place director of as many more, an introduction to a firm of smart lawyers in the city.

"They are the very people for you," this gentleman declared, "especially a fellow called Gettem, the junior partner. You enlist Gettem and the thing is done. And if I can be of any use to you in forming a board you know I'm at your service."

"Thanks, very much," answered Mr. Buncombe, mentally resolving that this distinguished "guinea pig" should *not* "assist him in forming a board." But he took the introduction and forthwith spread his case before the mind of Mr. Golightly Gettem, junior partner in the important firm of Spratt, Gudgeon, Hook and Gettem, Old Jewry Chambers.

Mr. Gettem was a stout little gentleman, a puffed out individual in fact. The very legs of him had a windbaggy look, round, shapeless and much of a thickness from hip to heel. Whether viewed behind or before, his aspect was that of a person who might visibly collapse with a hissing sound, were a pin run into his outer casing. In countenance, Mr. Gettem was as heavy and shapeless as in figure. The complexion was swarthy, the face clean shaven, the eyes small and peering, the mouth heavy. Owing to the extent and protuberant form of the cheeks, there seemed no nose worth mentioning ; but this defect in his anatomical construction did not prevent Mr. Gettem from using a pair of *pince-nez* spectacles, which stuck on the tip of his little snout not a second longer than the head was held back.

While Mr. Buncombe laid his story before this barrel of legal acumen, the said barrel sat back in its chair, alternately raising and lowering its round fat head, and dropping and picking up these *pince-nez* spectacles. When Mr. Buncombe had ended, Mr. Gettem said " I see," snatched up a pen, and began to draw a bird, or what looked like the outlines of a bird, on the blotting paper before him.

" I see," he repeated presently. "Then am I to understand, Mr. Buncombe, that yours is a good going concern?"

" To be sure ; I should just think so. Why, Mr. Gettem, I have made as much as five-and-thirty per cent. profit lately."

" Then why the devil do you want to sell ?" was the query, and up went the *pince-nez*, through which the keen little eyes peered straight into those of the ship-owner. They peered and saw nothing, for Mr. Buncombe turned his gaze upon the yellow patch in an estate plan which hung on the wall opposite.

" Why do I want to sell, eh !" he repeated.

" Yes. Why do you want to sell ?   It doesn't concern me to know, of course, not in the least.   Only lawyers are like doctors, don't you see. If they are to do any good there must be full confidence between them and their clients. Now, I take it, you wouldn't part with these ships if they paid you five-and-thirty per cent. to-day, or were at all likely to do so next year."   Mr. Gettem was not collapsible after all, then.

Driven into a corner after this style, Mr. Buncombe had to confess that there was a turn—a little turn in the tide of fortune.   " Profits are still good, Mr. Gettem," he protested, "and I see no reason why they shouldn't continue so, but the fact is the great profits of the last five or six years carried me away.   I have overbuilt myself, and it would require extra good profits to keep the thing going."

" I see," said the lawyer once more. " You want to cut and run before the bad times come. Quite right. I believe you can do it, too ; but you'll have to look sharp about it, for there are three or four more companies in preparation on the same lines. In fact, I'm busy settling the prospectus of one now, and it's such a race to be first in the field that the public will soon have too much of a good thing."

" Indeed," cried Buncombe ; "then there's not a moment to lose."

"Oh ! I don't say that. In this sort of thing it is often better to be second or third than first, don't you see. The public appetite grows with the supply up to a certain point."

"Hum!" said the shipowner, doubtfully.

"Oh, but it does, though. For instance, if this company I speak of comes out and proves a success, and it will do so, I have no doubt; I wouldn't touch it if I thought otherwise,—if it succeeds, I say, the people who miss it's shares will rush after the next lot of the same kind, and so on. Things always go in waves, don't you see!"

"Well, of course, you know best. I have had no experience of this sort of thing, and am naturally rather nervous about it."

"Quite so; that's quite right. But you would not be so if you knew me, sir. I never fail; never;" and the circular little person sat bolt upright, adjusted his spectacles, and took another stare at Mr. Buncombe, which seemed to refresh him like a pinch of snuff.

"Eh! well, I'm delighted to hear that," said Mr. Buncombe, jumping to his feet, "and, since time presses, hadn't we better discuss details a bit now."

"No, no, no, not to-day, if you please; I can't, don't you see; too busy. Send me an outline of your plan to-night or to-morrow morning, and come again, eh—say on Thursday, at three. That will save time for both of us."

Mr. Buncombe, in his impatience, demurred at this, but had to consent and obey. His scheme was drawn up that night—it was Tuesday—and on the following Thursday he again saw Mr. Gettem.

"I don't quite like your plan," said Mr. Gettem, in his sudden way, as Mr. Buncombe seated himself in the lawyer's room, to hear the verdict on the appointed Thursday.

"Eh, no, don't you, though?" the shipbroker answered with a start, and rather taken aback. "But it will do for discussion, won't it?" he added.

"Of course, certainly, of course, of course; only I like to start fair, don't you see, and if this proposal——" drawing forth Mr. Buncombe's carefully written sheet of foolscap as he spoke, "won't do at all, there's no good in saying it will, is there?"

"N-no, I should think not," gasped the discomfited shipbroker.

"To begin with," Gettem proceeded, "your capital is too small by a lot. You ought to make it a million and a half, at least."

"But God bless my soul and body," cried Buncombe, starting to his feet, "I don't want a million and a half. The public, I feel quite sure, wouldn't pay nearly so much for my fleet, good as it is."

"I didn't say they would. Perhaps they won't give half a million in hard cash. Nobody can tell, don't you see. But for that very reason, you must run into big figures. It looks well, and if your paid up capital is only half the nominal amount, all the better. Only let us have a good margin to come and go on, and plenty of shares for the vendor. They should always count for nothing to him in fixing the price."

As this appeared a reasonable proposition, Buncombe gave way, and it was arranged that the "authorised" capital should amount to a million and a half in ten pound shares. Only one million of this was to be issued to the public, and upon this five pounds per share, or half a million would be " called up."   The vendor was to secure the other half million in shares, credited with " five pounds paid " as part payment for his interest in the fleet, so that the capital would figure as seven hundred and fifty thousand paid up.   In order to give the people who found the money a sense of having to do with a genuine affair, it was decided that Mr. Buncombe should voluntarily agree not to put any of his shares upon the market for twelve months.

But then came the difficulty of the secret mortgages. " Those builders won't take my shares for what I owe them," Mr. Buncombe asserted, " at any rate not for the whole, and if the public don't subscribe I'll be rather in a fix, you know."

" Are you sure of that ? " said Gettem.

" Yes, sure enough ; I have sounded 'em, and they all say ' no,'—money down or fresh mortgages.   Now what I have been thinking is this," Mr. Buncombe proceeded, " could we not issue some terminable debentures, say a couple of hundred thousand or so of· five per cent. debentures, redeemable in five or six years.   Those builder fellows would take them, and as I know I can place privately a good many shares, it struck me that we could make a very fair show in the prospectus.   ' All the debentures, and so much of the capital already subscribed, and only so much left for the public,' that sort of thing, you know."

" Good, excellent, first-rate, if you can carry it out ; but don't you think we might trust the public to find the money to pay for the ships with shares alone ? "

"Perhaps, but in that case we should want six hundred thousand pounds at least paid up. Now the real question to my mind is, could we sell that amount of shares at a good premium?"

"At a premium! what do you mean? You surely don't suppose you can issue shipping shares at a premium?"

"Why not? Our books you know can be made to show a twenty per cent. profit, easily enough, for a given period; and from what you tell me I think that we might sell our shares at one hundred per cent. premium easily, if we don't offer too many, especially as I agree to hold mine back."

"No you couldn't; I'll lay five to one you couldn't. Besides, twenty per cent. is too much to promise. The bait is too big. You must not go beyond fifteen, else the kind of shareholders you want to catch won't bite. Your widows and parsons, and "poor gardeners," have come to think themselves too sharp to be caught with chaff, and twenty per cent. looks like chaff, don't you see. And you'll excuse me, Mr. Buncombe, I know, but for the life of me I can't see what you are aiming at. What the devil do you want with a premium?" As Mr. Gettem said this he raised his glasses to have another stare.

Mr. Buncombe did not like either the action or the query, but in the end he had to come out with his whole mind, and when he did, Gettem could not resist the temptation to jump up and shake the shipowner's hand with the energy of a dissenting deacon.

"By gad, you are a clever fellow, and no mistake," he cried. "I would never have thought of that now, 'pon my life I wouldn't. It's first rate, if we can only carry it out."

"We can only try," said the shipowner complacently, "and from what you tell me of the temper of the public, I think we shall succeed."

Briefly, the plan which so excited the admiration of the lawyer was none other than this:—In discussing the articles of association Mr. Buncombe had found that it would be rather a barefaced thing to constitute his firm perpetual and irremovable managers of the new company. It was, therefore, decided to constitute it the managers for five years only as an absolute thing. Thereafter dismissal could only take place on a three-fourths vote of the total body of shareholders. That was so impossible a vote to obtain as to make Messrs. Buncombe and Co.'s position almost absolutely safe. In order, however, to make assurance doubly sure, Mr. Buncombe hit on the idea of an issue of debentures ostensibly to pay off the shipbuilder's mortgages, actually to enable him to keep a good hold over the fleet. For should a good subscription list be made up for the shares at a premium, he proposed to utilize a portion of the money which would then come to him in taking up these debentures, paying off at the same time the mortgages held by the shipbuilders out of premiums or superabundant share capital. The debentures would, by that plan, fall into his own hands, and he could foreclose if the shareholders pushed him into a corner. By the large premium on the shares issued Mr. Buncombe hoped to have abundance of funds in hand for this and every other purpose, as it was easy for him to devote his spare money to any object he pleased.   He, in fact, stipulated that three hundred thousand pounds in cash should be paid to him over and above the fifty thousand shares.

No wonder that the lawyer was delighted with this clever plan.   When, however, his transports had subsided a little, his inquisitiveness returned, and he wanted to know what Mr. Buncombe proposed to do with the share premiums " furnished by outsiders," as he phrased it.

" Suppose we offer the shares at two pounds ten shillings premium, he said, on the promise of a 12 to 15 per cent. dividend, you will net two hundred and fifty thousand pounds.   What will you do with it ? "

" It won't be quite that, I think," said Mr. Buncombe. " We may have allowances to make, and some fellows will want time."

" I understand that.   But supposing, what will you do with it when it does come to hand?   A quarter of a million is a good round sum, you see, and it's the surest money you'll have, for I take it you expect lots of subscriptions for the regular capital in ship shares."

" Yes, of course, and so I had intended to put this premium money to an insurance and renewal fund, or something of that kind.   It would look well, you know— give an appearance of strength."

" Ah, so, so, that might do, sir.   Gad, it might do ; but then the question will arise, how about the premium on the fifty thousand shares allotted to the firm.   People will ask if you mean to pocket that hundred and fifty thou'?"

Mr. Buncombe smiled a serene, superior smile at this question, and, rising from his chair, took a brisk twirl round the room before he replied. Pausing in front of Gettem after this exercise, he remarked, in a quiet, casual sort of way, "The firm, of course, will pay up its premiums like the rest."

" Eh, the devil, no," exclaimed Gettem, fairly taken aback. "But I thought, my dear sir, you wanted to make money, not to give it away."

" I sha'n't give any money away," was the dry rejoinder.

" Eh, what ; and how the deuce are you going to pay your premium then?" demanded Gettem, once more staring with all his weasel eyes.

" Nothing easier. I'm surprised at your astonishment. But I suppose it arises from your small acquaintance with shipping affairs. Don't you see, Mr. Gettem, that we are in this position : our shares come to us five pounds paid. As you yourself have remarked, they count for nothing to us in the price of the fleet. It follows, therefore, that we can pay our premium with ship shares. By handing over so many of these to the company at a given value, we liquidate our debt to it, and swell the reserve to four hundred thousand pounds. It is a mere book entry, you know."

" So, so, I see," said Gettem ; "first rate, splendid in fact. Only your directors, if they understood the thing, might object to that plan."

"But I don't mean to let the directors understand anything about our affairs. They will be mere figure heads. Recollect, my firm are the managers of the fleet, and we do not mean to render fuller accounts to the company than we usually give to private owners. Why should we ?"

"Oh, no reason at all why you should, if you can get a board to submit to that."

"It must, my dear Mr. Gettem. It can't help itself. It will know no more about ships than I do about astronomy, never fear. Why, we may have to pay a dividend or two out of the reserve, to tide over a bad time, you know."

"And to let Buncombe and Co. dispose of their shares, premium paid, eh. Gad, you are a smart fellow, Buncombe, excuse me for saying so; a deuced smart fellow. You provincial chaps lick us all to fits when you lay on for a good try. I'm blest if you don't." Completely conquered, and abandoning altogether his superior airs, Mr. Gettem rose to his feet and reverently shook the great broker by the hand.

Thus masterfully was a great project brought into fit shape for presentation to the world.

CHAPTER XXXII.

THE NET FILLED.

ON these lines the prospectus was ultimately settled, only that Mr. Buncombe's courage rose to a height which made him demand three pounds premium on the hundred thousand shares offered to the confiding public. And the public paid.

But one difficulty had remained after the capital had been adjusted, and over it Gettem and the shipowner had several interviews. That was, how to form a board, and upon this momentous question Mr. Buncombe's genius again asserted its ascendency. The guiding principles laid down by him were—(1). That there should be at least one peer on it. (2). That all the directors should be ignorant of shipping affairs, and if possible stupid upon any business matters, and (3). That they should not be " guinea pigs "—mere hacks who lived by selling their names to all and sundry, but " men of standing and respectability."

" It would never do to have a Falstaff's regiment sort of board," he asserted over and over again, with emphasis, using a phrase he had picked up in a newspaper leader, and his obstinacy on this point rather disconcerted Gettem, who like all good company promoters, kept a private list of eligible candidates for guineas, whose appointment served mutual interests. His objections to the "peer" selected by Mr. Buncombe, represent his attitude towards the whole of the shipowner's nominations.

"Lord Powderhorn," he asserted "will never do; "poor as a rat, sir. His name stinks in the city; always hard up. You make a great mistake, sir."

"No I don't," retorted Mr. Buncombe. "Powderhorn's a selfish ass, and poor, and all that, but you can't say that he is merely a guinea pig. He is not on the board of more than three companies altogether, and one of them is a railway which doesn't count, as it is entirely an honorary affair. So his name can't stink much in the city."

"But I tell you it does," Gettem jerked out, "he has no credit with anybody. I have his 'kites' in my own possession sometimes, and might have them oftener, but that I have such a devil of a job to get 'em paid, for all the hold he has over a certain banker in Lombard Street."

"Pooh! I don't care a farthing for that. In fact, that is all the better for me. I shall get the man the more easily under my thumb. You don't tell the public that Powderhorn lives by accommodation paper and blackmail, do you?"

"No, of course I don't. Why should I? the public wouldn't pay me for the information?"

"Just so. Therefore, to all, except a few who don't count, Powderhorn is a most respectable peer, and that's why he's just the man for me. An earl for chairman will look well, and will help to draw the parsons and widows; such a respectable earl, too. Its the very thing."

As usual, when he had made up his mind, Mr. Buncombe overcame all opposition, and formed his board on his own plan. The event justified his confidence. It was a small board of six, but eminently respectable, containing, as it did, an earl as chairman, an ex-under secretary of state as deputy chairman, a great soda water manufacturer, of philanthropic tendencies, and a director of the bank to which Mr. Buncombe condescended to entrust his account. An "honourable" captain and a retired Indian civil servant, with "Sir" at his name, completed the cast. Not a man among them was a director of more than three other companies, and three out of the six were upon no other board. Gettem had suggested that either Buncombe himself or one of his partners should join the board, but the shipowner disapproved of that plan altogether. His firm were the "chosen brokers," pure and simple, of the great Excelsior Line, and there might possibly arise an awkwardness about their commissions if they, as interested parties, put a representative on the directorate.

"We keep outside," Mr. Buncombe emphatically remarked, "and let the board 'manage' us if it can. He! he!"

Mr. Buncombe's foresight was justified by events, as I have said. No sooner did the prospectus appear than the public rushed to subscribe. "Twelve to fifteen per cent." was a temptation no greedy mind could resist.

Q

Helped by excellent market tactics, so great became the pressure that Mr. Buncombe assured his friends he was reluctantly compelled to pledge himself to part, a year hence, with most of his own shares, which he did graciously at from three to four pounds premium. When all was over, and the Excelsior Steam Shipping Company, Limited, properly started, the proud Berborough ship-owner, once a poor pie wife's son, found himself possessed of a good paying brokerage business, as before, plus three to four hundred thousand pounds in hard cash, and two hundred thousand pounds in debentures upon the company's fleet. Well might his soul expand in joy within his bosom. Come weal or woe, henceforward his buttered bread was safe and his earthly glory sure. Half a million of realised and realisable capital, and all debts paid, plus a good commission business. Genius alone could have accomplished so grand a result in so short a time. Let us worship.

CHAPTER XXXIII.

THE BRAIN MARKET.

A COMMONPLACE person would have been disposed to rest and be thankful after so magnificent a success as that attained by Mr. Buncombe in the sale of his steam fleet. He, I need scarcely mention, had no such idea. On the contrary, as his wealth grew great, so did his ambitious mind expand. Like the mountain climber, no sooner had he surmounted one height than his imagination's eye saw others yet to climb. The exchange of half a million of debt he could not pay, except in depreciated ships, for as much in cash and debentures, was something no doubt, but to Mr. Buncombe it was but the means to an end. What, he began to say to himself, is wealth without "honours." For "honours," therefore, he henceforward strove, with all the energy of his active, powerful mind.

The first form this new passion took, was revived zeal in attendance on parliamentary duties. Mr. Buncombe's party was in opposition, and the aim of all pushing members of it was therefore to make themselves so conspicuous in debate, in obstruction, in the art of putting disagreeable questions that it would be impossible for the chiefs to leave them without office, when next the whirligig of time, and the fickle gusts of popular favour brought them to a division of the loaves and fishes. Upon this arduous task Mr. Buncombe entered with a fine phrensy admirable to look upon.

Some of my readers have possibly enjoyed the delectable pleasure of hob-nobbing with great or growing politicians in opposition, and will have remarked how gracious your tongue leaders then are to all and sundry.

Men they would pass with a curt nod, or with no recognition at all, when clothed in the glory and endowed with the salary of a Minister of State, they will stop to shake hands with. They smile and talk affably to the meanest wire-pullers and hangers-on, when in the nakedness and poverty of opposition. We have seen the great Launcelot Orchidion, that resplendent Autolycus, with his "come buy, come buy," whose sole mistress is democracy, whose only Lord God is the "State," in close intercourse with the bibulous Ted Lister, sweetly extracting from him what hints he could give towards guiding a "Statesman" in his next bid for favour. And as Orchidion did then, so do they all. In short, no sooner are the far-shining word-jugglers of politics detached by an adverse vote from the support of their official primers of the permanent bureaucracy, than they fall back upon the miscellaneous crowd of reputable and unreputable needy men with brains, who crowd the ranks of the literary profession. Unable to command the manufacture of speeches at the hands of official underlings, they draw upon the assistance of whomsoever fortune throws in their way.

Were you behind the scenes you might know, for instance, that the most telling "points" in Mr. Orchidion's more recent harangues were concocted by Ted Lister, between drinks, and that the resplendent Mr. Conduit fused them and gave them "literary form." It might come to your ears that a wild Irishman, full of Celtic patriotism and blood-drinking disloyalty elaborated the most cutting retorts upon the inviolability of church property, with which my Lord the Marquis of Trueblue delighted the bishops and clergy. The very ex-under Secretaries of State themselves frequently lean upon the mental resources of patriotic or benevolent society secretaries, reporters, leader writers, and garret residents in Grub Street. And how affable and polite they are to the men who have brains, be their coats never so ragged, their linen, if they happen to possess any, never so dirty. A Party in opposition affords a glorious spectacle of democratic equality.

Purse-swollen politicians now and then even pay men handsomely to write magazine articles for them on public questions, in order to establish that sort of reputation which may, they hope, lead them first to a seat in the House, and then to one on the Treasury Bench. Verily the world is wonderful, especially the English political world, where all great and good men serve the state for love, out of a spirit of pure patriotism. One's commonplace mind is lost in admiration as one gazes upon its convolutions.

But what has all this to do with Mr. Timothy Buncombe? Much. That exalted son of Mammon now

felt himself in a position to command all the brains in the
United Kingdom, and for a few months after the success
of his metamorphosis from a bankrupt to a plutocrat, he
spent money freely upon the production of speeches,
articles, questions, motions for papers, returns, &c., &c.
No ex-cabinet minister could have exceeded him in
profusion, and very few in affability.

It must not be thought, however, that he enjoyed this
profusion.   Mr. Buncombe preferred to be great thriftily,
and if he could get one man to do work for twenty
shillings, that another required five pounds for, he at once
gave the preference to cheap labour.   For a time, indeed,
he entertained hopes of securing all the assistance he
wanted practically for nothing, and to this end picked up
once more his son-in-law Weardale, a gentleman he had
found it of no advantage to hold much intercourse with
while consolidating his fortune.   A certain connexion
had always been maintained between the two families, by
the medium of mother and daughter, but Mr. Buncombe
himself took no active part therein.

When, however, a distended purse and political ambition,
as we may call it for want of a handier name, once more
fired the heart of the shipbroker, he remembered that
Weardale was a very clever fellow, and invited him to
dinner once and again, with quite a gush of condescending affection.

Weardale wanted to refuse these invitations, but his
wife overruled him.   "Let us go for the sake of peace,
and to please my mother," she said.   He obeyed and
went, he and his wife, and felt humiliated in going.   But

half aware though he was of the clever management by which Mr. Buncombe had suddenly become so rich, he nevertheless smelt dishonesty somewhere. It shocked him to hear sentiments of brotherly love for all mankind, and maudlin "equal rights for all" doctrines drop from the lips of a man who kept two magnificently-liveried flunkies and a grand butler to wait upon his guests, and who ate off silver plate. Moreover, with all his suavity and gush, Mr. Buncombe's attitude towards him was essentially patronising—the patronage of wealth—and it was with a half hesitancy, a half deprecating air, that he introduced his "son-in-law" to other guests when there were any. Oftenest it was "just a family dinner, you know."

Contempt, dislike, scorn, repulsion of the fiercest description, arose accordingly in the mind of the journalist towards this purse-proud relative, and ill fitted him for the labours which he soon discovered he was expected to bestow in return for his dinner. Mr. Buncombe, nevertheless, did his best to utilize Weardale's brains, because to buy them for a dinner was a cheap exchange, but the more he tried the more he was disappointed. Weardale did not refuse point blank to lend his father-in-law a helping hand; but he talked such pronounced Radicalism, and was altogether so impracticable that the politician could get no good out of him. He was far worse than Lister, in fact, for Lister could be made to do what he was told when sober, or partially so.

Weardale, however, turned everything upside down, so to say. When asked if he thought the present ministry would hold office long, his usual reply was, "It mostly depends on their mahouts."

"What do you mean by that expression, may I ask," Mr. Buncombe enquired, with his most dignified air, as the pair sat smoking alone together in the library one evening. "I have heard you use it several times, and I confess it did not strike me as being appropriate."

"I daresay not," was the dry response, "but the fact is, Mr. Buncombe, that to my mind your parliamentary leaders always look like a herd of tame elephants. Their private secretaries are their mahouts or drivers, and according as these are adroit or otherwise in conducting the beasts they bestride in the way the irremovable official hierarchy wish them to go, is the duration of a ministry—more or less, of course."

"Bosh," cried the shipbroker testily. "Ministries come and go at the bidding of Parliament, sir, and at nobody else's."

"All right. I do not care to argue the point ; you are welcome to that view, if it pleases you."

Whether it was the burning question of the consumption of one's own smoke, or that more terrible one, official liberty to drown sailors, or the unlimited power to restrict my neighbours' drinking, or the art of making bankruptcy a breach of the eleventh Commandment, or the necessity of tithes as a means to true godliness, or the advantage of prayers in the House of Commons, or "How to make all Irishmen happy," or the provision of larger scope for officialism, or the necessity that every infant born within the kingdom should be provided with three yards of flannel, or joyful " Autolycus " Orchidion's plan for bestowing on all men a share in their neighbour's goods, or henchman Conduit's motion that the claims of all foreign bondholders ought to be backed by a British force, as in the case of his pet example, the Nile valley, it was always the same. Weardale sneered and mocked and talked sedition until Mr. Buncombe felt sick.

CHAPTER XXXIV.

A BEAR THAT WOULDN'T DANCE.

ALWAYS the burden of Weardale's tale was: "We are
overgoverned, sir. What in the devil's name do we
want more officials for? The ideal of a free people is a
people that requires no government at all; but if things
go on as they are doing, no man in old England will be
able to lift his hand to his mouth without the formal
sanction of some damned Jack in office or other. It's
nearly as bad as that already."

Not much that was good for practical politics could
an ambitious M.P. extract from language of this
sort.

Mr. Buncombe's particular hobby, at that time, was
finance. It had been "borne in upon him," as the
Methodist would say, ever since his success in the matter
of the Excelsior Company, that he would make an
admirable Chancellor of the Exchequer. Hazy ideas
about taxation; the true way to obtain revenue without
the nation knowing it; protective tariffs for native
industry, warranted to fill the capitalist's pocket; and
such like, began to be cultivated by him in consequence
of this view of his gifts, and made him anxious before
shaking Weardale off, if it must be so, to obtain that

cantankerous fellow's help in the fabrication of a fiscal creed.

"Do you really want to play reformer now," Weardale demanded when this purpose was made known to him.

"Certainly; why, of course. This is an age of progress, you know. We can't sit still. The people demand something fresh, and must be gratified. It's mighty little I can see, though, and I would like to have your views."

"Mighty little you can see," shouted Weardale. "Why, good heavens, can't you see that the whole finances of the nation are going clean to the devil, sir?"

"God bless my soul and body," exclaimed Buncombe, "I can't see anything of the sort. Of course the Tories are running us into debt, but the nation is wealthy enough, and we can soon put things straight when we get back to office."

"Tories be——anointed," was the answer, "and Liberals too, for that matter. I tell you if you go on muddling as you are doing, many more years, we shall have a revolution. Mark my words!"

"Bosh! I don't believe anything of the sort."

"Well, well, you'll see. Do you imagine that the millions of poor, now that they can vote, are going to pay all the taxes, and let you swells pocket all the spoil? You are mightily mistaken if you do."

"Oh! I know, I know; you are all for denouncing the rich, because you haven't got much money yourself. The boot would be on the other leg if you had as much money as I have, for instance."

"Heaven forbid !" ejaculated the journalist fervently, and Mr. Buncombe blushed all over his face and bald pate. There was a moment's awkward pause, and then the shipbroker, more than half millionaire, renewed his demand for Weardale's plan of reform.

" It's all very well for you to denounce the rich, and cry out about unjust taxation, but let us hear what you would do suppose you were in office to-morrow ? "

" I know I could do nothing in office."

" Oh, bosh, that's not what I mean, you know well enough. Tell me what you think would satisfy the nation—that democracy you are always cracking up."

" I don't crack the democracy up—never did. The democracy is a stupid, confiding brute, except when it is hungry. Therefore I fear it, and therefore I keep telling all who will listen to me that we must open the door for a greater distribution of wealth, else a hungry democracy will one day rise and eat us all up."

" Never. Englishmen are too quiet and orderly. We never had anything here equal to the French Revolution."

" Thanks to our poor law, which, in its way, though, pretty nearly did eat the whole people up. But for it we should have had revolutions in plenty. It has proved a most excellent device, in virtue of which the lower middle classes pay insurance premiums against revolution for the benefit of the landlords and the plutocracy. It has saved us, individually, from the trouble of enacting Christian charity, too. A most excellent law."

" There you are again," cried Mr. Buncombe, angrily.

"Nothing but denounce, denounce. I don't see the good of it. Where's your remedy for all these wrongs?"

"There is no thorough remedy except in revolution—perhaps none in that."

"Well, but God bless my soul, man, you must have a theory, you know—something to measure the extent of what you call 'wrongs' by——"

"Yes, I have a theory, but it is so likely to remain a theory that it is scarcely worth stating," said Weardale, in a sad tone.

"Never mind, let's hear it. I'm anxious to look at these questions from all points, you know, and who knows but there might be something practicable in some of your ideas." Mr. Buncombe's desire to pick his son-in-law's brains seemed only to be whetted by all this fencing. Possibly he thought he would catch something with which to tickle up his constituents.

"I'm afraid I should only shock you more than ever if——"

"Never mind, never mind, go ahead. I can stand anything, you know,—from you, at any rate," he added.

"The fact is," said Weardale, slowly, "I hardly know where to begin, for no reform can take place without a complete decentralisation of the Government, such as is foreshadowed in Irish Home Rule, and the destruction of an insane spirit of imperialism. So long as Englishmen scamper round the world on land-stealing expeditions there will be no good government at home."

"Well, it's no good preaching that doctrine, anyway," interrupted Mr. Buncombe. "If we give up our empire, we may as well sell all our ships right off.　No party in the country dare go to the constituencies with such a cry as that."

"Just so, and therefore, nonsense though that fable be, what is the use of talking about good government.　With empire, with the tribute of empire pouring wealth into the country at every port, corruptions, social, political, and administrative will grow and grow until some fine day the whole rotten fabric goes to pieces with a crash. It would not surprise me in the least to see your vaunted democracy end in military despotism and the wreck of English liberties, before all is over."

" Never, never in this world," cried Mr. Buncombe, excitedly.　" The Empire of England is built on a better foundation than any the world ever saw before."

" It is built on some of the blackest crimes of treachery, cruelty, fraud, and rapacity the world has ever seen, if that is what you mean."

"Bosh ! You forget, sir, that England is a Christian State."

"Oh, there's where you are, is it," exclaimed Weardale dryly.　"All right ; hug your Christianity, and go to the devil with it, if you like.　I don't care."

" No, of course not, you are a pagan, I know.　I always suspected you to be an unbeliever, Weardale, but hang me if I thought you would avow it so unblush-ingly."

" Do you mean to tell me then that there is any relationship between your smug, well-paid clerical trades unionists in national pay, or your sleek pew-rented dissenting broadcloth mummers of holiness, and the religion of Christ. I never saw any."

"There you are again," was the impatient rejoinder. "I did not ask you to come here to discuss theology. With a sceptic that is waste of wind. I wanted to hear what you had to say on the immediate reform of the future. But I might have known I was a fool for my pains. You are too impracticable, Weardale, much too impracticable. God bless my soul and body, man, don't you see you stand in your own light. I might help you to a good thing if you'd only give me a cue or two."

"Much obliged, I'm sure, but I'm a bit of a Bohemian, you see, and prefer to wander as the spirit moves me. 'Good things' are rather a bore."

"Ay, that's just where it is. There's no doing anything with you. Man alive, can't you see that it might be worth my while to find you a seat in Parliament, and a great thing for yourself too, for that matter. Gad, you might be a cabinet minister, Weardale, with your abilities."

"Heaven forbid," again ejaculated the journalist.

"Well, well, as you please—only I think you are throwing your chances away, I'm blest if I don't, and I'm sorry to see it both for your sake and for your family's."

"Thank you, my family will do very well, I hope. I'll try at least to rear them honestly, and give them honest employment."

"Oh, hang it all ; yes, of course. But that's not the question. God bless me, won't you see that it would be more in accordance with the fitness of things if your sons and daughters took a position in the world suitable to their relationship to me? You don't mean them to be grocers or butchers, do you? Or, perhaps, you count on getting a lump of my money for them. That's the way of poor relations, I know," he went on brutally, Weardale the while sitting stock still. "But you make a mistake, sir, you make a mistake. I shan't waste my fortune on people who don't know how to take advantage of their privileges." Mr. Buncombe said this while jerking himself about the room, and his tone grew angrier as he went on. It was his way of venting his disappointment. But he had gone too far. Weardale sprung to his feet as his father-in-law ended, and stood facing him with a flushed face and flashing eye.

"I trust, sir, you did not invite me to your house to-night with the deliberate intention of insulting me," he asked, in a voice which, though calm, vibrated with emotion.

"Eh! what, what, no, no. God bless my soul and body, you know. Hang it all, man, sit down, sit down. I was only a bit riled, you know, you are so impracticable."

"Because," Weardale went on, without heeding, "because I refuse to accept the insult. Neither myself nor my wife have ever counted upon receiving a penny at your hands, sir, nor have my children been taught to look to you as in any sense their earthly providence. We are not of those whom you can cast off and take up again as caprice or self interest may dictate. Therefore your taunts have no power to make me ashamed.

Anger and contempt they may produce, but not self reproach."

"Well, well, my boy, drop it, drop it," said Buncombe, in a wheedling voice. "Hang me, you know I didn't mean anything, only you riled me a bit. Sit down, man, sit down, and tell me what you think of Orchidion's latest motion. He has brought in a bill, you know, to provide a knife and fork out of the consolidated fund for every child born in the United Kingdom. Is that worth supporting, think you, eh?"

"Bah!" said Weardale, flinging himself back in his seat with a look of disgust, as much as to say "What a fool I was to get angry at a vulgar humbug like that." For that was the disrespectful fashion in which he occasionally alluded to his father-in-law.

This little outburst, however, had had the effect of rendering Mr. Buncombe more circumspect, and by dint of a little manœuvring, he at length drew forth a monologue from Weardale, on what he was pleased to call his ideal of government.

I shall not inflict this monologue on the patient reader. To what good, indeed, for as Mr. Buncombe kept protesting, it was not practical politics. The journalist was an out and out Republican and decentraliser; a free-trader also, and of so thorough a type, that he would, forthwith, have abolished all customs duties, and all liquor excise, forcing the nation to go back to the rent of its land for revenue. No wonder then, though Buncombe blessed himself, and cursed himself, and squirmed, and "boshed!" and danced

R

through the apartment. "All drink consumption should be regulated by licenses alone, under the control of provincial houses of Assembly, without whose authority the supreme Parliament should have no power to raise any taxes, except direct taxes on land and property. "I would sweep away some of the permanent departments altogether," said Weardale, "and cut the rest down to a tenth of their present force. Those who would not work then could starve."

As for what he called "that mockery of Christianity," the Church of England, it was to be completely disendowed, it and the universities, and great public schools, and the whole of the money accruing to the people by this act, together with the whole of the incomes of guilds and ancient corporations of London, and throughout the country, used to provide a free liberal education for all ranks and classes of the community, according to their wants and capacities. What was left ought to go to sustain hospitals and feed the poor. Thus at one stroke the criminal thefts of a trades union of selfish, pagan, pelf-hoarding clergymen, and their hangers-on, all the corruptions of universities, where jobbery and imbecility mocked at wisdom and common sense, together with the hideous deformities of the poor law, would be swept clean away. Hoarding Lord Bishops and mockers of all that is loftiest and best in human nature, would then be relieved from the painful necessity of having to accept livings, fat, if possible, at the hands of some "beastly" king or king's lickspittle toad-eater, or fawning king's mistress; or of buying and selling cures of souls on principles analogous to the most infamous forms of "stock jobbery." Deprived of its stolen property, the Anglican creed, which masquerades as the one true Christian church, would be free to vindicate its divine sanction by the means appointed of the Master it now mocks with its droning rituals and llama-like praying machinery. And so on.

In his hatred of the lazy, "living"- trafficking, soul-darkening arrogant, and self-seeking parsonhood of England, Weardale was as fierce as in his contempt and scorn for the swarming, life-stifling, eat-all bureaucracy. Towards both, his attitude of hostility yielded in nothing to that of the communards of France. "Neither truth nor plain dealing will prevail in old England," he said, "till these sources of falsehood, fraud, and corruption are driven from the face of the land. Till that work is accomplished, our vaunted freedom is a delusion, our 'progress' a progress towards the bottomless pit that swallowed the mighty empire of Rome and all empires before it."

Buncombe listened, disgusted. "There is nothing of any good to me in all this," he cried, when Weardale had finished, "nothing whatever."

"I told you so before I began," said Weardale with a laugh.

"But I wanted hints, man, hints. I want to attack the Tories on their finance, don't you know. Hang it all, there must be some good way of making a telling attack on their extravagance."

" Doubtless. You can make telling attacks on the finance of all Governments. Poor devils, your so-called Governments, with their First Lords, their Chancellors of the Exchequer, their secretaries and other talking machines, can do but as they are told. They must find money, and perpetrate or connive at jobs, as their masters order, and take the curses accordingly."

"Yes, yes, of course, I know all that, but the question now is an attack on Tory finance, don't you know."

" Ah, as to that, my dear sir, you must find some fellow to help you whose brains are for hire," laughed Weardale, and that was all the satisfaction his father-in-law could get out of him. The poor man felt aggrieved, almost duped. His dinners had for once brought him no return, and he was reluctantly forced to the conclusion, that if he wanted 'hints' he must go, as Weardale had said, where they were to be had in exchange for cheques or current coin of the realm. That decision reached, it naturally followed that Mr. Henry Weardale soon ceased to be invited to family dinners, and the two men from that time forward fell completely apart.

Even Beatrice Weardale learned to feel that it was best so, for the atmosphere of the grand mansion in Prince of Wales' Terrace was ill suited to her tastes and habits, still less adapted to be a place of resort for her children. Not that she came to this conclusion without a painful wrench. A true heart clings to a father, and still more to a mother, be they never so unworthy.

CHAPTER XXXV.

TO BE OR NOT TO BE.

MUCH though he spent, and hard though he worked, Mr. Buncombe's ambition was not gratified when next his party came into "power." It was disgusting. The chiefs entirely overlooked his great services. In vain did he thrust himself under their noses in the lobby of the House. They passed him by with a friendly greeting or a nod, but with never a word about "office." "We might have offered him something for form's sake," the patronage secretary of the party was afterwards reported to have said, "but to tell the truth we were afraid to do so. He might have accepted." They did not so much as ask him to second the address. That sublime function was bestowed upon an ego-rapt Quaker, of an arrogant-humility air, whom it so completely overwhelmed that the poor fellow has ever since been half demented with the belief that he is a heaven-born word-ruler destined yet to shine above all men in playing upon the national wind instrument.

If true, the remark of the patronage secretary was none the less heartlessly cruel. But if the leaders of the party did indeed abstain from this motive it showed their wisdom to be considerable, for that Mr. Buncombe would have accepted any office, however humble, is beyond question. Gradually, then, this hard-working man, whose voice had so oft and so long worried the Tories during the session preceding dissolution, felt his hopes die away within him. Others far less rich, and, in his opinion, far less worthy, were preferred before him. To his party he was a man of no account. Why was this? Alas, it is a long story, too long to tell in all its sad details.

For one thing, however, it has to be admitted that the great manager of the Excelsior Steam Shipping Company was not popular in the House. Nobody liked him much. His manners were a *bizarre* mixture of cringing and insolence, and although he made tolerably passable harangues he was never able to convince those who stayed to listen to him that he believed one word of what he said. That in itself was an immense drawback. A similar failing had helped to wreck Lord Brougham, and Mr. Buncombe was, on the whole, a less gifted man than that grandiose lunatic.

Still rude, coarse-grained, thick-hided, brazen-tongued, pushing, insolent, corrupt, vulgar men do, under our admirable constitution, get office now and then, and behave therein like tolerably well-trained elephants, as Mr. Weardale would say, consuming their provender in a more or less circumspect manner, with due interlude of trumpetings, and Mr. Buncombe's exclusion did not necessarily flow from his unpopularity and lack of following alone.

There was another reason. His last election had smudged him. The compact with the Powderhorn interest held good in a way, but that interest proved unable to control the Tory party in Oldhills. Consequently Mr. Buncombe, to his horror and amazement, found that he must contest his seat once more. He had lulled himself to sleep in a false security, and, believing himself free from all danger, had rather neglected the Oldhills electorate. Perhaps he thought that they would be so proud of his displays in Parliament that they would keep his seat safe for him whether he "nursed" the borough or not. Whatever his motive, he ceased to spend on local charities, local flower shows, local treats and fads to the extent he had done when a newer politician and a poorer man. So Oldhills betrayed him, and decided to have a fight, in order that a little money might circulate.

In the end Mr. Buncombe kept his seat, but at the cost of a great deal of money. Not, of course, that he ostensibly spent much. He was far too astute for that, but the promises he had to make for the future, the sham volunteer canvassers he had to come to understandings with, the meaning winks he had to distribute to dissenters, ambitious of possessing new school-rooms or Gothic chapels ; and to high church parsons in want of altar pieces, stained glass windows, &c., &c., meant in the end quite as much money as it would have cost him to have prevented a contest, while the acknowledged costs came upon him as an additional fine.

This was cruel, and what was worse than all, the Tories, who understood a thing or two, in the rage of their defeat, set to work to get up a petition against Mr.

Buncombe's return. They were in the full swing of this new, money-spending manifestation of constitutional privileges at the time the victorious party was showering the gifts of office on its leaders and their henchmen. Nothing in the end came of this cry of vengeance. It was said by the evil tongued that Mr. Buncombe purchased the enemy's leading witnesses. But clearly it would have been altogether wrong for the pure-minded, white-handed chiefs of the party; men like Mr. Orchidion, and Lord Steer, and Sir Algernon Drivel—right honourables all—to commit a portion of their honour to the keeping of a man likely to be unseated for bribery. The mere hint of such a thing was sufficient to make them turn their backs upon him.

This is why, ostensibly at least, Mr. Buncombe was left out in the cold. It was a great hardship, I, as his humble biographer, might even go so far as to say, a great wrong, but there he was. The pathway of emoluments, dignities, and honours was closed against him. All the money he had spent, the breath he had used up, the nights he had watched, the subjects he had "crammed," were as much wasted as if he had passed the time on the treadmill, and flung his gold into the common shares of the Excelsior Company.

Shall I try to paint Mr. Buncombe's rage, his despair and sorrow? Not a bit of it. Readers can imagine all that, each in the degree of his capacity. There is not the least danger of overdoing the thing. All I am concerned with is, not the passions which rent this valiant bosom, but the energy with which, one road to advancement barred, the strenuous shipbroker took another.

Of course he sulked for a time, and for a time also threatened to become disagreeable to those who had overlooked his merits, but that did not last long. Mr. Buncombe soon saw that he was making himself ridiculous and, what was better to the purpose, that he lost more by mulishness than he could possibly gain. And inasmuch as he was not a man to be baulked in his ends by spite of party, or any common feeling of that kind, he soon desisted from all outward signs of chagrin, in order to discover a way of repairing his defeat. He even went so far as to apologise publicly to the Right Hon. Launcelot Orchidion for having spoken slightingly about that gentleman's famous knife and fork endowment bill. It did not go nearly far enough, Mr. Buncombe had declared, with a sneer. In his opinion, to be complete, it ought to provide a flannel petticoat for every girl of two years old within the kingdom, as well as a goose and plum pudding to be furnished, post free, on Christmas Eve, to all who applied in their own handwriting within the previous fortnight.

Taking a leaf from Weardale's book of sarcasm, he had proceeded to point out that so complete a reform would not only enable the bureaucracy to add fifty thousand pounds a year for salaries to the civil service estimates, as Mr. Orchidion calculated, but would afford scope for a great many more backsheesh and secret discount operations. And if press of work at the year's end involved the employment of extra labour, it would be easy to draft men, at overtime pay, from the do-nothing and muddle-all Board of Trade, or brain-destroying education offices. In short, Mr. Buncombe had urged, the "reform" would be much more thorough and satisfactory if carried out as he ventured to suggest.

This speech had been made in the first spasm of his disappointment, when his heart was sore within him, and Mr. Orchidion had resented it, not so much perhaps because it savoured of mockery—his sensibilities were not keen—as because it had the appearance of touching upon his peculiar prerogative. He was the one man living who knew how to make the backs of the dull-witted multitude bend to the yoke. "Mine is the only great soul," Mr. Orchidion in effect said, "that knows the right carrot to dangle before the eyes of this great long-eared beast Democracy;" and he forthwith declared war against the shipbroker.

His enmity might have mattered little to Mr. Buncombe had the "party of progress" been in opposition, but it was altogether a different affair now that the Right Honourable Launcelot Orchidion had become a powerful minister of the Crown. Orchidion, unappeased, meant no more fat freights for the Excelsior Company, to mention but one result. This was an imminent danger not to be trifled with. So the much-enduring Timothy saw the error of his ways, and before Parliament had been many more days in babbling order, he publicly purged himself of his sin by making an abject apology.

So far well, but where were the honours and social advancement he courted? No nearer, alas, than before. This was melancholy. Mr. Buncombe, however, did not despair. There remained open to him the system of feeding his way to a higher grade of society, and no sooner had his mind recovered tone after his parliamentary disappointments than he commenced a series of entertainments unrivalled in splendour.

All sorts and conditions of men and women—within the charmed circle of Society, of course—were invited to his dinners, and a good many of them came. His receptions were less successful, but still well attended, and he would have felt himself making way towards a peerage, or something of that sort, had it not been for Mrs. Buncombe, poor woman. At least it was her he blamed.

Never in all his life before did Mr. Timothy Buncombe regret so keenly as in these months the unfortunate marriage he had made. His wife, he felt, was vulgar. She dressed badly, spoke badly, grimaced badly, and, worst of all, she had never been presented at Court. A more glaring defect than that it is impossible to imagine. Lacking the Royal Hallmark, Mrs. Buncombe was no better than a Zulu; in fact, not nearly so good. Had she been an unlettered savage from the wilds of Africa, a tattooed Maori, or a scalp-wearing red Indian, Society would have crowded round Mrs. Buncombe, pinched her, thumbed her blanket or her skin, stared at her, laughed at her, humoured her, and made itself charmingly ridiculous for her. Being, however, a mere Englishwoman without talents, less coarse than Lady Betty

Tangle, and not "compromised" in any way so as to be
interesting ; unable to swear like the Duchess of Hay-
cock, or to don tights and dawdle through maudlin plays
like Mrs. Ethelberta Maypole, the wife of a pawnbroker
and usurer of aristocratic connexions, Mrs. Buncombe
was a female of no account. Her guests snubbed her,
her son and daughter laughed at her and ignored her,
her very husband blushed as he beheld her struggle to be
agreeable to the dawdling mob of both sexes which
gathered at her receptions.

Young Callow was often at Prince of Wales' Terrace.
It was rumoured that he was "sweet" upon Evangeline
Buncombe, and doubtless he or his parents coveted her
father's gold.   Young Timothy Buncombe was a kind of
chum of his. "My Lord" and the shipbroker's son
played billiards together, lost money on horses and at
cards together, hunted down pretty ballet girls in company, and got drunk now and then to vary the monotony
of existence. Between whiles they amused themselves
by baiting Mrs. Buncombe at her own dinner table, and
in her drawing-room, amid an amused and applauding
crowd of male and female " bloods."   It was so easy to
put the burly little woman in a temper, and make her
forget her manners and her always uncertain grammar.

Any outburst on her part sent her husband to the
rescue, and as often as not his attempts at pacification
only brought the lightning of his wife's wrath down on
his own head. On one such occasion the exasperated
woman declared before all the assembled spectators that
her husband wanted to be rid of her. Her reason for so

thinking was that he had never sought to present her to the Queen.

"He has been and gone and kissed the Queen himself," she remarked, "and I call it a downright shame as he's never took me to see her."

This was true enough, all except the kissing. Mr. Buncombe had been introduced to the sacred presence of Majesty, early in his parliamentary career, in order, as he said, to utilize the Windsor uniform he had been obliged to buy, before he could accept the Speaker's invitation to the regulation parliamentary dress dinners. Since then, as a matter of course, he had been at levees, and his superiority in this respect was a standing grievance with his wife.

It was a grievance he would now gladly have removed, but nobody of his acquaintance would willingly take the responsibility of presenting her. Lady Powderhorn was quite willing to perform the rite for Evangeline, but would have nothing to say to Mrs. Buncombe, and none of Mr. Buncombe's other friends were a bit more ready.

It was not exactly because Mrs. Buncombe was vulgar that they displayed their reluctance. Indeed, mere vulgarity has nothing to do with fitness for the charmed circle which surrounds majesty. Had lofty manners and high-toned conduct been essential, most of our sovereigns would themselves have been disqualified from attendance at their own shows. It was Mrs. Buncombe's general appearance that stood in her way. She "looked so dreadfully like a charwoman," Lady Powderhorn said, and her view was the view of all, though what their precise idea of a charwoman's appearance was they never condescended to say. But they dreaded her capacity for making herself odd, and felt that if she did aught ridiculous while in their charge, their nerves would receive a shock too great to be endured.

CHAPTER XXXVI.

A WOMAN GREATLY DARING.

MATTERS were in this unsatisfactory position when Mr. Buncombe began to systematically eat his way upwards, or rather to make the eating of others, at his expense, a means to his one end and aim in life. He soon found it uphill work, uphill and "deuced expensive," as he told his wife.

"Then why don't you get a title right off, Mr. B.?" she contracted a sort of habit of saying, and quite early in their notoriety and title hunt they had a squabble over it. "I'm sure I'd buy one, if I were you, and then I would get to a levvy in spite of 'em."

"No you wouldn't," was the rough retort, "and don't talk nonsense, my dear. It doesn't become you."

"I talking nonsense. That's like your impudence. I ain't no more talkin' nonsense nor you are, and I'm sure I don't see why I should worrit myself to death seven days a week to please them snobs you bring here. Buy a title, I say, and be upsides with 'em, right off."

"But, my dear, you can't buy a title in England. Titles are only given as a reward for public services, you know."

"Then how did Lord Whinstone get his, I'd like to know? And there's that baronet chap you had here last Tuesday, what's his name — Winkles, Winnocks or something, I'm sure *they* never served nobody but themselves, and not much of that. How did ninnies like them get titles?"

"Oh, Whinstone changed parties, you know, and besides, he is a kind of jackal to a powerful railway director, and he was thought to have some brains of his own. That seems to be a mistake, but the mischief's done. Besides, he had a wife who was somebody, you know, my dear. As for the baronet ——"

" Bother the baronet. I don't care for the baronet, or for you neither. What I say is as you can get a title if you like, only you like better to see me sat upon and laughed at, because I ain't a wife as was 'somebody.' But I'll be upsides with you yet, just you wait a bit. I'll get to a levvy whether you like it or not. I ain't a-going to be made a fool of by you nor nobody else.

" He, he, he ! That you won't, my dear, that you won't, he, he !" sneered Mr. Buncombe, with a deprecating shrug of his lean shoulders.

" What are you laughing at, Mr. Buncombe, ain't I as good as you, I'd like to know, for all I ain't 'somebody.' Who are you, to laugh at me, the wife of your bosom. You ought to be ashamed of yourself. No, no, in course not. That would be too much to expect. You want to be rid of me, I know, but I'll be even with you yet. I'm not the one to put up with no more of your nonsense, not me."

" How you do go on, Mrs. Buncombe, making yourself ridiculous. Don't you know that women never go to levees, only men."

"Gammon. I know better. Don't the Queen go, and ain't the Queen a woman ? Eh, Mr. Buncombe ?"

" Yes, yes, my dear, but, hang it all, you know, that's different. Of course, the Queen is the head of society, and the fountain of all honour, and can go where she likes. But that does not alter the fact that gentlemen are presented to Her Majesty at levees, and ladies at drawing-rooms, don't you see ? "

"Ah ! that's it, is it. That's what you're a-laughing at. I made a slip, did I ? I ain't used to high life, I ain't. I'm not a lady, I'm not. But I don't care, Mr. B. Drawing-room or levvy, I'm a-going to see the Queen, and you are going to buy a title,—you can get it somehow, I know quite well."

" Humph !" said her husband, " that's all very fine, but if I had a title to-morrow you couldn't go to Court all by yourself. Somebody must introduce you, you know."

" Well, do it yourself. You've been there, and the Queen knows you, I suppose."

" Bosh, that's just what I can't do, my dear. No man can present his own wife to Her Majesty. You must find a lady who has been admitted to Court herself to do it for you."

This statement struck Mrs. Buncombe " all of a heap," as she afterwards told Eva, her daughter, and redoubled her chagrin and impatience under the slights to which she was subjected by the fashionable *canaille* who enjoyed

S

themselves at her expense, by the kind permission of her husband and children.   In short, so hot did the worthy little dumpling of a woman make life for the loungers sometimes, that long before the season was over Mr. Buncombe felt that the sooner he again altered his course the better.

Clearly this purchase-of-title-by-entertainments plan was destined to no better success than the brilliant parliamentary career business.   And then his wife persisted in laying all the blame on her non-presentation at Court.   It seemed to her that this ceremony would in some fashion or other endow her with the power to sit upon the snobs.   Mr. Buncombe's despair, however, was limited to an abandonment of the hope of obtaining a title by private dinners and receptions.   So long as Mrs. Buncombe continued to be what she was, while the great presentation at Court question remained unsettled at all events, it was mere waste of money to persevere in this course.   Than that nothing could be more certain, for Mrs. Buncombe grew daily more difficult to control, and several times had bounced out of the room before all the lounging assembly.

CHAPTER XXXVII.

ROYALTY WITH A COLD IN ITS HEAD.

BUT there still remained a good third of the fashionable season, and it occurred to the great shipbroker that he might be able to entertain lofty strangers in another fashion, at a less cost to himself, and with even greater chances of success. He decided to fall back upon the resources of the Excelsior Steam Shipping Company.

A few pages back a remark very like libel has been dropped about this splendid undertaking. Hasty readers, and others, might go away with the idea that the company had come to grief and disappeared. Nothing of the kind. It had ceased to pay dividends to the outside shareholders, and possibly enough might never resume that useful practice; but as a great trading concern, and as the source of an income of between twenty and thirty thousand pounds a year to Mr. Buncombe and his partners, the company, whose head quarters were in London, was as flourishing as ever, and likely to live. Hope, too, kept its shares at a good price, though dividendless. Shareholders were unable to believe that a fleet of such splendid ships, bought regardless of expense, all glittering in gilt and shining colours, could fail to yield them any return; so they held

on in hope.   But Mr. Buncombe had not thought it wise
to retain many of his shares.   They had been "sold
forward," and now, two years or so after its creation, the
company's finances were low.

For this very reason, as Mr. Buncombe remarked to
the chairman of the Board, Lord Powderhorn, who
always received his fees, it might be an excellent
advertisement to give a few entertainments on board the
company's newest vessels.   Two were nearly ready, and
one had just been delivered by a Clyde firm to replace
an unfortunate wreck.

His lordship agreed, of course, with this view, in his customary urbane manner.   The manager's word was law to
him, it saved so much trouble.   But he did not quite grasp
all that Mr. Buncombe meant by entertainments on
board ship, until that excellent man told him to try and
obtain the presence of a Royal personage to grace the
festive scene.   Then he rather wished he had not so
readily consented.   However, with the best grace he
could, he set to work to hunt up Royalty, in order—
though that of course was not stated—that by this
method, if by no other, as he now saw, Mr. and Mrs.
Buncombe might obtain a title.

All this is very commonplace, you may say.   Perhaps
it is, but so is life in general.   I merely contend for the
wonderful pluck and perseverance of the hero of this
history—qualities which title-hunting can display as well
as fly fishing.   Nothing baulked him, or turned him aside
from his purpose; and his wife, to her credit be it said,
was as eager as he could possibly be.   A title would

salve all her heartaches. By means of it she thought her admission into the charmed, mystical circle, which surrounds majesty, sure. And there was less annoyance promised, both to husband and wife, by these ship-in-dock demonstrations, than in private dinner giving. The expense was nothing at all, because the company bore it. Being viewed in the light of an advertisement of its excellent ships, the board naturally saw no objection to carrying the cost of the luncheons to the debit of the working account. Mr. Buncombe would have felt justified in doing so, whether the board had thought of objecting or not.

It was, however, one thing to try and catch Royalty, and quite another to succeed. Aided as he was by an earl, Mr. Buncombe had felt no doubts upon the point, and gave orders for a first entertainment of great magnificence. Paragraphs about the coming event appeared in the newspapers, and the shipbroker's hopes ran high. So did Mrs. Buncombe's, so did Evangeline's, and so, perhaps, the junior Timothy's, as far as his dulled brain admitted of any such emotion.

All were doomed once more to disappointment. Whether Lord Powderhorn lacked zeal, held back as he would be by his wife's dread of the ridiculous, or whether Royalty, having at that time no new endowments to beg from the public purse, felt permitted to rest from the toils of universal obsequiousness and enjoy itself, I know not; but Royalty could not, would not, come. Neither in the first, second, third, or fourth degrees would it consent to put in an appearance on board the splendid new mail steamer *Lady Powderhorn*, just delivered to the Excelsior Company at fifteen per cent. profit to the "managers."

This was chagrin upon chagrin, and for the first time in their lives, perhaps, Mr. and Mrs. Buncombe realised that Royalty really was after all human. From the excuses made they discovered that not only could Royalty tire itself out like common bipeds, but that it might be afflicted with a running at the nose, or a colic, or sciatica, or a sprained thumb, or a boil in the back of its neck—in short, Royalty was after all astonishingly commonplace.

And, strange to say, its amusements or occupations were fully as numerous and fully as Royal as its ailments. "Princes of the blood," it may be understood, pride themselves in maintaining the sport-loving traditions inherited from the forest prowler of Anjou, the Rhine blackmailer, the Scotch or Welsh cut-throat and cattle lifter, or whatever other ancestor they are pleased to acknowledge. To shoot with guns was a Royal prerogative. And though there was no legitimate shooting in the month of April, though Royal personages could not yacht then, though the hunting season was at an end, yet Royalty might be as busy as it was sick. It had still, while resting from its severer labours, occasional speeches to make glorifying its revered father, a foundation stone or two to lay, water works to open, museums to consecrate, dinners to eat, state balls and concerts to give, all in spite of the running at its nose and the sciatica. Above and beyond this medley of occupations or diseases, had it not always also the gentlemanly sport of horse-racing to cultivate and squander its tax-provided

salaries upon. The "Derby," and the "Oaks," and Ascot
loomed immediately ahead at the very moment when
Mr. Buncombe commenced his importunities. He was
mad to imagine that Royalty, well or ill, could desert its
proud position among the dæmons of the ring in order
to drink his champagne and eat his ices. What was the
music of the finest string band procurable for money
compared with the pandemonium of book-makers,
welchers, thieves, blacklegs, touts, and gentlemen who
made horse-racing glorious? What indeed! Mr. Buncombe displayed none of his customary astuteness in
pitting his modest "spread" against attractions like
these,—plus mere common-clay diseases.

The first strategic entertainment at the expense of the
Excelsior Company was thus foredoomed to be a failure
from Mr. Buncombe's point of view, although attended by
a brilliant crowd of fashionable idlers and others. Lord
and Lady Powderhorn were there helping Mr. and Mrs.
Buncombe to do the honours, and his Lordship almost
outshone the shipbroker in the splendour of his nautical
get up, although I rather think Mr. Buncombe's white
ducks had the advantage. Among the guests were a
needy marquis, out at elbows, and eager for directorships,
but considered too light fingered even for that trade ; two
Tory peers, and a viscount, who had professed Radicalism
in his plebeian days, but whose politics were now piebald;
sundry baronets, including a hide and tallow man, who
had been Lord Mayor of London, and who professed
Toryism, tempered by a gift for "preaching the Word."
These were Lord Powderhorn's guests. Mr. Buncombe

brought for his share a right honourable peddler, who alternated the occupations of consuming the emoluments of a cabinet minister with excursions in the domain of what is called finance,—a gentleman that is to say who deigned to take fees and luncheons, proper to the trade of director when not a "pillar of the State," at five thousand pounds a year. Besides this distinguished person, Rooster, by name, there came three under-secretaries of State, a few members of Parliament of circumspectly Radical proclivities, and no less than ten great departmental dignitaries, backed by a judge, wise in all laws but the decalogue. All were accompanied by the due proportion of females. The company was not motley in one sense, for all were gentlemen and ladies in their own esteem, but wondrous mixed withal, and eke most gorgeous in the petticoated division thereof.

One guest was there whose presence served to keep the hearts of the Buncombe family from melting within them in sorrow. It was an "equerry" of Royalty, captured by Lord Callow, a meek creature to look upon, but one who rejoiced in a fighting title. This being was placed at table by Mr. Buncombe's left hand, with a slight disregard of social rank, and so graciously did the host behave to his guest that, before the toasts, of which there were three, had been all spoken and swallowed to, he began again to hope the day had not been spent in vain, nor yet the Company's money. Who knew but what the servant might yet lure the master into the toils, and then! Ah, what visions may not crowd a fancy stimulated by champagne cup.

CHAPTER XXXVIII.

A GLIMPSE OF HEAVEN.

BUOYED up upon this, not perhaps unfounded, hope, Mr. Buncombe decided to persevere, and arranged for three more entertainments in the course of the summer. His pluck was all the more laudable that Lord Powderhorn deserted him, meanly and basely deserted him, and fled to the country after the second demonstration, instigated doubtless by his countess. Lord Callow, however, remained dawdling round Evangeline, and by the help mainly of Lord Callow, and of the Hon. Captain Brabazon Lambkin, a director of the company, nobly descended for a generation and a half, no falling off was visible in the quality of the guests, but the contrary. At the third entertainment success so far crowned efforts as to produce what may be called a royalty of the fifth degree — a doubtful highness and his wife — whose presence made the Buncombe family feel that they were getting warm.

At the fourth and last entertainment the success was greater still. Royalty in the third degree appeared in duplicate — a haughty lady with a fine insolence of manner, and great staring powers, accompanied by a husband whose acquaintance with the English language was too limited to permit free conversation. In the presence of these sacred beings Mr. Buncombe seemed a man who had that morning left his back bone at home. He was all bows and scrapes, and the wreathing smiles of his wife played second to his own fixed grin of joy, in a manner rarely surpassed here below. It was all "your Royal Highness, yes," and " your Royal Highness, no," and "would your Royal Highness condescend," and " might your Royal Highness permit me the pleasure,"— beautiful to see and hear. The words, of course, came from Mr. Buncombe for the most part. Mrs. Buncombe contented herself with purrs and nods and ever rippling smiles, for the terror of death had been put upon her that morning to beware of her grammar.

" To think, my dear, that we should be going to entertain princes of the blood," her husband had repeatedly observed.

" And now, my dear, you must be careful of your tongue, you know, to-day. Who knows what depends upon the success of our little entertainment. Don't say ' them things,' or ' ain't,' or ' not have nothing more,' or ' as how.' Try for the love of me and speak what little you do say grammatically, and always remember to say ' your Royal Highness.' Won't you now, there's a dear?"

For once Mrs. Buncombe took advice, and so well did she observe her orders, that strange guests might have taken away the impression that she knew as little of her native tongue as the male royalty, whose heart she strove to reach with her dimpling smirk.

Surely labours of this kind were destined to attain success. More must be coming than the gracious "I tank you, sare. E-ch—, it vas ein luncheon sehr gut gekocht," with which the male highness took leave of his host? The fame of the feed was in all the daily papers, and even drew a paragraph from the *Golden Calf*, which hinted that the presence of "royalty," in the third degree, on board a ship of the Excelsior Line might have some connexion with a new arrangement of the divinely appointed English government of India. Glories of this kind were never going to end by leaving Timothy Buncombe, Esq., M.P., plain "mister."

They should not have done so. They had no business in this world to do so. It was against all sense and reason that they could do so. Nevertheless they did. The *débris* of the great feast disappeared, the good ship *Hesperides* departed on her first voyage, the "season" of Society's moths and butterflies came to an end, the town emptied, life became dull, parliament a nightmare of the dog days, "supply" a galloping burlesque, and Mr. Buncombe was plain Mr. Buncombe still. I think if he had had any hair left he would have extracted it from his pain-racked head in a violent manner, when the fulness of the iniquity of this shameless neglect and ingratitude on the part of royalties was borne in upon him. Having none worth mentioning, he bore his sorrows in what looked like manly silence. Mrs. Buncombe was tragic enough for two.

"Take me out of this horrid place," she cried. "I can't abide London any more, the nasty dirty hole. Let's get

away to the country and forget our disgusts.   I hate the
thought of it.   And that impudent wretch, Lady Powderhorn, to run off and desert me so.   It's like her nasty,
stinking pride," and so on.   Let us hasten to draw a veil
over the harrowing scene.

CHAPTER XXXIX.

THE SWEET SADNESS OF A SUMMER SEA.

IN the dawdling seclusion of Scarborough, Mr. and Mrs. Buncombe recovered heart and tone. They were alone together once more in their lives. Timothy, junior, had gone to shoot in Scotland, with Callow and one or two other gentlemen of no occupation, he finding the shooting; and Evangeline had turned aside on her way north, to visit her sister, the seed crusher's wife, on whom troubles were looming.

So the parents were alone, and as they loafed on the sands, or lolled about the seats on the cliff, their hearts opened to each other in sweet converse after a little time. At first the talk was jagged and brief, for the wounds of the spirit were raw.

"We must find some other way of getting on, Mr. B.," the sturdy matron was given to observe. "Them lunches evidently ain't the thing."

"Yes! indeed, we must," her husband would answer in a melancholy voice, and there the matter lay.

The wealth-compelling shipbroker's spirit was uneasy. Politics! what were politics to him any more, or the sound of debate? In all the clang and roar of party he had taken his share, and for all he had obtained thereby, he said to himself, he might just as well have striven with the melancholy ocean. A curse on politics. He thought they meant titles and honours, and behold they were but as a shrivelling, skin-cracking, death-dealing east wind.

This was the first hue of the mind. It was not a just one. Politics had done more for Mr. Buncombe than he could then bring himself to admit. But that he was able to write M.P. to his name, it is probable that his Excelsior Company would never have floated with the success it did. An M.P. may not in popular esteem count as much in the company-making business as a lord or "right honourable;" but it ranks higher than a common baronet, or still commoner knight, and it is thousands a year more valuable than mere J.P.

By the thaumaturgical power of these two letters, Mr. Buncombe had obtained ready access to the most exclusive of the party clubs, and the entrée into gilded drawing-rooms, to beam amid the glancing human foam that floated there ; not to speak of the supreme honour of passing now and then before the eyes of Royalty in old-world livery. It was unjust, therefore, to despise the gifts of the democracy and free institutions, as he was then disposed to do. He might never have become a second Silas Brown even had he not written himself down M.P. ; but assuredly his income might have been docked by some twenty-five or thirty thousand pounds a year. Putting it on a vulgar money basis, the lower of these sums equalled three or four times over all he had ever spent on Oldhills, so that the return was at least three

hundred per cent. on his investment. Thus advantage-
ously through his M.P.ship, had he been able to convert
his liabilities into a fruitful asset.

When of unclouded mind, Mr. Buncombe's natural
love of justice must have made him ready to acknowledge
the advantages of his position. Just then, however,
his mind was darkened by disappointment, and all the
past was distorted by its fuliginous vapours. His wife
was much more elastic in temperament, and while she
grumbled, did not cease to ruminate on some new plan.
Royalty she felt, they both felt, was still their only hope.
It, in one or other of its presentments and manifestations,
is indeed always the hope of the politician neglected or
cast aside by his party—always unless the slighted one is
prepared to spend freely on party objects, which men
who feel themselves wronged rarely are. Something
may be got by "ratting," too, but Mr. Buncombe as yet
prided himself on his consistency.

Ratting, moreover, to be effective, can only be resorted
to now and then. Two men of the party had gone over
to the enemy already, in the course of last session, and
that was as many as said enemy could hope to be able to
reward at their next scramble. One of the two, it may
further be explained, was a creature so exceedingly
unclean of soul and speech, that his volt-face had
temporarily thrown unusual discredit on the practice.

Had he been willing, then, Mr. Buncombe felt that
there was no opportunity, nothing to be gained by joining
the outs. They had a large and increasing hungry horde
of their own to provide for.

All that was left for him to do was to play the part of the soured political follower. Such an one, if possessed of money, spends it not upon party objects. If he opens his pockets at all, it is to build almshouses, or to found a free library or a mechanics' institute, or to present a town with a park, as a trap for royal favour. All this and much more will the sulky man do rather than subscribe to procure seats for his ungrateful colleagues of the Palaver Hall, and Mr. Buncombe was in this respect neither better nor worse than his neighbours.

As his mind cleared it reverted to his wife's suggestion to buy a title, repudiated with scorn at the time it was first advanced. After all, he began to ask himself, must not a title be bought? And then the idea would force itself upon his notice that he had all the time been trying to effect this very " deal," as Americans would say, but that he had been bent upon doing it " on the cheap." That was quite Mrs. Buncombe's view—shrewd little dumpling that she was.

" I've been thinking," she remarked one morning, as she sat watching her husband drawing a rough outline of a coronet in the dusty path with his stick. It was an hour or so after breakfast. Sombre and abstracted the shipbroker had started to lead his wife down the zigzag of the spa gardens on the south cliff to the sea shore. But they, as by mutual consent, paused at the nearest seat, and sat down beneath the grateful shade of the rustling leaves—grateful already, for the day was hot. Through openings in the swaying branches in front of them they caught glimpses of the sea, shimmering in the sunlight of a cloudless August day.

Where they sat they felt sheltered, and to minds content with themselves, the sounds that reached their ears in their shaded wayside seat would have been soothing and sweet as a message from a fairy world. Mingled with the sighs of the light land breeze among the leaves came the measured breaking of the waves on the sandy beach, dominating the leafy music, and giving it a cadence soft, calming, regular, like the breathing of the spirit of nature at rest, and dreaming passionless dreams in its sleep. It was a day of healing to the heart-weary, and, insensible as Mr. Buncombe was to "mere scenery," as he would have said, he could not help feeling a sense of grateful ease of mind steal over him. There was less irritability lodged in his mind, and he listened to his wife without his usual half-deprecating, half-mocking smile when she took up her parable.

"I've been thinking," said she, "and I don't see as we have gone the right way to work. You should have spent a lot more money, Mr. B."

"Perhaps I ought to, but I didn't feel that I could afford it."

"Nonsense, Mr. B., what's ten or twenty thousand pounds to a man like you. We'd never miss it, I'm sure, and I would give that twice over to be 'my lady' any day."

"Well, well, my dear, that may be all very true, but I don't see how I'm to lay the money out now. I'm not going to give it to those blackguards of ministers. I'll see them at Jericho first."

T

"But couldn't you get yourself made Lord Mayor of London, now, Mr. B. I see as all Lord Mayors get titles, and Lady Mayoresses go to see the Queen at Court. That wouldn't cost you so much, would it now."

"Bosh, my dear," but he said "bosh" without impatience. "You don't understand. I couldn't be Lord Mayor of London right away if I tried. You've got to go through a regular course, and get elected an alderman, and then wait your turn. I might be dead before my chance came, even if I managed to get the city voters to elect me. No, that won't do."

Little debates of this kind became more frequent as the days slipped by, and they usually ended in the discomfiture of Mrs. Buncombe. Defeat, however, only quickened her ardour, and made her read and rack her brains for ideas. Her zeal and perseverance bore fruit at last.

CHAPTER XL.

WOMAN'S WIT WINS.

"I SAY, Pappy," she exclaimed at breakfast, about a week after the Lord Mayorship proposition had been ignominiously rejected. "I say, Pappy," and the Pappy betokened a return to old plebeian familiarities; "I've got an idea at last. Why don't you present the people of Berborough with a public park?"

"Eh, what, my dear? God bless my soul and body, what next, I wonder? You must be mad, surely. Where have I the means of presenting Berborough with a public park?" and Mr. Buncombe laid down his fork, oblivious of the bit of bacon on the point of it.

"There's that land you are always growling about, you know," proceeded his wife, "the land by the river as you bought ever so long ago, and as you thought the docks people would have wanted, but didn't. Now, I say, give 'em that for a park."

"What on earth put that notion into your head?" demanded Mr. Buncombe, turning half round on his seat to stare at his wife in wide-eyed amazement.

"Well, you see, I keep a-thinking and a-thinking, and reading the papers, and I've noticed as how the men as give parks mostly get titles to themselves. Then it struck me as you might just as well give 'em this bit of land. You know you always say it'll never be no good to you."

"But, God bless my soul, Penny, woman, it's a long flat bit of ground, half marsh, half sand. The Berborians wouldn't have it at a gift. It would cost more than it is worth twice over to reclaim it."

"Oh, but I've thought of that too, Pappy, and I read in the paper only this morning as how a man named Hoggins, Alderman Hoggins it was, of—of—I don't remember the place—Slopperton, I fancy ; but it don't matter. I know his name was Alderman Hoggins, and he has been made a knight or a baronet, or something as makes him Sir Alderman Hoggins, all because of a few acres of land he gave his town for a park. The paper was a-sneering at him, and said as how it was two for himself and one for the town, and that was what put the idea in my head that you might do as much by your land, and kill two birds with one stone."

"I don't follow you, my dear. What was it this alderman is said to have done ? "

"He drained the land, they say, and made drives through it, and laid out nice streets all round it, where people can build villas with a nice view over the park. But I'll fetch the paper and you can read it for yourself," and away Mrs. Buncombe trotted up stairs to her bedroom, whence she presently returned with the newspaper in her hand.

Her husband took it with some eagerness, and read slowly and meditatingly the paragraph his wife pointed out to him. When he had finished he dropped the paper on his knees and sat pondering, forgetful of his coffee and toast.

"My dear," he said at length, "I believe you are right. That's a good idea of yours, not half bad at all, worth thinking about, in fact. Really now, Penny, my dear, you are a cleverer woman than I took you for, and I believe it can be done. In fact, it's first rate, and we may kill three birds with it, eh, my dear?" and the cold stiff man actually gave his wife's hand an affectionate squeeze across the angle of the table.

The fat little woman was ready to dissolve with pleasure and self-congratulation.

"Ah, I always thought you would come to appreciate me some day, Pappy," she exclaimed, with a giggle quite girlish, which puckered up her knobby red cheeks, hid her eyes and made her little dot of a nose look like the end of a miniature walnut.

But her husband's exhibition of incipient effusiveness was already over, and he took no notice of this demonstration. His mind was following up his wife's suggestion, and measuring its value. For the space of I will not absolutely say how many minutes he sat silent, summing the matter up. And as he thought, his features gradually assumed a look of cheerfulness.

"Yes, it will do, my dear," he said at the close of his mental review. "Capital, in fact. Upon my soul, Penny, I can't think what possessed me, never to think of that before. Eh, little woman! and to think the idea should have first occurred to you. Why, do you know, I believe I might have saved all that money I spent at the last election on my seat for Oldhills, if I had only done as you now suggest. Gad, it's first rate, my dear, and you're a regular little brick. By making part of that land a park I believe I'll not only secure the title you are so anxious for, but a safe seat for Berborough, as well as perhaps a good return on what I have long considered a very bad investment."

Mrs. Buncombe listened and smirked and purred her satisfaction, till feeders at neighbouring tables, had they cared to look, might have taken her for a very experienced widow receiving propositions for yet another match. Her husband's delight equalled her own, and when they strolled into the town later in the day, he insisted on marking his approval of her conduct by the present of a massive gold bracelet.

His mind once made up, Mr. Buncombe proceeded to business with his accustomed energy, and in the course of the following winter his park was made. It formed a long strip of ground on the north bank of the Berborough estuary, about sixty acres in extent, bounded on the landward side by a broad sweeping drive, behind which lay a ribbon of ground, from thirty to ninety feet broad, which, huge boards informed the public, was to be let in plots on building lease. The park itself was drained and artistically laid out with shrub-covered mounds, winding pathways, a cricket ground and tennis lawns.

At first the Berborians wondered what this digging and planting and sewer and street laying meant, and could make nothing of it, for Mr. Buncombe kept his own counsel, until the work was nearly completed. Most of the citizens did not even know that this barren waste was his, until the contractor to whom the work was let made the fact public. Then, when the possible object of this expenditure of capital began to be suspected, there were not wanting cavillers and envious people who gave it as their opinion that " Old Buncombe must be up to some deep game." These, however, were creatures who did not require pretexts for hating the successful shipbroker and M.P. Rivals of his in business some of them had been once on a time, but they had long ago fallen behind him, and the higher he soared the more they affected to be shocked at his character.

All the meanness of such folk counted as nothing with the multitude. When in due time Mr. Buncombe sent a letter to the mayor of the town, intimating that he had prepared a little present for his beloved native city, " where so many happy days had been spent, and where the foundations of his fortune had been laid," the enthusiasm of the common people overbalanced every other feeling. The local press exhausted its vocabulary in sounding the praises of the " generous, noble hearted donor," and with one acclaim it was decided that he should have a public reception of the grandest, at the expense of the ratepayers, on the day of the opening and dedicating ceremony. It was also decided that the pleasure ground should be known for all future time as " Buncombe Park."

One thing only was wanting. The people of Ber-borough had overlooked it in their first hour of delight, but Mr. Buncombe, nay, Mr. and Mrs. Buncombe had not. At the earliest opportunity afforded him by the proposal to hold high revel on the day when the park was to pass into the custody of the corporation, Mr. Buncombe had hinted softly, and by the way, as it were, to the mayor, that it might be an excellent thing to get a royalty of some sort to "open" it.

"Yes, certainly, just the very thing," the mayor had written back, adding, however, the suggestion that Mr. Buncombe himself should send the invitation.

Mr. Buncombe did not see this at all, and posted off to Berborough to interview the mayor on the subject. It was so much better to do that than to write letters. The two great men soon came to an understanding. Both coveted honours ; both deprecated any self-seeking, and each saw through the other's game. But it was impossible for Mr. Mayor Pankhurst to deny the force of the park donor's argument. Mr. Buncombe did not wish to approach royalty directly again, because his recent disappointments had left a soreness. That was his true reason for hanging back, but the one he gave to the mayor was that it would be much more appropriate either for that functionary to send the invitation to royalty direct, or to get the senior member for the borough to do it in the name of the town itself.

As finally arranged, the mayor sent the invitation through the two borough members, and urged them privately to do their best to procure a favourable reply.

I am not sure that this was good tactics, still less sure that the members appealed to felt hotly zealous to further the aims of Messrs. Buncombe and Pankhurst. They did, however, make the wishes of these men, or, rather, the wishes of the borough, as it was phrased, known by devious channels to royal minds, and the result was a qualified success. No male of the necessary quality could come. One was in the wars, with the baggage of a fighting force ; one was at sea, one on the continent, visiting his Westphalian or other relations. It was most unfortunate, and might have been disastrous but that there were several females of unadulterated royal blood available. After a little persuasion one of these consented to grace the ceremony with her presence for an hour on the auspicious day. This was not what the mayor and Mr. Buncombe had hoped for, but it was better than nothing. The golden key ordered for the park gate, and as a perquisite to the functioning royalty, would not be entirely money wasted.

In due performance of the pledge given, the female royalty came, attended by a priest, a husband, and a select squad of male and female toad-eaters, and great was the joy of Berborough. Flags waved from every window on that drizzly May morning, brass bands cracked men's ear drums with their lusty braying, volunteers marched, and nobly courted their death of cold in the east wind ; civic dignitaries, in robes and chains worthy of a cathedral service of the first order, read addresses, bowed the knee, bared the head, and grovelled like slaves before the presence of a stoutish, heavy-featured female in fur and feathers, and proud Mrs. Buncombe, all purple and jewels, handed over the golden key on an embroidered velvet cushion, while the crowds shouted as if they were bidding welcome to a new Messiah, riding, not on an ass, but resplendent in a carriage and four.

In the evening the inhabitants of the workhouse had a supper of beef and potatoes at Mr. Buncombe's expense. This emphasised his love for the common folk, so much exalted that day, and taught the world at large that the fountain of all food-giving human bounty lies fast by the British Throne !

Royalty and its train gleamed an hour before men's eyes, and then, it is to be presumed, went home happy. The volume of huzzas was at any rate of gratifying strength, and the throne, all know, will stand for ever, if the breath of the people do but encompass it with the due amount of hoarse roaring on all public occasions.

CHAPTER XLI.

DIGNITY AND IMPUDENCE.

AT last zeal and devotion met fitting reward. Common mortals would have thought so, at least, but Mr. Buncombe being uncommon, was not satisfied. Royalty had acknowledged his claims to honour at its hands, but a malign ministry made the honour small.

"Her Majesty has been graciously pleased to confer upon you the honour of—KNIGHTHOOD," an understrapper of the Prime Minister's had written, and, for the space of a week after the receipt of this communication, Mr., or, as we must now call him, Sir Timothy Buncombe, was tempestuous. It was dangerous to approach him, and, as for attempting to congratulate him upon the glory which had fallen on his shoulders, it would have pleased him better, I verily believe, if his friends had offered to fight him. He swore, in private, at the ministry, and appeared to think that a scurvy trick had been played upon him.

"In fact, it's next thing to a disgrace," he told his assembled family, when the letter had been read.

"But I'll be 'my lady,' won't I, Mr. B.?" remarked his tender better half.

"Don't say Mr. B. any more ma," remarked the son

and heir. "You must call the Guv'nor 'Sir Timothy,' now, you know."

"Hold your tongue, all of you," cried the new knight with a scowl. "I say this letter is a disgrace after what I have done for the party. But I know whom to thank for it. That old black-my-boots, sneaking scoundrel, Cravenmore, the patronage secretary, has been and served me this dirty trick. He always was a mean hound, and bore me no good will. But I'll unmask him yet, the sweep that he is, see if I don't."

"But you don't mean to say 'no thank you,' do you, now, Pappy?" exclaimed Mrs.—I beg pardon, Lady— Buncombe in a wheedling voice.

"'Pon my soul and body, I've a great mind to. It would serve the devils right. Really, I've a great mind to."

"Oh, no, you won't, though," chimed wife, and daughter, and son, in chorus. "You'll do nothing of the sort, father," Timothy, junior, proceeded. "Why, damn it, you know, that would be a beastly shame, by Jupiter it would. Those fellows would only laugh at you for being such a confounded ninny, don't you know. I wouldn't give them the chance, if I were you ; a title's a title, any way—always something gained, the first step, you know. I know lots of fellows whose guv'nors were only knights to begin with who are now baronets or peers. I'd see those skunks in kingdom come before I let them know what I felt about their cussed spite, blest if I wouldn't."

These were words of wisdom, the force of which it was impossible that the new knight should not feel even in the midst of his wrath, and as the young hopeful was powerfully backed by his mother, the dispute ended in the despatch of a gracious reply, full of " humble duty," " sense of the great honour conferred," and so forth.

This occurred on a Tuesday, and for the rest of that week Sir Timothy seemed to be more galled than glorified by his new dignity. "Only a knight," his whole attitude seemed continually to cry " only a knight," and he displayed a sulky carelessness about the way people addressed him, which hurt his wife's feelings above everything. Servants were constantly lapsing in their mode of addressing her, and saying "yes " and " no," or " yes ma'am " and " no ma'am " instead of " my lady " this and that.

She scolded these careless, unworthy creatures with all the length of her tongue, and was most careful always to address her husband as " Sir Timothy," in public ; but the domestics were either too wilful or too stupid to take the hint. So when the Sunday came round, the excellent little woman decided to bring the subject forward in family conclave after dinner, in order to induce her lord and master to address an admonition to the servants that night at family prayers. The Buncombe family always had prayers on Sunday nights when the head of the house was at home. Formerly prayers had been read daily, night and morning, but as the earthly grandeur of the now quasi-noble shipbroker increased, superstitious practices of this sort were put in the background, and might have been discontinued altogether but for the consideration due to intimate matrimonial relations with the church. A man who had a daughter wedded to fifteen hundred a year, plus tithes and burial fees and a genuflecting biped in embroidered magician's togas, could not be supposed guilty of outward contempt for all forms of religion.

Prayers then were read before the assembled domestics of the Buncombe household on Sunday nights, and mindful of this orderly custom, Lady Buncombe urged her husband to seize the opportunity this habit afforded to address them on their behaviour. Sir Timothy was a little reluctant at first to entertain the proposal.

" But you must, Pappy dear," his wife wheedled, " I'm sure you don't want them vulgar wretches to be treating me disrespectful as they have been doing. Only this very morning I had words with my maid, because she kept saying ' yes'm ' and ' very well'm ' all the time she was a-doing my back hair. I said to her, says I, ' Mary, my dear, you mustn't go on so. I ain't a ma'am no more ! ' ' Lawks,' says she, as pert as a parrot, ' what be you, ma'am,' says she. ' I'm my lady, ' says I, as dignified as I could, and what do you think ? the girl just sniggered and said, ' Oh, lawks, I'm sure'm, I allus forgets.' That put me in a rage, and I scolded her till I was all of a tremble and not fit to go to church. I'm sure I never heard a word of the sermon all the time for thinking on it." Here the good lady proceeded to wipe tears from the corners of her eyes, and her husband struck in with a—

" Humph ! But what the devil am I to say to them, my dear." Sir Timothy took a good many more liberties with the devil and other nondescript deities—

Jove, Jingo, Gad and the like—since his new honours had fallen on his shoulders. Probably he considered this free and easy mode of speech to be a mark of high breeding.

"Say! Why tell 'em as how they've got to call you 'Sir Timothy,' and me 'my lady.' You can lead up to it, you know, by reading a prayer about doing our duty in our station, and paying respect to them as is above us in authority. There's one in the book somewhere, I know."

"Humph!" exclaimed Sir Timothy again, in a tone which seemed to intimate that he supposed he must, but didn't at all like the job.

To a husband, however, obedience is generally the better part of discretion, and knowing this by long experience, Sir Timothy judged it prudent that night to carry out his wife's commands. When, therefore, the servants rose to file out of the room at the sound of the final "Amen," he cried in a tone altogether distinct from that in which he had drawled the words of prayer: "Wait a moment, my good people, I wish to say a word to you?"

The servants glanced at each other and at the speaker, half uneasily, and silently seated themselves again.

"My good friends," resumed Sir Timothy, when stillness had again fallen on the domestics ; "for you are all our good friends, I hope—faithful according to your stations in life. You are aware, of course, of the eh— high honour which our Gracious Sovereign has been pleased to bestow upon my unworthy self. She has lifted me by her favour out of the ranks of the common

people as it were, and placed me amongst the nobles of
the land. It's a great honour, for which I need hardly
say to you that I am profoundly grateful. But
it is like all honours, it brings its duties and responsi-
bilities. To me it conveys the order, as it were, to live
worthy of a loftier station ; and to you, my good friends,
it brings the duty of changing the mode in which you
address Lady Buncombe here and myself," and he waved
his hand gracefully towards his wife. "As you can
understand, I do not myself care by what name I am
called. Timothy Buncombe I am, and, please God,
plain Timothy Buncombe will do for me to the end. At
the same time, as you will no doubt quite understand, both
Lady Buncombe here and myself would feel that we
were not doing our duty towards our Gracious Sovereign,
whom God long preserve, were we to allow the titles of
honour she has bestowed on us to be in any way slighted.
Now my lady tells me that some among you do not
seem yet quite to recognise this important consideration.
You still address her as ma'am, and perhaps, for aught I
know—I can't say I have noticed it much—you address
me with a plain 'sir,' just as usual. It is quite natural
you should, my good friends, quite natural—I am not
blaming you at all. I have not the least wish to do so.
But—eh, at the same time, you know—eh, it is just as
well you should understand what form of address Her
Gracious Majesty has prescribed for people in our
station, and, I may say, expects in the circumstances.
Pray understand that I don't complain. Far from it ;
but—eh, it is just as well—eh—the fact is that you ought

always now to address Lady Buncombe here, not with 'ma'am,' but with 'my lady." You must say 'Yes, my lady;' 'if you please, my lady;' 'shall I do so-and-so, my lady;' always 'my lady,' recollect. It is an indication of lack of respect to do otherwise, which I'm afraid it may be impossible for my lady and me to overlook, if you persist after this in saying 'yes, ma'am,' and 'no, ma'am.' As for myself, it follows, of course, that I should always be addressed as 'Sir Timothy.' Not that I care, you know, but you, eh—can see, of course, that it would be impossible for me to retain about me servants whose mode of address would betray to my friends that my household was wanting in respect for Her Majesty, through their way of speaking to me. Therefore, remember it is 'my lady,' and 'Sir Timothy,' henceforth, and see that none of you forget what is right and proper. Now you may go. Good night!"

Silently, and with faces as expressionless as masks, the group of domestics rose and filed out of the room; twinkling eyes alone betraying emotions dangerously akin to mirth in one or two cases. What they said and did, and how Lady Buncombe's maid, Mary, laughed till her nose bled, down in the housekeeper's room, are matters which do not concern this history.

Upstairs, when left to themselves, Lady Buncombe congratulated her husband on his speech. "It was just the very thing, my dear Pappy," she said; "and so nice and smooth like."

"Ah, I thought it too smooth, by Jove," remarked Timothy, junior. "I'd have given it 'em hot, had I had to do it, for their devilish impudence, and serve 'em right too. I'll lay five to one the underfootman and three of the maids were laughing at you all the time, dad."

"Do you say so," exclaimed the orator. "Damn it, if I thought that I would bundle them out of the house, neck and crop."

"Oh, no, they didn't ; and you won't, Pappy," observed Lady Buncombe. "It will be all right, never fear. I know the maids. They may snigger and laugh, because they are giddy young monkeys ; but they won't go agin your orders, never fear. And I don't want new servants just now with the season a-coming on. They'd worrit me to death, they would." And so the matter rested.

CHAPTER XLII.

A VOW UPON PASTEBOARD.

WERE I morally inclined what a beautiful homily I could now lay before the reader on the vanity of human wishes. No glory without affliction, a title not enjoyable without chagrin ; a Knight and his Dame put out of sorts by their very domestics. There you have a theme capable of filling many pages, and I shall be delighted if somebody else fills them in somebody else's book.

I am merely a historian, and as a historian I am compelled to disclose the melancholy fact that the sorrows and troubles of the great Buncombe family over their title and its duties and privileges, did not end with their domestics. These were effectually brought to a state of superficial order and obedience by Sir Timothy's admonition, as his wife said they would be; but the first drawing room of majesty subsequent to the receipt of the new dignity was no sooner announced than the vexed question of presentation at Court came immediately to the fore.

"I must be presented now I'm Lady Buncombe," Sir Timothy's better half had declared, and there was no denying the force of the argument. But to admit that in no way conduced to bring my lady a step nearer the performance of this wonder-working ceremony. The question, "Who will present Lady Buncombe to majesty or majesty's deputy," was as difficult to settle as before, for a wicked, fashionable world, crooked of heart, and venomous of tongue, refused to consider Penelope Drabble as Lady Buncombe, one whit more aristocratic or refined than she had been as plain "Mrs."

The wicked human froth of Belgravia and Mayfair, on the contrary, took increased pleasure in retailing stories illustrative of the oddities of word and deed uttered and performed by the new accession to the ranks of the gentry. Lady Powderhorn herself, a woman whose husband lay under many pecuniary obligations to Sir Timothy, of which she reaped her share of the benefit, took malign delight in showing her friends a certain visiting card whereon the words "Lady Penelope Buncombe" were beautifully engraved. This card she declared had been left at her door by the new knightess, on her return to town, and conveyed to her the first intimation she had received that Sir Timothy Buncombe had married an earl's daughter.

Unhappily, Lady Buncombe had unquestionably committed this mistake in her innocence of heart, but it had been discovered by her husband or daughter, and the cards destroyed before a dozen of them had passed into circulation. Of that dozen, unfortunately, Lady Powderhorn received one, and, with a malice most reprehensible, the proud peeress made the most of it. For the best part of a fortnight this card was the delight of her mornings and her evenings' sweetest joy.

" She went too far with it though, at last ; when she chaffed Timothy Buncombe, junior, at one of her receptions, publicly chaffed him in the presence of a crowd. The young man was too feeble, or too under-bred shall we say ? to retort upon her ladyship as he might have done, but he bottled up a good deal of wrath in his bosom, and carried it home to his father.

" I say, Guv'ner," he remarked next morning at breakfast, " Can't you stop that wretch Lady Powder-horn's tongue ? D' you know she had the cheek to laugh at the mumsy there in public, last night. I was never so much flummaxed in all my born days, by the Lord Harry. You should have seen how her tribe sniggered when she remarked to me, that she supposed she ought to congratulate me on having discovered high connexions. Callow himself grinned all over his face, the dirty little weed that he is."

" Eh, what, God bless my soul and body, Tim, you don't mean to say that Lady Powderhorn made game of your mother, before your face."

" Of course I do, and mighty uncomfortable she made me, I can tell you."

" And didn't you stick up for your family, sir ? Gad, I'd have given it her hot."

" You're welcome to do it, then. I'm blest if I'm going to get up a wordy cock-shy with a woman, and a peeress, too. She has got a devilish sight too sharp a tongue for me, that shemale."

" Oh, Tim," groaned his mother. " I may be a peeress, too, some day, and I think you might have said a good word for your mother, considering all as I've done for you."

"Oh, the deuce, mother, what could I say? You know you've been and gone and made an ass of yourself with that blasted card. You couldn't expect me to deny that, could you? If you will play the fool, it seems to me you must take the consequences," answered Timothy.

"Just so, just so," interrupted his father, "most dutifully spoken, my son. It's a pity the servants are not here to see how respectful you are to your mother. It isn't worth your while to stand up for her, of course not."

"Oh, hang it all, now, dad; you know I didn't mean that. What's the use of going on at a fellow like that?"

"No use at all, I admit. My son is a gilded youth; born with a silver spoon in his mouth, don't you know; can't be expected to stick up for his mean progenitors," Sir Timothy went on, venting his chagrin on his innocent boy, because it was useless to do so on the mother.

The chided son and heir made no further answer beyond thrusting his hands down to the bottom of his trousers pockets, and looking sulky. His mother blubbered and wiped eyes already inflamed with the rubbing of her handkerchief. Evangeline, her breakfast finished, sat with her head down, manufacturing bread pellets out of the crumbs on the table. Silence, broken by sniffs and muffled sobs, fell on the group.

Presently Sir Timothy roused himself, and getting to his feet, exclaimed; "Devil take me if I'll stand this sort of thing any longer. I'll speak to old Powderhorn about it this very day, and if that malicious fool of a countess of his won't consent to present you at Court, my dear, I'll make it hot for 'em. Oh, yes, I'll let 'em know which side their bread is buttered on, never fear. Impudent, gambling, penniless gipsy that she is ;" and with that the knight hurried from the room on his way to the city.

Parliament was sitting at this time, but Sir Timothy rarely put in an appearance there now. He had no longer an interest in politics. They were nothing to him compared with the hunt and toil after social advancement, and unless he made up his mind to join that American land jobbing syndicate which Powderhorn and a few needy kindred spirits were organising, in which case the lobby of the House might be a convenient spot for catching subscribers, it was not probable that he would be found at a dozen divisions in the course of the current session. Oldhills he had made up his mind should see the colour of no more of his money, so it was unnecessary for him to be particular. Politics, in short, were, in his own phraseology, "bosh," but he was determined that his wife should now go to the Queen's drawing room come what would. The dignity of knighthood made that step perfectly indispensable.

CHAPTER XLIII.

A NEW "COMMISSION" BUSINESS.

"Oh, by the by, Powderhorn, I want a word with you." said Sir Timothy that same afternoon, as the directors of the Excelsior Company were rising to go their several ways, after consuming the sumptuous lunch provided for them three times a week out of working expenses.

"All right," said my lord, turning back from the door and sitting down again. Powderhorn was a tall, heavy man, not ill favoured but for the hungry, hunted look of the eyes, and the perfectly selfish expression of the mouth. Meeting him in the street you might have mistaken him according as his duns were at his heels or not, either for a bankrupt fleeing from his creditors, or for an auctioneer on the watch for bids. In dress he was careless after an elaborate style which betrayed the old Dandy, and amid all his sorrows and impecuniosities he had never fallen so low as to be compelled to pawn the massive watch chain at which he ostentatiously dangled the gold passes of a railway director. That chain with its appendages, his crimson necktie, and his large fishy eyes, were the most conspicuous points about him. Nay, I forgot, he was also knock-kneed—a physical characteristic which moralists say accounts for many things. Seating himself near the great manager, "What is it?" he demanded in an abrupt way, such as he might use to an unfortunate creditor. " Any new game on ? You are not going to ask me to pay my debts, are you, Buncombe, because I can't, you know; devilish sorry, but I can't." This last remark was probably drawn out by the preoccupied, not to say threatening look on the knight's face.

"No, no, I was not thinking about your debts," Sir Timothy answered. " It would do me no good if I did. Besides, we have settled all that, you know, unless, of course, Lady Powderhorn wants to break off the match."

" Whew !" whistled his lordship, half to himself. " Her ladyship has been at her tricks again, has she; then I'm in for it. What, in the name of Moses and Aaron and the whole tribe of Jews, has Lady Powderhorn been up to now," he demanded in a louder tone.

" Oh, nothing, nothing at all ; only amusing herself in a mixed company, at the expense of my wife and son ; that's nothing, of course," sneered the knight, the scowl on his face deepening.

" Curse her, for a sharp tongued fool," ejaculated the earl. " But I say, Buncombe, you are not going to mind that, are you. Damn it, you know very well I never back my wife up in these escapades, and you are not going to visit her sins on my head, I trust."

" Not if you can make her obey you so far as to present Lady Buncombe at court," answered Sir Timothy, coming brusquely to the point. " If you can't do that the sooner we square up and part company the better."

"Well, Buncombe, I have again and again tried to get her ladyship to do that same, and you know how I have succeeded. For the life of me I cannot see why she shouldn't yield on this, to me, trifling affair, but women are as obstinate as pigs when they take a notion in their heads, and I really can't promise. I'll have another try to please you, if you like, but it will only produce a row, I know. My wife has some confounded prejudice or other against yours, and that's the truth. You needn't cut up rough over what I can't alter."

"Yes, yes, I know. No one knows better than I do. My wife is a good woman, a very good woman in her way, Lord Powderhorn ; but there's no denying the fact that I made rather a mistake in marrying her. I was young and ignorant of the world then, and made a *mésalliance*, having no parents to advise me. I am perfectly willing to admit all that ; but though she is a bit underbred and ignorant, she isn't a fool, Lady Buncombe isn't, and with a little coaching can be trusted to go through the ceremony as well as the greatest lady of the land."

"I don't doubt it for one moment, my dear fellow. In fact I have often said as much to my wife, but all to no purpose ; and to tell you the truth, I'm sick of the job," said the peer peevishly.

"Humph, a good deal hangs on it though, Lord Powderhorn. Not to speak of the money transactions between us already, there is that match between your son Callow and my Eva. You can scarcely expect that my family will let me send my youngest and best loved child into a family by whom she would be despised."

"Oh, but, my dear Sir Timothy, that is to be quite a love match, you know. Callow is clean floored by your daughter, and whatever his mother might say or do, they would be all right."

"I'm not so sure of that, by Gad. Besides, Eva is a proud girl, not at all like her mother. She takes after my family, and is high spirited and generous. It's just as likely as not that she will refuse Callow altogether, whether she loves him or not, if she finds her mother made game of, as she was at Lady Powderhorn's reception last night. She was in a rage over it this morning, I know."

"Curse it, no. It shan't come to that, I give you my word of honour, it shan't. I will overcome my wife's scruples somehow. She must not be allowed to play Hell and Tommy with our plans and family interests in this fashion. And yet, for the life of me I cannot tell how I'm to bring her round."

"Could we not bribe her somehow?" asked Sir Timothy, with a shrewd guess at the cause of the peer's hesitation.

"Bribe her? How do you mean? Do you suppose my wife would take a fee for doing the needful to yours? Rather gross that, I fancy."

"Nonsense, Powderhorn, you needn't flare up over a mere phrase. I didn't mean that I should strike a bargain with Lady Powderhorn, so much cash for so much work. Not at all. What I rather implied was whether I couldn't assist you to smooth over any small financial difficulties she might have. If our families are to be united, you know, I may just as well do a little in that way now as later. There's no social law against a husband bribing his wife. Eh, Powderhorn? That I should bribe your wife; God bless my soul, no."

"Ah, that's it, is it? Demme, that's not a bad idea, Buncombe," answered the peer, all gloom vanishing from his countenance. "I never thought of that"—he had been thinking of nothing else. "It is not likely I should, either, having no money to pay up with. As sure as God made me I never was so hard up in my life, the rents of my estates won't pay settlements and mortgages. I've pawned most of my securities—those worth any-thing, you know, and can't get along after all. So I'll be bound my wife has debts, and I rather fancy she did a little business with ' my uncle ' lately on her own account. That necklace she wore last night, I am quite sure, was paste. But how much would you be disposed to fork out, Buncombe, supposing I did attempt to bring her round with the chink of gold? I'm some thousands behindhand, and can do nothing."

"Ah, well, I'm game for a thousand or two, say not more than four thousand at the outside. I'm not particu-lar, you know, as long as the thing is done, and peace restored to my family circle," said Buncombe, with an affectation of cheerful alacrity easily seen through.

"Then, my dear fellow, I believe the thing is as good as done. I know I can take her ladyship on a weak point when I speak of money. It will make everything smooth. And I say, Buncombe, I suppose if I do the job for two thousand or three, you'll give me a commission, won't you? Ha, Ha!"

"Don't mind if I do," was the answer, after a moment's hesitation. "In fact, you may as well say four thousand right off, and if you can arrange for less with Lady Powderhorn the balance will be yours."

"Hooray," exclaimed the noble huckster. "Hooray, then I shan't lose an hour, Buncombe. I'm off to the battle, good bye," and away he went, so greatly delighted with the fee attached to his mission that, instead of going west by the underground railway, as usual, he took a cab home.

CHAPTER XLIV.

A MARKETABLE COMMODITY.

A CERTAIN amount of delicacy was requisite on the part
of Lord Powderhorn in broaching the subject of Lady
Buncombe's presentation. To have mentioned it abruptly
would have driven his wife into a rage, and while her
mind was agitated by passion the promise of money
down might have been scouted.

Happily the noble pair were dining out that night, so
that his lordship had plenty of time to meditate his plan
of attack before the hour for a connubial *tête-à-tête*
arrived. When at last he and his wife were alone in her
ladyship's boudoir, where they often had a little dish of
scandal together before seeking their dressing-rooms, the
first observation he made had apparently no connexion
whatever with his " mission."

"Harry," said he. His wife's christian name was
Harriet, but he called her Harry when they were friends.
" Harry," said he, " do you know I'm devilish hard up.
Can you give me any money ? "

" Good God, Powderhorn, are you mad ! where should
I have any money to give you.   I am at my wit's end for
a few hundreds myself," was the retort.

" But I thought you had raised some on the last of

the family jewels. Wasn't that a paste necklace I saw you wearing last night. It seemed to me rather garish."

"Oh, you noticed that, did you? I felt sure of it, though the jeweller swore to me that at a little distance no one could tell the necklace from diamonds. But what could I do? I lost nearly a hundred pounds at cards last week at Lady Snaffle's, and my milliner has been dunning me for money like a very Jew for months. After all, the old miser wouldn't give me more than two hundred and fifty pounds on the diamonds, and I'm just as hard up as before."

"Devilish awkward that, Harry, devilish awkward. Demme, if I don't think we shall end in the workhouse. I can't raise another farthing, and you know my land might as well be in the moon for all it yields me in these times. It's just my cursed luck," and his lordship hung down his head, like a man at his wit's end. His wife shrugged her shoulders and gathered her dressing-gown closer round her bosom, but made no reply.

"Look here, love," Lord Powderhorn resumed, "can't we hurry up that marriage with old Buncombe's daughter? It's devilish hard in a way, I know, but the brute has lots of money, and will pay like a man for the privilege of having a lord for a son-in-law, ha, ha!"

"I hate the very name of Buncombe," cried Lady Powderhorn, with energy. "And if I didn't, I believe the girl hates Jack." Jack was known to the vulgar world as Lord Callow. "He says she has another flame some-where, and won't have him if she can help it, the stuck-up minx. Of course, her indifference has turned Jack's head."

"Yes, I know all that ; but you are wrong about Eva. She had a fancy when in her teens for some underling in Buncombe's office, but the old rogue nipped the thing in the bud and sent the ambitious youth abroad. He would have no more '*mésalliances*' in his family, he said, the upstart purse-proud old fool, ha, ha!" Lord Powderhorn's laughs were, so to say, barked out in a manner resembling the speech of a French doll—dry, and short, and heartless.

"Just like his insolence ; but that reminds me, Powderhorn, there is a daughter of his married to some low fellow or other, isn't there ? "

"I believe there is. Some scribbling blackguard, I've understood. Fancy I met him at Buncombe's once. But after all, you know, Harry, my love, what the devil does that matter ? We shan't marry the whole family, and Buncombe, I feel pretty sure, has cut that lot himself. At least, I never see either the scribbler or his wife there now, or hear their names mentioned. They are an advantage to us in one way, in fact, because they won't get much of the old man's brass. More to divide among the others, in fact, for old Bunny's not the chap to foster poor relations."

"There's something in that. Will his knightship come down handsomely, do you think ? "

"He won't give *us* much, Harry ; you leave the tight-fisted old skinflint alone for that. But he talks of settling fifty thousand pounds at once on his daughter

should she marry Jack, and I daresay I might get him
to lift a mortgage or two, he's so deuced keen on the
connection."

"Well, but that won't do much to keep us out of the
bankruptcy court. Fifty thousand isn't much, is it?
What might it mean a year?"

"Oh, perhaps two thousand, perhaps rather more.
It's all according to how it is invested."

"Then Jack and his girl will want all that for themselves, and we shall be as bad as ever, Powderhorn."

"No, no, not quite that, my love ; we shall at least be
delivered from Jack's extravagances. He has cost me no
end of money since he came of age, you know. Devil take
him, what with betting and gadding about, I do believe
the fellow spends two thousand pounds a year as it is."

"Lord, so much as that. Then marry him, Powderhorn, for God's sake, and leave him to his own devices,
I thought he only cost you a few hundreds."

"Ha, ha ! That's all you know about the thing, Harry.
But I didn't say I had *paid* all his debts, did I ? He owes
a few thousands, I fancy ; in fact, I know he does, and
old Buncombe will have to pay these debts, so that the
couple may start fair. I have no doubt he can get Jack
a few directorships in the city too, in order to eke out his
living. All depends on how we treat the chap ; and
that reminds me, by the by, haven't you been rather
rough on that dumpling of a wife of his lately ? "

"What, the Lady Penelope Buncombe joke. Oh,
good gracious, Powderhorn, don't talk to me of that. I
thought I should have died with laughing when that

X

card of hers was handed to me. Don't talk to me of
that sausage roll of a creature. I loathe the very sight
of her."

"Tuts, Harry, my love ; that's not reasonable, you
know. If we are to take in the daughter we must
tolerate the mother."

"But you have just told me that we were not going to
marry the whole family."

"Neither we are, but that does not alter the fact that
we must make the most and the best of the connexion,
and brave it out before Society if necessary. It's the only
way to keep Society from laughing at us. You only give
it the cue when you make game of the dumpling."

"Do you think so ?"

"I'm sure of it. You make a mistake altogether in
turning that little dot of a creature into ridicule. It
shows your friends that the connexion galls us. I
wouldn't do that for a fortune, were I you."

"Ah, I never thought of it in that light. Perhaps there's
something in that. But then, you know, I'm afraid of the
little wretch asking me again to present her at court ?"

"And why shouldn't you, pray ?"

"Why shouldn't I ? Good God, Powderhorn, you don't
mean to insinuate that I should drag that bolster of a
creature through the crowd at a drawing room."

"Yes, I do, though. Demme if I see any good reason
why you shouldn't."

"Oh, Powderhorn ! "

"I grant you the woman is vulgar, and all that, but
she can be made to behave. She isn't a fool, you know,

and after all there are lots of women just as low bred and vulgar as she is who yet go to court,—Mrs. Montague Emanuel, for instance, the greasy little Jewess, presented last year by the Marchioness of Rabbitwarren."

"Oh, Powderhorn! How can you think of such a thing. I'm sure I shall die of shame."

"Devil a fear of you, Harry, my love, you'll excuse my saying so, for there is money in it."

"How, money in it! Do you mean to say that old Buncombe would pay me to take his wife to a drawing room. The insolent wretch."

"N—n—no, not exactly that, but there is no denying, love, that your obstinate refusal to have anything to do with his wife has riled him, and made him anxious to conquer us. And, of course, a vulgar, low-bred fellow like that knows only one way of gaining his end—money. It is always ' What's your price?' with damned cads of that sort. So he hinted only this morning that he didn't mind if he tided us over a bit till the iron trade improved, or the luck somehow turned, if we could manage this little piece of business for him. He could get no peace at home for it, he said. It was all very vulgar and low, I grant you, but then, Harry, we are so hard up that I don't see why we shouldn't take the fool in his humour. I really don't."

"I hate the idea of the thing. Why, the wretch is sure to dress herself like a nigger at a camp meeting, and I shall be laughed at till I am fit to die of shame," retorted her ladyship, who now saw the meaning of this conference.

"Oh! no, you won't. You can stipulate about the dress to be worn, you know, and then the girl, your future daughter-in-law, will be with you, of course. She is presentable enough, and the small, squat, dumpling Buncombe will be hid behind her daughter's tall form. Oh, it can be managed easily, if you'll try. The girl, you know, must go to court, at any rate, and it will be best that her mother should do the first presentation. And if I tell you that Buncombe is squeezable to the tune of a thousand or two, that's worth a little annoyance and trouble in these times, isn't it, my dear?"

"But the parvenu won't hand over a thousand or two, will he?" exclaimed her ladyship, with a surprised look.

"I'll guarantee he will. Just you leave it to me, Harry. I'll see that the money is forthcoming."

"It's worth thinking about, certainly. A couple of thousand pounds or so would, in fact, carry us comfortably through the season, and keep off the Jews."

"Of course it would. Well, you shall have two thousand, my love, if you can manage this little business. I'll wring the money out of the brute, never fear. It's vulgar in a way, you know, but I don't see why, if our station and privileges in Society are marketable commodities, we shouldn't live a little by them when the luck in other ways goes against us. That's my view of the matter, and now you just go ahead, it will be all right."

With many wry faces, and sighs, and head shakes, Lady Powderhorn at length agreed that this was perhaps the best course in the circumstances, and so, the compact sealed, they betook themselves to bed.

CHAPTER XLV.

RED OR BLUE?

NEXT day his lordship communicated the decision of his wife to Sir Timothy Buncombe.

"It's all right, Buncombe," he said, "her ladyship sees the error of her ways, and will make amends. You can tell your womenkind to get ready for the drawing room."

Sir Timothy was so delighted with this news that he insisted upon giving a dinner, "just a little family dinner, you know," to the Powderhorns, in order to sanctify and seal the bargain.

Lady Powderhorn would have avoided this feast, as she instinctively avoided everything belonging to the Buncombe tribe, as she named the great shipbroker's family, but her husband's calculating shrewdness over-ruled her.

"You can take the chance this offers to arrange about the dresses, you know, Harry, and as there will be no one there to see your tortures except Callow, who is blind, and myself, who won't look, I think you can go with an easy mind."

Poor Lady Powderhorn. Originally she had been by no means a selfish or bitter minded woman. But her beauty and her parents' ambition had been her ruin. Her father was a needy baronet, the descendant of a be-baroneted physician, and when his only daughter, Harriet Gertrude Mumbles, grew up, tall, graceful, finely formed, Greek featured, and sweet as a moss-rose, his wife and he put her in the market against a title. She was knocked down to Lord Powderhorn, then Lord Callow, and thirty years of intimate association with this selfish, mean-spirited, greedy and needy peer had made her over again, had changed her into the narrow, bitter, excitement-loving, sharp-tongued, scornful woman we have seen. Traces of her early beauty still lingered around her and sustained her pride. No court hanger-on and toad-eater of them all could carry a higher head, or sustain more gracefully a splendid court garment than she. It was, therefore, gall and wormwood for her to be forced to take a being like Lady Buncombe under her wing. But necessity is a cruel nigger driver, and the murmur of many duns, empty pockets, and a black future, forced her to submit.

It was with a smiling countenance then, and a gracious air, that her ladyship accompanied her husband and son to Buncombe's family feast of love, and her heart in a sense grew light within her, when she found that, as Powderhorn had said, no guest was there save those Buncombes she already knew. None were, in fact, available. The Weardale connection was now altogether too low; the clerical tie was better, but far away, and therefore loose; and as for the Fosters—corn dealers, seed crushers, etc.,—they were as bad as the Weardales, for Foster had lately failed, and was now living in retirement on the jointure prudently settled by him on his wife,—out of his creditors' means, as it turned out,—when he married.

No, the Buncombes had now no family available, except Timothy, junior, and Evangeline. The others were as dead to the knight and his dame on an occasion like this, as were Lady Powderhorn's two little ones, whom a merciful heaven had called to their long sleep in infancy.

So it was quite a successful family feast. Callow, lisping, gawkish, brainless youth, was in his seventh heaven of delight, knowing himself now the accepted of Evangeline. Timothy, junior, chattered for two in order to keep Lady Powderhorn from being shocked by his mother, and the earl and the knight had abundance to say about city affairs, the new land-grabbing American syndicate, the sins of other magnates, or cat's-paws, of finance, and the general dearth of good directorships, where a well furnished table added sweetness to the fees.

All went beautifully until the ladies retired to the drawing room, and began to discuss the all-absorbing question of the approaching presentation. Upon this subject Lady Buncombe proved tractable at all points, except that of dress. She was quite willing to undergo daily drill in deportment, and frequent lessons in the routine of court ceremonies; but her obstinate little mind stuck fast at the gown. She had seen a gorgeous costume in some milliner's window, and set her affection on something similar. It was a robe composed of a pink petticoat, and a crimson train.

In vain did Lady Powderhorn try to persuade the dame that these colours would be unsuitable for her high complexion. The more the peeress tried persuasion, and the more Evangeline echoed the peeress's sentiments, the more convinced was Lady Buncombe that these colours and no other were just what she would have.

Lady Powderhorn's temper was rising fast to boiling point at this pigheadedness, and as her vivid imagination pictured the guy her protégée would be in such a garb, beads of sweat gathered on her brow. "Oh God," she whispered to herself, "how can I ever go through with it."

In all probability an explosion would have occurred if the gentlemen, prompted by Callow, whose taste for wine was smaller than usual, had not appeared on the scene with unwonted promptitude.

The moment he entered the room, Lord Powderhorn saw that something was up. His wife's face was flushed, and her lips compressed. Her little feet drummed nervously on the carpet, and her hands clasped and unclasped with spasmodic irregularity.

"Well, ladies," cried my lord, "have you fixed it all up, as the Yankees say, garments and everything, eh, Lady Buncombe?"

"Lawks, no," that personage answered, "we can't hit it off about my dress, your lordship. Her ladyship there says as how the dress I want don't suit my complexion, and she wants me, your lordship, to put on——What is it, your ladyship?"

"Nay, I don't want to coerce you in the least," said Lady Powderhorn, in a cold tone ; "I merely made a suggestion to you, thinking that perhaps my experience in these matters might give it some value. You like reds, it seems, and they are beautiful, no doubt, with some complexions ; but I feel sure that you would look much better in a dress composed of a sapphire blue train over a pale blue satin petticoat. But then that's only my opinion, you know."

"Well, and I say blues don't suit me ; at least I don't like 'em. They're too cold."

"As you please, Lady Buncombe. I have no wish to dictate to you, none in the least."

"Tuts, Bosh, Eh ! Excuse me, your ladyship, but my opinion is that Lady Buncombe here can't do better than take your advice. What can you be thinking of, Penny," Sir Timothy added, turning to his wife, "setting your opinions up against a lady of taste and fashion like the countess. Drop it, my dear, drop it, and be thankful you've got so good a guide."

Lady Buncombe screwed her mouth and looked sulky, but her husband went up to her, slapped her heartily on the back, and whispered "Don't be a fool. Do you want Lady Powderhorn to throw you up ?" at which query a look of alarm crossed Penelope's flat features, and she at once grasped the situation.

"Well, well, if Sir Timothy wishes it, I'm sure I've got nothing to say. It was only my fancy, you know, and your ladyship knows best, I'll allow," said she, as graciously as a baulked woman could

"That's right," cried the knight, in a loud, thickish voice. "That's right; I knew you'd be sensible, I did." He had taken in a fair amount of champagne and sherry downstairs, and spoke more vulgarly than usual. "And, now I think of it, if you wouldn't mind the trouble, Lady Powderhorn, why not order the dresses for all three yourself, you know. You can then have them made to suit your taste, and, since it's quite a family affair, just send me the bill for the lot. Eh, will that do?"

Lady Powderhorn demurred a little to this for form's sake, and hinted scruples, but ended by yielding to Sir Timothy's well played importunity.

"Now that's settled," the knight ended the debate by saying, "you go and give us a tune or two, Evey—just loud enough to let us old folks talk comfortably, you know. It will be a chance for you to turn over the leaves, Callow; eh, my boy. He, he!" Thus all danger of a rupture of friendly relations was avoided, and an important series of negotiations brought to a satisfactory conclusion.

CHAPTER XLVI.

THE FIFTH HEAVEN AND A GOLDEN HOLINESS.

AFTER so many disappointments Lady Buncombe reached the height of her ambition at last. And when the great court ceremony was performed, she could not help wondering what the fuss had been all about. Had she been a woman of a reflective or philosophical turn of mind, she might, indeed, have extracted a fund of amusement from the scenes in which she had her share. Strange scenes they were. A mob of half-naked women crowded and pressed their way towards the presence chamber, their bare bosoms rent and heaving with all the angry passions which move humanity in its primeval savage state, and likewise in its state civilised. Scorn, hatred, malice, contempt, envy, back-biting, slander, disgust, vulgar pride, rivalry, shamelessness—all were there.

Well might Lady Buncombe stare with all her eyes at what she saw, and forget in the wonder and amazement that overtook her narrow intellect, the drilling she had received. Happily it mattered little. Few noticed her in the crowd, and her stay in the presence of royalty was too short to afford royalty's toad-eaters much opportunity for their favourite pastime. The Countess of Powderhorn did her best to hurry her protégées, and when she had presented the mother, and the mother the daughter, and the flurried march past was ended, she felt her soul relieved of a great burden.

On the whole, too, Lady Buncombe behaved very well. She bobbed instead of curtseying, to the delight of those who noticed her, but it was all done so quickly that she had no time to commit any great absurdity.

Only when the trio were retiring did a stage whisper of hers send a cold shiver down Lady Powderhorn's back.

" I say, your ladyship," cried the little woman, waddling up, with her heavy train leaping along behind her, " is that the Queen ? I thought she was a stout little woman like me, only older."

" Hush, you——hush ! hush ! " replied the countess in an imperious tone. " Come away, I'll explain afterwards," and they got safely off.

Unsophisticated Lady Buncombe did not understand that majesty in person, when moved at all to attend these acts of worship, rarely stayed more than half-an-hour. Half-an-hour was quite enough acknowledgment for majesty's salary and perquisites, and the Buncombe party were much too late to be received by the apotheosis of Society's excellencies in person. Majesty was quite right. Any deputy of authentic royal blood was good enough for the mob.

For a few minutes after this was explained to her, Lady Buncombe's face wore a dissatisfied air. Possibly she felt disappointed, not only at missing a chance of gazing on the face of the being who exercised divine attributes over the church and the plutocratic swarm in virtue of a

Parliamentary licence, but at having no means of comparing the person and deportment of majesty with her own.

When, however, she read in the fashionable journals the next day, that Lady Buncombe had been presented by the Countess of Powderhorn, and Miss Evangeline Buncombe by her mother, and saw a full description of her own and her daughter's dresses inserted, for the customary fee, in the court paper, joy welled up in her soul. She had reached her fifth heaven at last—I think heaven's stages go by odd numbers—and had nothing in this world left to pray for except a peerage. This newspaper paragraph was her mental food and drink—her soul's sweet rest for days and weeks. In her happiness she felt disposed to pinch herself to see whether she was really awake, and an inhabitant of this lower world.

She bought two dozen copies of the blazon roll of her fame, and gave one of them to Mary, her maid, to take down to the kitchen, where it afforded delight and instruction of a kind she, simple creature, thought not of. Another she felt disposed to hand to the butler, but did not know how Sir Timothy might relish that step; so she contented herself by laying a copy in the hall, another in the library, and a third on the dining-room sideboard, casually, as it were, so that all might have an opportunity of reading the catalogue of her own and her daughter's splendours.

She lived for many days like one in a dream, and spoke softly to herself, communing with her own heart, one of the elect of majesty.

"*Me*, Penelope Drabble, Lady Buncombe, *me* at court, among all them duchesses and countesses and princes and big wigs. What would aunt Cutler have thought of that?" Thus was she always whispering to her own heart, and the thought made her more amiable, less querrelous in her manner and speech, than her family ever saw her before in her life.

What a contrast her own and Eva's position was to poor Beatrice's, she could not help thinking, now and then, or to Penelope the younger's, the wife of a fellow who had gone bankrupt. Ah, it was a good world, a sweet world, a joyful world to live in, this world that surrounded and propped a throne.

Who does not envy Lady Buncombe this sweet pleasure? How different she is in her simplicity of heart from that way-worn fashion's slave, Lady Powderhorn. No delight arose in her soul that she had been permitted to look on the face of royalty, even deputy royalty, and live. That to her was nothing. The privileges and corruptions of her class were held to be identified with these court ceremonies, this worship of idols, sometimes afflicted with a running at the nose, and she submitted to her fate as in duty bound.

But her heart did not rise within her as the trio left the presence and shoved their way to their carriage, unless it was in thankfulness that all was over, without a scene. When in the welling joy of her silly little heart, Lady Buncombe proposed that they should all go next day "to the photographer and get themselves took in a group," Lady Powderhorn had so little sympathy with her protégée as to reject the suggestion with unfeeling coldness. She had no mind, proud pensionary, hired bearess leader of Sir Timothy's though she was, to perpetuate what she called her degradation in a picture of that dangerous kind.

It must be confessed, however, that the countess did not allow Sir Timothy Buncombe to inflict these outrages upon her for nothing. She received her two thousand pounds; but perhaps a suspicion, justifiable enough, crossed her mind that her husband was not dealing honestly by her, and that she might have had more if she had been obdurate. Whether on that ground or another I do not propose to decide, but certain it is that on some ground deemed by her sufficient, Lady Powderhorn extracted a bonus or additional solatium peculiarly agreeable to her lacerated feelings. Sir Timothy had, when swayed by the generous bonhomie induced by abundant libations of stimulating wine, gallantly ordered her ladyship to send the bill for all the dresses to him. Her ladyship obeyed with admirable promptitude, and took occasion to include in the account, by private arrangement with her dressmaker, the bulk of an old debt of her own. This explains why Sir Timothy Buncombe cursed a little one morning at breakfast, and seemed for an hour or two totally unappreciative of the glory attained by his wife. The exact amount he was called on to pay for the three dresses was five hundred and sixty nine pounds three shillings and fourpence.

A large sum this undeniably, but then what could an upstart shipbroker expect? Did he think that he was going to be admitted within the pale by the great and noble adorers of majesty's attributes without paying his footing? He was altogether mistaken if he did. "All things are possible to the man with his pockets full of gold," is the principle upon which the bulk of the nobility and gentry of England habitually act, but that implies that the gold has to be spent. Of what use is it to be noble, and great, and privileged if one cannot levy blackmail? That was the employment of those whom nobility, falsely or otherwise, claims to be its ancestors, and such excellent examples ought to be followed.

And after all did not these little tastes of sorrow serve but to make the joys of a lofty station more sweet? When Sir Timothy's immediate goal was reached, and his wife made blessed, the momentary pain at spending money was soon lost in a sense of deep satisfaction. At last Sir Timothy Buncombe was somebody, had made his way in the world, and become a man of mark. The M.P'ship and many things else had paid.

Not that the great shipbroker's satisfaction was complete. Far from it. In his heart the conviction rankled that he had not yet been blessed according to his deserts. But that did no more than stimulate him to still further exertions. When next the topsy-turvydom of politics should decide to enact the tragedy of a dissolution, he meant to contest Berborough on the strength of his "generous gift" of a park, and whether the fight ended in triumph or defeat it was his design to try for a peerage. Only with a peerage did he feel that he could sit down and rest and be thankful, and for some time past he had been quietly getting the mortgages of a spendthrift, heirless landowner into his hands, with a view to securing an estate cheap from which to draw his title.

These are Sir Timothy's hopes for the future, hopes I must leave him to realise, as I doubt not he will. He is a man, as everybody now understands, who never lets the grass grow under his feet, never forsakes an aim once it has laid hold of him. So he will succeed.

At the very time when it is necessary for us all to part company, he is fully engrossed in the labour of catching a bishop—a real live *lord* bishop with five thousand to ten thousand pounds a year,—all complete, in tight smalls, a sanctified apron, and most mystical hat, garb without which the " Church " must perish, and Christianity fade before Nihilism, Atheism, Budhism, and all the demons of old Chaos. This holy functionary is wanted by the knight to perform the magical incantation over the heads of John Gosling, called Lord Callow, and Evangeline Buncombe, in order that, as we are taught in the mysteries of priest-craft, the Divine All-father may be constituted a binding party to their marriage bargain.

That he will succeed in this pursuit also I have not the least doubt, in spite of the anxiety of the bishops to be up and doing, so that they may escape with their plunder before democracy claims its own, for not only has he abundance of money, and therefore of godliness according to the clergy, but has himself a daughter rich in the Church. And Lord Powderhorn is bound to second him cordially in his labours, a circumstance which should itself suffice to capture half a dozen bishops,

since his lordship—patron or huckster of five livings—
is well known as a great pillar of the Anglican communion.
Money he cannot give it when it sends round the hat,
dissenter fashion; but his name is always at the service
of the bishops and clergy when they raise the cry,
"God's heritage is in danger."

Look out for him and you are sure to find this distinguished bankrupt, city leech, and society panderer,
well up in the list of names appended to protests against
"spoliation," etc. A gospel with money in it is within
the grasp of his lordship's comprehension, and he is
faithful according to his lights.

Sir Timothy Buncombe will, therefore, bag his bishop,
may even, spite of tithe-rescuing pre-occupations, find
the catch so easy as to abandon it, and try for an
archbishop with fifteen thousand a year, and lace ruffles
of extra holiness.   His ambition is boundless.

"And are you going to leave the hero of this history
at this point," I hear the reader cry.

Yes, assuredly, why not?

"Why not? Why, because it isn't fair. In spite of
all your disgusting admiration for the fellow, he is an
undeniable rogue, a thief and a villain, and you are going
to leave him in the full enjoyment of the fruits of his
crimes. It isn't fair. Justice cries out against you."

Nonsense, worthy or other reader.   Your mind has
been vitiated by a course of sentimental novel reading,
mingled with still more sentimental sermon-swallowing.
You think there is justice done in this world upon the
wicked. Permit me to assure you that, than this, there

cannot be greater stupidity. The days of the wicked-and-the-green-bay-tree poetical sentimentalists, have passed away long, long ago, and Freebooter David, the Jew, or whoever it was who imagined that taking simile, was a being of most limited understanding and experience.

Nowadays, let me assure you, this world is made mostly for the people called "the wicked." So much is this the case that I should have felt myself guilty of a mean sacrifice of truth, had I allowed Sir Timothy Buncombe to be overtaken by what old fashioned people will call his "sins." No, no, nothing of the sort. Sir Timothy flourishes, Sir Timothy sees the widows and the decrepit, the needy and the greedy, who bought his company's shares for an income, weep, and it may be starve, and cares not one brass farthing for the sight. They cannot touch him ; his money is his own by the law of the land. Why should he suffer for the sorrows he has caused ? Do robbers and thieves of the loftier breed ever suffer in this world ? Nay, verily. Nowadays at least, the green bay tree withereth not. It is they that seek its shade who die.

Grumble not then, O reader. Know thou that in this modern era men steal under the blessed dispensation of limited liability and a funded debt. The crimes of the cunning man are laid upon the back of the simple. He who is wise in his generation lays his debts at the doors of the poor-spirited, the ignorant and the lowly, in exchange for money down, and invests the proceeds in real estate or the three per cents. Happy age.

But is there no retribution at all or anywhere? Ah, ask me not. I cannot read the future, and I dare not speculate about the end towards which drifts this sublime system, whereby the poor increase in poverty, paying the debts of the rich, and posterity is endowed with the obligations born of this generation's lavish selfishness and of the plutocrat's crimes. It may wind up in a great world-melting, civilization-destroying, universal bankruptcy, wherein even holy, tithe-blessed lord bishops will fail to find sure footing, and a safe place for their ruffles, their aprons and hats. It may and it may not. Again must I plead that I am not a prophet. Enough is it for me that the M.P. and ship-broker, whose fortunes I have followed till glory burst upon his head and was reflected from the ruddy face of his wife, is in no danger of collapse. His company may go to the wall, but he stands secure. Unless I mistake not, he—weathering all storms of fortune, defying all hate and malice and envy—is destined to die in that exquisite odour of sanctity, indicated by a will proved " under a million,"—in the glory of the peerage. Happy man.

ABEL HEYWOOD & SON, PRINTERS, OLDHAM STREET, MANCHESTER.